He saw the woman's eyes widen and ducked, trying to avoid what he knew was coming. The club crashed down on his shoulder rather than his head. That was all the fight he put up before a fist like a mallet drove into his gut, doubling him over. In the far distance he heard the maid complaining. The answer she received quieted her. The back door closed. Lucas saw that through tears caused by pain. The roar of blood and the fierce hammering of his heart filled his ears.

He wished he had been totally deaf so he wouldn't have heard, "Kill him?"

Titles by Jackson Lowry

THE GREAT WEST DETECTIVE AGENCY
THE SONORA NOOSE

THE GREAT WEST
DETECTIVE AGENCY

JACKSON LOWRY

BERKLEY BOOKS, NEW YORK

THE BERKLEY PUBLISHING GROUP
Published by the Penguin Group
Penguin Group (USA) LLC
375 Hudson Street, New York, New York 10014

USA • Canada • UK • Ireland • Australia • New Zealand • India • South Africa • China

penguin.com

A Penguin Random House Company

THE GREAT WEST DETECTIVE AGENCY

A Berkley Book / published by arrangement with the author

For information, address: The Berkley Publishing Group,
a division of Penguin Group (USA) LLC,
375 Hudson Street, New York, New York 10014.

ISBN: 978-0-425-27243-5

PUBLISHING HISTORY
Berkley mass-market edition / October 2014

PRINTED IN THE UNITED STATES OF AMERICA

10 9 8 7 6 5 4 3 2 1

Cover illustration by Bruce Emmett.
Cover design by Diana Kolsky.
Interior text design by Kelly Lipovich.

1

Tonight he would get rich or die trying. Lucas Stanton looked across the table at the drunk rancher who had been bleeding money for the past hour. The more he lost, the more reckless he became. He had seen this before but seldom in a man who owned a ranch covering half of Middle Park, or so went the rumors.

He motioned to the bartender for another round. The rancher drank without regard for how the potent liquor dulled his good sense, if he had a whit. Lucas saw Lefty, the one-armed barkeep, deftly pouring two more shots, both from the same bottle, then stuffing the cork back in the bottle and bellowing for the drinks to be delivered. Two barely touched glasses of whiskey still sat in front of Lucas, but he would gladly pay for more. He was a professional gambler and knew his limits. What the rancher sought to prove tonight mattered less than cleaning him out. It wasn't anything personal. It was just business.

A pretty waiter girl came over with the drinks and winked at Lucas, her long eyelashes fluttering just enough to look sexy. He smiled. Claudette might actually be from France. Not cosmopolitan Paris as she claimed but possibly from the southern part of the country. A farm? A harbor town? If he won big—and he already had most of the rancher's poke in front of him—finding out her true origins might prove a pleasant cap for the night.

Lucas adjusted his cravat, then smoothed nonexistent wrinkles from the velvet lapels of his fine coat. It would have cost a hundred dollars or more, but the tailor had owed him for recovering money bilked from him by one of Denver's cleverer confidence men. Outwitting a swindler had caused a small warmth inside, but that was nothing compared to what he felt now with close to a thousand dollars on the table and more to come.

"You ought to quit, boss," a marmot-like man behind the rancher said. "You lost plenty already. And you know what the missus said about—"

"Shut up," the rancher snapped. He knocked back the whiskey and glared at Lucas. He had to close one eye to focus properly. "I got him smoked. His luck can't last forever."

"Boss, you've lost most all of—"

"Get the hell out. Now. You're not my conscience. I know what I'm doin'."

Lucas watched the small cowboy nervously shift from one foot to the other, then retreat, running out the fancy etched glass doors imported from Europe just for the Emerald City Dance Hall and Drinking Emporium. Those had set back the owner more than five hundred dollars and were small works of art with fancy lettering and suggestive feminine silhouettes. The place was the pride of Denver and boasted the prettiest girls and strongest whiskey. Tonight the piano player actually hit the right notes as he hammered out "Sweet Sixteen." That catchy tune had even the shyest wranglers paying a dime to many of the women for a dance. Boisterous laughter rolled like thunder off the Rockies from the dance floor at the rear of the saloon. Heavy smoke from both tobacco and poorly trimmed coal oil lamps swirled in the air, turning the interior into an imitation of San Francisco's Barbary Coast on a foggy night. Men drank and propositioned the women, and Lefty carried a beer keg as easily as any man with two arms.

This was his milieu. This was his night. This was the night Lucas Stanton got rich.

Lucas did a quick count on the rancher's chips, then pushed out that many and said, "I got to call, sir. You have the look of a man with a big hand, but my mama said I never had a lick of sense."

"She was a smart woman," the rancher said. He stared at the mound of money and chips, then said, "I'll raise."

"Sir?"

Lucas rocked back and shifted to one side, wary of the man's belligerent tone. He carried a Colt New Line .22 revolver in a coat pocket. The two-inch barrel allowed him to slip it easily, quickly into his grip, even if the small caliber didn't afford much stopping power across a table. It worked better as a belly gun; ram it into the foe's stomach and fire. If the slug didn't stop the target, the muzzle flash might set fire to his shirt.

His cards lay facedown on the table, and his right hand hovered within inches of his hideout pistol. The rancher ran his fingers around the edges of his five cards, then tapped them.

"I'm raisin' the limit."

"You have nothing more to bet, sir," Lucas said. He sat a little straighter in the chair. The raucous sounds around him faded. The spilled beer and tobacco and sweat no longer affected him. He even ignored how Claudette shoved her chest out and threatened to pop free of her low-cut dress as she bent over, trying to sneak a peek at the rancher's hand.

"I got this. Deed to my ranch. It's worth a hundred thousand dollars."

"I don't have enough to cover that. All I have is a few thousand." Lucas knew to the nickel how much he had. Twenty-two hundred dollars.

"Then you lose." The rancher reached out to pull in the pot.

Lucas moved like a striking snake and caught the man's wrist.

"We were playing table stakes. Chips. Cash. If you put up a deed, I have to agree to it, and I won't since I win the pot if you have to fold."

Lucas wanted the money on the table. He would be five thousand ahead. The rancher had only to stand pat and the best hand would carry the day. From the way the man's forearm tensed, he wasn't inclined to let the hand play out like that.

"I'll put up the deed against all you got on the table. And your coat. I took a fancy to that the minute I walked in."

"You aren't asking for my pants, too?"

The rancher looked a tad confused, then shook his head.

"Don't want your fancy britches. All your money and your coat. Against the deed."

"You must have a powerful hand to give odds such as those," Lucas said. "A hundred thousand dollars against what cannot amount to more than three thousand. Those are odds even a greenhorn would reject."

"I got the best hand and want to win as much as I can."

Lucas looked around. Laughter still rattled the saloon

windows, and the piano player had moved on to the raunchy "Honky-tonk Asshole." But a couple dozen customers and almost as many of the working girls circled the table. The Emerald City saw its share of high stakes games, but nothing like this for some time. More than getting rich, Lucas could add to his reputation with a win.

The rancher might be drunk, but he was determined that his hand was the best. Even snockered the way he was, the man certainly didn't think a pair of deuces would take the pot.

"I share your sentiments, sir," Lucas said. "Winner takes all? Is that the bet? What's in the pot plus your deed against all the money I have on the table?"

"Yes."

Lucas nodded.

The rancher let out a whoop of glee and dropped his hand onto the table. A sigh went up from the crowd.

"I been working here for three years, and I never saw four aces show up like that before," Claudette said. She heaved a big sigh, sent her ample bosoms shaking, and turned away. Her interest in Lucas disappeared in a flash of aces.

The rancher reached for the pot but again Lucas stopped him.

"You haven't seen my hand yet."

"Hell, man, you can't beat me. You were careless and showed a trey. No matter what you got, you can't beat me."

"I was careless showing you the three," Lucas said, lying. He had made sure the rancher saw the card. It was all part of the game's ebb and flow, enticing the highest bets possible. "You neglected to see the other cards."

Another gasp went up around the crowd.

"He's got a straight flush, deuce through six of clubs."

"You are beaten, sir."

Lucas pushed the man's hand away, scooped up the money in a pile, and then reached across the table to collect the deed to a ranch. Even if it wasn't worth what the man claimed, Lucas knew he could parlay it into a considerable sum. A hint of a gold strike on the land would let him divide it up into hundreds of smaller tracts, each worth more than a thousand to an avid prospector.

"You can't have the Rolling J!"

The rancher shot to his feet, staggered, and regained his balance, then had his six-shooter out and held in a surprisingly steady grip. Determination burned through the haze of alcohol.

"Please, sir," Lucas said. He had no chance to draw his own weapon. Exchanging a .22 round with a .45 had to be a bad bet. Even if the situation had been reversed, his Colt New Line out and the rancher's Peacemaker in its holster, he would have been at a severe—and deadly—disadvantage.

"I don't know how you did that, but you cheated."

"Sir! I did not."

"You're not taking the deed to my ranch!"

Lucas saw how the circle of customers around him widened. They were torn between getting close enough to see a gambler take a bullet in the gut and being in the line of fire themselves. Self-preservation won out for most of the crowd.

"My reputation, sir," Lucas said, steering the rancher away from anyone who might overhear. The man pulled away so he could keep his six-shooter leveled at Lucas's gut. "Please. Listen to me. Let's talk this over."

"There's nothing to talk over."

"I can't just give you back the deed, not when everyone thinks I have won it fair and square. My reputation, my honor! Besmirched! Everyone would think they can lose to me and do nothing but ask for their lost wager to be returned. I cannot make a living that way. But I have no real interest in your ranch."

"Then I'll keep it and—"

"Please, understand, sir. I can't *give* it to you. My reputation as a gambler would suffer." Lucas moved around the table but didn't get too close. The way the rancher's finger whitened with tension on the trigger showed how close he was to dying. "You value your ranch, I value my reputation as much. However, I have a solution so we both come out winners. I have no desire to own a ranch. Why, I am unsure which end of a cow the grass goes in, though I do think I can find where the digested product comes out. Such a business has no appeal for me since I spend my nights swilling bad liquor and fending off soiled doves as I deal faro or indulge in a game of five-card draw."

"I can keep my ranch?"

"And I will emerge with my reputation intact as a high-stakes gambler. I propose a single draw, high card wins. I will put the deed I have just won against your stake. You do have something more to bet?"

"No, it's all there." The rancher motioned with the pistol but his aim returned to dead center on Lucas's chest. "I don't have anything to put up."

"Well," Lucas said, pursing his lips and looking intent in thought. "That's not really true. You have that fine six-gun. A brand spanking new Colt Peacemaker, isn't it? You put it up against the deed, we draw, and high card wins."

Lucas watched as the proposal rattled around behind the man's bloodshot eyes.

"I'll win? You can make sure of that?"

"I am a professional gambler. Knowing the odds is how I make a living."

"All right," the rancher said. "Let's do it so I can get the hell out of this gin mill." He spat toward a brass spittoon and missed. Only the cowboys getting chaw on their boots moved. More than one surged forward to get retribution, but the promise of a second act in the card game caused their partners to hold them back.

Lucas edged back around the table and then announced the wager loudly enough to draw back the crowd. He wasn't surprised to see Claudette return. If she would stand behind him, her ample fleshy Front Range pressing outward might distract the rancher, but Lucas hardly needed that.

"The turn of the card will decide who wins the Rolling J Ranch. The deed is bet against about the finest six-gun I have ever seen." Lucas motioned for the rancher to put the six-shooter on the table next to the deed.

He shuffled, pushed the deck across for the rancher to cut. The man made a big show of doing so, then pushed the deck across the table using a shaking finger. Claudette had placed a fresh shot of whiskey at his elbow. The rancher knocked the liquid popskull back. He tried to put the glass back on the table and missed. It hit the floor with a loud ringing sound and rolled away.

Other than the piano player continuing his assault on anything he played, there wasn't a sound in the room. All attention focused on a single table. Lucas was aware of how the crowd sucked in a collective breath and held it.

He kept his eyes on the rancher. The man wobbled a bit and almost followed his shot glass to the floor, then caught himself on the table edge and pulled it closer. Lucas scooted his chair after the table. The nickel-plated Colt gleamed on the table next to the sweat-stained deed. The pile of chips and greenbacks had been shoved aside, as if mere money no longer mattered.

For Lucas Stanton it didn't.

"Draw," he said.

The rancher cut the deck and peeled off the top card. He flipped it over. A gasp went up. Jack of clubs. The rancher grinned ear to ear, and the crowd's pent-up breath released in a huge gust like a chinook gusting off the Montana Crazies.

"Smoked you good."

"My turn." Lucas moved fast, cutting the deck and slipping a card to lay facedown. He slid a fingernail under the edge, then flicked his finger. The card stood on edge for a moment, then dropped.

The rancher gaped. Lucas moved like a striking snake, shoving the deed onto the pile of money and chips—and grabbing the Colt.

"I couldn't lose! You said—"

"The queen of diamonds will beat you every time." Lucas slipped his finger around the trigger as he hefted the gun. "Why don't you leave now that you've lost?"

"You can't take my ranch!" The rancher surged to his feet and leaned forward. He looked down as Lucas lifted the cocked six-shooter and aimed it at the man's exposed chest.

"I'd offer you a drink as consolation, but you have had too many already. Good evening."

"You haven't heard the last of this!"

The rancher forced himself back and staggered away, shoving customers out of his way as he exited the saloon. Lucas waited until he had vanished before gingerly lowering the hammer and placing the six-gun on the table. The piano was still the only sound to be heard. Lucas knew what had to be done.

"Drinks for everyone. On me!"

Lefty had already begun pulling bottles of whiskey from

a case under the bar. He knew as well as Lucas what had to be done to keep the peace in the Emerald City.

The gambler found himself pummeled as everyone wanted to slap him on the back, but this died down fast when Lefty began pouring at the bar. The only one remaining was Claudette. Her lips brushed his ear as she whispered all that she would do for him. Later. After they left the saloon and were alone.

Lucas had to laugh. What she had to offer was fine and he had wondered what it would take for him to find out, but the night was young, he had a pile of money and the deed to a big ranch, and there were so many in the saloon wanting to gamble. Lucas laughed heartily. Lady Luck was his whore tonight. Others would gamble with him—and he would win!

2

A few minutes after he lost the deed to the ranch to a merchant he thought was bluffing with his full house, Lucas also lost Claudette's attention. She increasingly left his side to take drinks to others in the Emerald City and even ran an errand for Lefty that took her away for almost a half hour. In that time Lucas burned through the pile of chips with bets he shouldn't have lost and had only a few greenbacks left. Not only Claudette but Lady Luck had abandoned him. He tried to be philosophical about it. He had quite a run before the cards turned against him. Memory of owning a huge ranch somewhere out in Middle Park would stick with him for quite a while.

After losing yet another hand to a cowboy with a knack for drawing to inside straights, he leaned back and looked around the saloon. He carefully took out his watch, opened the case, and as always, stared for a moment at the picture of the woman in the lid, before deciphering the time. Most of the painted roman numerals were gone, leaving him only the large brass hands and a few specks to guess at what was revealed.

"What time is it, Mr. Stanton?"

"Time for me to quit," he said to the young cowboy. "It's telling me if I stayed for just one more hand, you'd be in possession of what I have left."

He squared up the stack of bills, riffled through them, and got an idea of his night's profits. For all he had won and then lost, it was skimpy. He had begun with a hundred-dollar stake and now had only two hundred. Still, any profit was better than none at all.

"Lefty, see that my friend gets a drink on me."

The barkeep inclined his head, then repeated the gesture. Lucas left the table, settled his elegant jacket across his broad shoulders, and carefully put his hands on the sticky bar to lean forward as Lefty whispered, "You owe me for the round you bought after you won."

"A hundred dollars should cover it," he said, counting out the bills onto the bar.

Lefty's huge hand slapped down and snatched away the roll of greenbacks. With surprising dexterity, the one-armed barkeep counted out all but seven singles. These he shoved back toward Lucas. The gambler smiled ruefully, then tucked the bills into his vest pocket across from his watch.

"You owe me more but this will do if you come in and deal faro for a couple hours tomorrow night."

"Not for free!"

They dickered until Lucas squeezed the promise of a fifty-fifty split from the man. Working halftime for the house wasn't to his liking, but he stood to get back his stake and not end up a loser.

"You got a bonus comin' for the work, too," Lefty said. The man's pale eyes glowed with an inner light that had less to do with a desire for money than lust. This told Lucas what he needed to know.

"When did Carmela get back to Denver?"

Carmela Thompson had a voice like a morning dove and a body to make it difficult for any man to notice her true singing ability. Lucas had crossed paths with her a dozen times or more, often spending as long as a week in the same emporium before she continued her concert tour throughout the West and he moved on to another cow town or boomtown where miners valued a moment's thrill at the poker table over actually winning. For all the times they had worked under the same roof, he and she had never spent a night under the same blanket.

It wasn't for lack of trying on Lucas's part either. He knew he was a handsome man, dressed expensively, and preferred the finer things—when he could afford them. The last time he and Carmela had met had been in New Orleans. He had been flush and willing to spend lavishly. She was as willing to receive his largesse and had proven to be a witty conversationalist and a lady who would be as at home with the crowned heads of Europe as she was in a dive. Lucas cherished their time together, but somehow she had once more escaped his net of compliments and gifts intended to win a woman's heart.

He remembered too well standing at the foot of Poydras Street, near the dock, watching as she took the captain's hand to help her onto the riverboat going north to Saint Louis. The sternwheeler had rounded the oxbow crescent in the river and disappeared for more than ten minutes before he had shaken himself free of her spell and gone in search of company at one of the myriad cotillions always filling the Vieux Carré with uplifting music during the winter months.

That night he had found a willing Creole belle with midnight hair spun up in a fancy whirl dotted with pearls, a beguiling accent, and rouged lips that begged to be kissed. He had also found her lover, who carried a *colchemarde*. The sword cane had a wicked edge and an even deadlier tip, which Lucas avoided only through a spot of luck as the cuckolded lover slipped in the black loamy street in his haste to slay his paramour's coxcomb.

After that he had seen Carmella twice again, the last time on the stage at the rear of the Emerald City Dance Hall and Drinking Emporium not six months earlier.

"Her tour isn't going well?" Lucas asked.

"A sellout wherever she goes. I had to offer twice what I paid before," Lefty complained, only there was no hint of outrage in his voice. Like Lucas, like so many others, he would pay any price to be in the same room as Carmela Thompson.

"Does she still travel with . . . what's his name?"

Lefty grunted.

"Her and the lawman had words when she was here before. I offered her a permanent job and to get rid of the marshal so he wouldn't bother her again."

"She turned you down, of course."

"Yeah. She said being in one town too long gave her the collywobbles."

"Moreover," Lucas said, "she is more than capable of getting rid of unwanted bodies on her own."

Lefty shot him a hard look, then laughed and slapped him on the back hard enough to rattle his teeth.

"You know her too well."

"Ah, not well enough, but rest assured I will return to the Emerald City to deal faro and to appreciate her dulcet tones."

"She sings pretty good, too."

"Good night." Lucas touched the brim of his bowler hat and strutted toward the rear of the saloon. The piano player sprawled across the bench with a pretty waiter girl's head in his lap. Both had passed out.

Lucas considered playing a quick song to see if either of the dreamers stirred, then decided against it. He hopped up onto the stage and pushed through dirty curtains. He paused for a moment looking out over the mostly deserted Emerald City. When Carmela sang, they would be packed shoulder to shoulder. The waitresses would be working at a dead run to keep the thirsty men in whiskey and beer, and in the moment Carmela swept onto the stage in her lavish costume and struck a pose, for that moment there would be silence. Her smile would ignite catcalls and suggestions both heartfelt and improbable from her audience.

Then she would sing.

Lucas let the curtains fall into place, blocking off the room. He would be across the room at a faro table. His view of her performance might suffer, but her song always cut through the loudest of cheers. Quick steps took him behind the stage to the pair of dressing rooms. Lefty already had a crudely painted sign with Carmela's name on it nailed to one door. He reached for the doorknob, then pulled away. He saw no reason to go into the empty dressing room now. And when Carmela occupied it, an invitation to enter was not likely to be forthcoming.

A man could dream.

Lucas settled his bowler hat at a jaunty angle and went out the back door into a long, narrow alley. The brick wall facing him belonged to another saloon, but he avoided the

Points North because the owner was a son of a bitch and made no pretense of running an honest game. Lucas matched any other gambler's dexterity and ability to deal seconds or pull any card from the deck he wanted, only he never cheated. It was beneath his dignity.

He pressed his hand against an empty coat pocket. The rancher had even lost in a fair high-card showdown. Lucas regretted not keeping the man's Peacemaker. It had been a fine shooting iron. As clearly as if he still sat at the table, he played through the hand where he had lost it in a bet against eight dollars and a small leather pouch that might have held gold dust.

"I should have known two pair, jacks and eights, wasn't good enough," he chided himself as he came to the end of the alley and looked up and down the deserted street. Even in Denver's wildest, most notorious sections along Tremont, 4 A.M. proved the boundary of human endurance for gambling, booze, and women.

"Hey, you! Stop!"

In the deserted street at this time of morning he knew better than to loiter. With two men shouting at him and pointing, he reacted instinctively. He walked briskly, then broke out in a run for the doors of the Erstwhile Saloon and Hotel down the street. Lucas skidded to a halt, then shot a look behind him. The two men who had lain in wait outside the Emerald City's front door were still running for him. Worse, coming out of the Erstwhile Saloon and Hotel were two more men he recognized.

The rancher and his weasel of a sidekick pushed back their coats to expose six-shooters hanging at their hips. It hadn't taken the man long at all to get another smoke wagon.

"You're going to give it back!" The rancher drew the

six-gun and cocked it. In the quiet night it sounded like a massive clockwork ratchet falling onto a cogwheel. "I'll cut you down if you don't stop!"

Lucas lived by his wits and figuring odds. Talking his way out of this predicament didn't look like an appealing prospect.

"I lost it," he shouted over his shoulder as he ran south along the side of the Erstwhile.

All the doors were secured for the night. He might bash in a window and try to enter that way, but the hotel had a reputation of dealing with unwanted guests that afforded him a slimmer chance of survival than avoiding the rancher and his hired hands.

He darted down a side street, only to find the two who had waited at the saloon were ahead of him. They had taken a side street to cut off his escape. With a deft twist, he changed directions and plunged into deep shadows and large piles of garbage. Lucas dodged the worst of the rotting debris, though he scared away some of the more cowardly rats. Two as large as house cats fixed red eyes on him, bared their fangs, and dared him to take away their early morning repast.

Vaulting a crate, he hit the pavement on the far side and slipped. Garbage on his boot soles turned every step into one on ice. He skidded about, caught himself, and found another alleyway cleaner than the first. He pressed into a doorway, heart hammering. Forcing himself to breathe in slow, deep drafts settled him somewhat and kept his pursuers from hearing heavy breathing. He reached into his pocket and drew the .22-caliber pistol. Against men hefting .45s, it seemed ineffectual, but the rosewood grips reassured him. A tiny bullet to the head ended a life as surely as a heavy 250-grain hunk of lead through the heart. All he had to do was make every shot count.

All he had to do. All . . .

He held his breath and pressed harder against the door when the rancher stopped at the mouth of the alley, looking around frantically.

"Dammit, he was here a minute ago. How'd you lose him?"

"How'd *you* lose him, boss? You was closer than Relf and me."

For a moment Lucas thought escape would be easier than he anticipated. The rancher lifted his heavy .45, pointed it at his henchman, and cocked the weapon. The report as it discharged made him wince. But the ranch hand who had mouthed off to his employer still stood upright in the street. The rancher had fired past the man's left ear.

"You deafened me. I cain't hear nuthin'." The man clapped his hand over his left ear and swung around. Lucas prepared to fire if the man saw him as he looked down the alley. The nearness of the rancher's bullet robbed the henchman of concentration. He wasn't in any mood to look for the quarry. He turned back, hand still covering his ear. "What'd you go and do that for?"

"To get your attention," the rancher said. His words slurred. He hadn't stopped drinking after he left the Emerald City. "Don't stand around and lollygag. Find the bastard! Find him or I'll fire you so fast yer ass'll scorch!"

The deafened cowboy and his partner set out down the street, leaving the rancher and his whining conscience behind. Lucas considered a shot to put the rancher out of his misery, when he heard the scrawny ranch hand's complaints.

"Boss, what you gonna tell the missus? She's not gonna take it good you lost the Rolling J in a poker game."

"I didn't lose it. He cheated me out of it. He was dealing off the bottom of the deck. You saw him. You saw that, didn't you, Justin?"

The rancher thrust out his belly and bumped against the skinny man, shoving him into the middle of the street. A distant gas lamp provided enough illumination for Lucas to get a good shot at the rancher. He lifted his Colt New Line, steadied his hand against the door frame, and put his thumb on the hammer to draw it back for the shot. Just as he would have taken the shot, the other cowboy, Relf, stepped around and provided inadvertent cover for his employer. Lucas relaxed his trigger finger because this situation was handled by a better tactic than gunning down the rancher's hired hands. Cut the head off a snake and the body dies. If he took out the rancher, his wranglers would light out running and never stop.

Lucas wasn't a cold-blooded killer, but circumstances sometimes dictated the way he had to behave. Odds were better shooting the rancher than letting him go on his merry way.

He swallowed hard. The rancher's idea of merry entailed a necktie party if he didn't get his deed back. Since Lucas had lost it to someone he hardly remembered—the cards were vivid in his mind, the other gambler less so—he was in no position to turn over the deed. He couldn't even tell the rancher where to find the man who now boasted of owning the Rolling J.

The way the cards had turned that night, the deed might have changed hands a half dozen more times.

"Jist tell her you don't know how that fella got the paper," Justin said.

"He's not likely to ride up all alone. He'll have Sheriff Gonzales with him."

"Gonzales hates your guts after you—"

"Shut up. You're not telling me anything I don't know. That's the reason that gambler'll take possession of the ranch with the law backing him up."

"Well, if we jist kill him, that'll be all right, won't it?"

The rancher muttered and paced about, casting a long, dancing shadow from the distant streetlamp.

"Hell, I don't know. Why'd you let me do a damned fool thing like betting the ranch? You know how I get when I've been drinking."

"You said you couldn't lose."

"He cheated me. That's the only explanation. I can get Judge Setrakian to swear out an arrest warrant. That'll hammer a bung into his hole for sure."

"The judge is on the far side of the Front Range. It's two days back, maybe three if we haul our supplies, too."

"I'll haul something and it won't be supplies."

Lucas lowered his pistol and tried to will himself invisible. The rancher peered straight at him. The heavy shadows hid him from all but an owl's eyesight.

"He must have gone down this alley. Where else could he have gone?"

"I don't know, boss. He—"

"Down this alley. Shoot anything that moves."

To emphasize his point, the rancher triggered another round. The slug struck brick and whined away into the darkness. Lucas couldn't keep from flinching. He straightened and hoped that he hadn't been spotted. The rancher left him no choice but to shoot his way out.

As he raised his Colt, a shout came from the far end of the alley.

"Ain't down here, boss."

Lucas almost choked as his gorge rose and clogged his

throat. The other two cowboys were coming from the opposite end of the alley. He was caught between the two pairs of men. He suddenly knew how a walnut in a nut-cracker felt. They had him boxed in, and shooting his way out with such a puny pistol gave him terrible odds.

Footsteps from both directions came closer to his hiding place.

3

Bullets or edged words weren't going to save him. Lucas looked up and saw no chance of getting to the roof of the building or the one on the other side of the alley. He spun and tried the doorknob. Locked. With the sounds of footsteps coming toward him from each end of the alley, he dropped to his knees and pressed his face close to the lock. Deftly taking two slender steel strips from his collar—no need for collar stays if he ended up in a coffin—he probed about inside the lock.

If it had been more complex, he would have been caught. As the rancher came within a few paces of the door, Lucas slipped the lock, spun about, and leaned heavily on the door. Lifting one foot, he pressed it against the door. Every screech of unoiled hinges and feel of air from inside the building gusting past caused him to cringe. The door clicked shut as the four in the alley converged.

Lucas spun about, not caring if he ruined his pants, and

pressed his back against the door. He reached up in time to grab the doorknob as someone outside checked to see if it was locked. Lucas's palm was sweaty, and hanging on to the knob caused a strain all the way up into his shoulder, but he hung on for dear life.

Muffled words came to him through the thick wood door.

"He didn't go inside. The door's locked. You idiots sure he didn't get past you?"

"Aw, boss, nuthin' got by us. You're always bad-mouthin' me and Relf and we about had the most of it."

Lucas heard inarticulate shouts that faded. The four men walked out of the alley, going back toward the street. He gave a huge shudder, then laughed in relief. He pulled off his bowler hat and tossed it onto the floor in front of him. Eyes closed, he banged his head against the door a few times to convince himself he had survived. After swiping sweat from his forehead, he got his legs under him and stood. Finding his knees unusually shaky, he braced himself for a moment until the last vestiges of panic disappeared. He lived by his wits. Avoiding shoot-outs with irate ranchers was a far superior course of action than shooting it out.

When his hands no longer shook, he bent over and used his two steel strips to lock the door. He felt safer with the bolt once more thrown. Any of the men on his trail could break the door down with a single kick, but it gave him a sense of safety nonetheless.

False security could be more dangerous than none at all, but Lucas willingly accepted whatever flimsy ward against confrontation he could find.

He edged through the darkness and found shelves with supplies. Working more with his nimble fingers than sight, he rummaged through some of the boxes. Lucas recoiled when he touched something big and hairy in one. He held the box at arm's length and moved to a doorway leading to a small office. Light from a gas lamp down the street filtered in to let him see what he had found.

He frowned as he held up a handful of hair. Instead of a scalp taken in battle, he held a theatrical wig. He had seen a fine production of *The Tempest* at the Broadway Theater with less expensive wigs. Poking through the box revealed tubes of theatrical makeup and things that would do Carmela Thompson proud. Sliding the box back onto a shelf, he looked around the storeroom, thinking he had broken into a theatrical agent's office.

The contents of the other boxes puzzled him. He found envelopes filled with dust. Running some between his thumb and forefinger told him it was grainier than ordinary sand, but not enough to be specially marked. Tapping out some into his palm and holding it up showed no telltale glitter as he would expect from gold. Whoever ran this office seemed to keep worthless dust. The other boxes contained nothing more than office supplies and several different styles of shirts.

Lucas examined the clothing with a jaundiced eye. For every expensive shirt, there were two work shirts. Checked flannel more in keeping with a miner's outfit was stuffed in with denim shirts he had seen worn by railroad workers. The one frilly-fronted starched dress shirt worthy of a high-society cotillion was two sizes too small for him. He left the clothing and other odds and ends and went into the main office.

Two desks almost filled the room to overflowing. A tall wooden file cabinet between them had a drawer partially opened. Lucas idly leafed through the files inside, not bothering to read any of them. Whatever went on here no longer interested him. He had spent enough time for the rancher and his hired hands to have retreated to a saloon to continue their bender. Or since dawn challenged the feeble gas lamps out in the street, they should be feeling hunger pangs and need breakfast. This was the situation Lucas found himself in.

A night of drinking, even moderately as he did, was no substitute for solid food. He went to the front door and tested the knob. It was securely locked. He pulled the slender steel strips out and began fiddling with the lock. More complicated than the back door, this lock finally yielded to his skill. He had apprenticed himself to a locksmith for almost eight months to get a steady income and a place to sleep as he gained experience gambling. This had worked out well for him on both counts. There were few locks he could not understand and open quickly. And he had learned odds and reading people over the long nights spent gambling.

The door opened and Lucas stepped out. He froze. Then he slowly backed into the office again and silently closed the door. When the rancher and his right-hand man marched past, Lucas sank down below the plate glass in the door. From this angle the rising sun caught gold letters and turned them into a flaming banner. He read backward.

GREAT WEST DETECTIVE AGENCY.

He had burgled the office of a detective. That explained the wig and the different styles of shirts. The operative fancied himself some kind of Allan Pinkerton, wearing disguises as he went about his investigation. From the simple furniture and sparsity of decorations, the detective—the Great West Detective Agency detective—wasn't rolling in the money.

Like a prairie dog, Lucas popped up, looked around, saw his enemy, and sank back. The rancher was nothing if not persistent. Lucas fancied himself to have that trait, but he saw how it could be difficult for others to endure. He wished the rancher would give up and go home.

Legs pulled up, he put his head on his knees for just a moment, then came awake with a start. He had dozed off. From the look of the sunlight causing the lettering to form a banner of shadows across the far wall over the desk, he had been asleep for a half hour. Another quick look outside showed more people stirring now. Denver was waking and commerce began.

He saw nothing of the rancher or his three cowboys. Heaving a sigh, he opened the door and stepped out to take a deep breath. It felt good to be alive. He pulled the door shut behind him, then froze when a sharp command pinned him to the spot.

"Stop!"

He moved his hand to the bulge where his Colt was stashed. Lucas half turned, then forgot the pistol and instead concentrated on getting his clothing in as good order as possible. The woman rushing toward him had a most delightful bustle. Raven-wing dark hair had been tucked under a wide-brimmed hat more suitable for a day in the country than business in the city, but the rest of her outfit had cost a pretty penny. The fine material flowed about her, hinting at the outline of the well-curved corset beneath, the skirts whispered sweet nothings, and her petite shoes clicked rapidly against the cobblestones.

"Don't go. I need to speak to you!"

Lucas made certain she spoke to him. He touched the brim of his bowler hat and bowed slightly.

"How may I be of service, miss?"

"Don't close your office. Not yet." She pouted. A strand of black hair like delicately spun midnight drifted across her bright blue eyes. She brushed it away without noticing she did so. Lowering her chin, she looked up at him. "Please. I need your expertise."

Lucas silently pushed the door open and ushered her into the office. He grabbed a chair and held it for her. A hint of perfume caused his nostrils to expand in appreciation.

"Spikenard," she said.

"I beg your pardon?"

"My perfume. Men always notice it. It is made from a plant found only in Nepal, in the Himalayas."

"A very rare scent, to be sure. It fits you."

"How do you mean?" She looked at him and batted her eyes, the long dark lashes moving seductively.

"A rare perfume for a woman of rare beauty." He flashed her a smile that melted feminine hearts. She smiled almost shyly, but a sadness tinged the woman's bow-shaped lips.

"I feared I would miss you when I saw you leaving."

"For you, I will stay open around the clock."

Lucas forced himself not to reach for his watch to check the time. The real detective and owner of the agency would show up anytime now. The streets showed the traffic expected in a thriving frontier town and the capital of a newly minted state. More riders went in the direction of the capitol building than otherwise, but heavily laden wagons began the daily deliveries necessary to feed thirty thousand residents. So much activity meant any self-respecting businessman would be out and about in it to rustle up the most revenue possible.

"You are so kind. I am sure I am keeping you from very important work."

"Not at all," Lucas said. "How can I assist you?"

"Well, sir—"

"Lucas Stanton," he said, immediately realizing it wasn't smart to give her his real name. "Rather, you can call me that since, of course, I often use assumed names to solve my clients' cases." He had learned to stop yammering when he realized how badly he floundered with a lie. He did so now. He leaned back and made a gesture that he hoped kept her talking so he didn't have to.

"I am Amanda Baldridge." She sat primly, with her hands folded in her lap and eyes downcast.

"Miss Baldridge, I—"

"Please, call me Amanda. My needs are so . . . personal. Such familiarity—and may I call you Lucas?—puts me more at ease over a most disturbing matter."

"Lucas is fine," he said. "What is the nature of this problem?"

"He was kidnapped!"

Lucas sat up. He had not expected anything serious.

"A missing person is best dealt with by the Denver police. They have the manpower to conduct a real search."

"I went to them immediately and a sergeant at the front desk was very rude to me. He laughed, then threatened to have me thrown out!"

Lucas understood a lawman wanting to wrap his arms around such a delightful package as presented by Amanda Baldridge. He frowned a little when he came to the quick conclusion there was more than the woman was telling.

"Who is this missing gentleman? How long has it been since the kidnapping?"

"Yesterday morning," she said, taking a handkerchief from her sleeve and dabbing at her eyes. For the life of him, Lucas saw no tears yet the woman sniffed and continued to brush her eyes, carefully avoiding any ruin to her makeup.

"Why don't you give me the full details?"

"Are you going to write all this down?" She looked at

the bare desk. Not even pen and ink marred the vast expanse of polished wood.

Lucas tapped the side of his head and smiled in encouragement. Amanda nodded in understanding.

"When I awoke yesterday morning, he was gone. He is always beside me in bed, under the covers."

Lucas listened less to what she said now and concentrated more on her lovely features. Although she didn't wear a wedding ring, that meant little in these modern times. What distressed him was the longing in her voice for her missing paramour.

"I thought he had gone outside for breakfast."

"Outside?"

"If I haven't prepared something special for him, he goes out to kill something. He's so cute."

"Your husband is cute when he is killing?"

Amanda looked up, startled. Then she smiled wanly and dabbed away some more nonexistent tears.

"He is not my husband, Lucas. I cannot imagine what you were thinking! He is my puppy. Tovarich is a Russian wolfhound."

"Your dog?"

"My itty-bitty little puppy."

"The police wouldn't look for a lost dog?"

"That is right. It is so cruel of them, because Tovarich was stolen. He was spirited away by evil men. I just know it."

"Was anything else stolen from your room?"

"No, nothing. Only Tovarich."

Lucas refrained from asking if there was something special about the puppy. The love in Amanda's voice almost approached reverence.

"Do you know anyone who would steal your dog?" He left it unsaid what men on the frontier would have taken rather than the dog if they had sneaked into her bedroom and found her asleep.

"No. I have driven myself quite crazy trying to imagine who might have stolen my puppy dog."

Lucas held back his opinion that, no matter how lovely she was, Amanda was crazy as a bedbug. The dog had run off or, more likely, become the morning meal for a coyote or a pack of wolves. Although wild animals avoided Denver because of the influx of people, they also came to live off the garbage. Nosing through a pile of rotting meat from a slaughterhouse was easier than tracking down your own four-legged meal. And only the night before he had seen two rats which would prove a match for any small dog.

"Here is my address. It is a boardinghouse."

She fumbled in her purse, found what she wanted, and passed over a scrap of paper with an address written on it in pencil.

"There might be a neighbor who saw a man or men with your Tovarich yesterday morning," he said, not believing a word of it. Lucas tucked the paper into his vest pocket and stood. "I hate to be abrupt, Amanda, but I was on my way out."

Her nose wrinkled, and she dabbed more at her eyes. All the while she studied him from head to toe.

"You are going undercover?"

It took Lucas an instant to realize how disheveled he was after his late-night escape from the rancher and his henchmen. His pants were torn in places, and his once elegant coat had been smudged in more places than he could count. A good cleaning would return it to respectability. And he ought to tend to that right away since he wanted to look sharp for Carmela Thompson's debut that night.

He wanted to look sharp for Carmela. After too many brushes with her in the past, it was time to press his advantage for a lengthier encounter with a woman who didn't sleep with her dog.

"Please don't mention the way I look," Lucas said, moving behind her and holding the chair as a hint for her to leave. "I sometimes adopt a disguise for the purpose of a case."

"There won't be any need to do so when you go to find the men who stole Tovarich."

She preceded him to the door. "Will this be enough for a retainer?" She held out a wad of greenbacks large enough to choke a cow. "It's only a hundred dollars. I can give you that much more when you recover Tovarich and return him to me."

Startled by the large sum, Lucas instinctively held out his hand. Amanda dropped the greenbacks into it.

"I'm so happy you will take the case, Lucas. You must begin the search as soon as possible. I don't want those thieves to take Tovarich to some faraway place where I will never see him again."

"The case I intended to work on is quite pressing," he said. He closed the door behind him and considered locking it. To do so without a key required him to use his lock picks. Amanda might believe he did this to show off. Instead he decided to leave the door open. There wasn't much to steal in the office.

"I feel you are a dependable man, Lucas. You will do your best." She cast a quick look at the door. "You and the Great West Detective Agency."

She reached out shyly and put her hand on his arm, then turned away and hurried off. All he could see was the sway of her bustle. He took a couple steps, then stopped to look around the business district for any laundry where he might get his coat cleaned. Something about the man and woman coming toward him made him step to one side. His instinct was vindicated when they stopped in front of the agency door.

They were plainly dressed, nothing too expensive. But clean and neat. Lucas thought they might be wearing their Sunday-go-to-meeting clothes, but not knowing them better kept him from making this assumption. The man's brown suit had been tailored to fit, though his shirt cuff peeking out was worn. He wore a string tie that did not match his coat, though the color difference was subtle. He might not even have noticed, but Lucas did. The man wore no jewelry other than a gold wedding band. He didn't even sport a gold watch chain or fob.

The woman's gray dress was similarly unembellished with even a broach or locket. Her hand moved restlessly, but Lucas caught the golden flash of a wedding ring that matched the man's. Both were of a height a few inches shorter than Lucas's own five foot ten. The man was beginning to sport a beer gut, but the woman was thin as a rail and likely as tough. She had that look about her.

The exact opposite attitude showed in her husband. Lucas had seen men bossed about by women before. There was no question who wore the pants in this family.

He touched the slip of paper with Amanda's address and then the hundred dollars she had given him. He had no reason to look for a lost dog and one likely to have become a meal for a hungry predator, but honor required him to do something about her plight. Hiring the detectives from the agency satisfied his honor and possibly returned the dog to its owner. He started for the couple, then turned and pretended to watch a fight across the street.

"Not here yet. Where can he be, dear?"

"How should I know?"

The woman scowled. If a smile had ever graced her lips, she might have been attractive. Lucas would never classify her as more, not even pretty. Her angular features reminded him of a schoolteacher he had hated. Even the chopping motion made with her left hand was similar. But this was not Miss Draper. That harridan would be sixty now, and this woman wasn't a day past thirty.

"It makes no sense, putting an ad in the newspaper for assistants and then not being here to interview us."

"You'll make a great detective with logic like that," she said. The sarcasm flowed thicker than honey but nowhere near as sweet.

"How long should we wait for him, dear?"

"As long as it takes. This is the only job you're qualified for."

"And since there are two office positions open, we can work together."

Lucas kept from laughing at the man's tone. He mixed wistfulness with outrage. If his wife noticed, she made no comment about working together.

Lucas took his hand away from Amanda's address and the money she had given him. The two in front of the detective agency wanted jobs; they didn't work for the Great West Detective Agency and would be unable to find the missing dog with any more skill than he had at his disposal. And if Lucas was any judge, skill would have nothing to do with finding the dog. It would be pure luck.

He was willing to use up some of Lady Luck's largesse

for a hundred and the promise of more later. Besides, he needed something to keep him occupied while the laundry worked to clean his coat for the evening's tryst with Carmela.

Lucas went off whistling "The Cuckoo's Nest" as he hunted for a shop capable of cleaning his jacket without leaving spots or holes.

4

With his coat being cleaned and his remaining clothing torn and stinking of garbage, Lucas saw that he would get nowhere in the neighborhood where Amanda lived and the dog had been stolen. Matching the woman's obvious wealth, the well-kept boardinghouses lining the street spoke of society a notch above where he dwelled. Even walking down the middle of the street garnered unwanted glares and more than one woman closing her door. The sound of a locking bar dropping into place quickly followed.

As he walked, Lucas appeared not to be too attentive to the details of Amanda's house. It was a two-story house with a neat lawn and a lawn jockey in front for the visitors to tie up their horses. He suspected only Thoroughbreds were so tethered. A smile crept to his lips. That might describe the occupants of the house, too, but he had no real information about that. Who in the boardinghouse might steal a young lady's puppy dog? Unless he barged in, he would never find out. His quick trip down the street had already drawn the attention of two policemen. As he sped up, so did they, closing the gap between them.

He had dealt with lawmen all over Denver and knew many of them by name. These two might have been employed as specials, guards restricted to patrolling this single neighborhood. The residents might easily pay for the added protection. If so, he needed to speak to them to find what had happened the night Tovarich disappeared. The two guards might be a part of the theft—or had been paid off to look the other way.

He cut down a street to his right. They followed at a run now. Lucas had learned nothing and wasn't going to find out any more without appearing as if he belonged here. He saw no point in being caught and interrogated. He ran faster than either of the policemen, but they seemed determined.

Panting, he finally reached a spot off Larimer Square where he could catch his breath without being beset by men with wooden clubs or slung shot, that nasty piece of iron hung on the end of a chain Lucas avoided whenever he could. As he recovered from his run, he watched the street traffic. Everyone headed in one direction, drawn by a deep bass voice extolling virtue and rectitude. He followed and then moved into the middle of the crowd for further anonymity. Being coshed by the specials was less likely if he hunkered down and seemed as attentive as the others pressing shoulder to shoulder with him. The feigned interest became real when he recognized the man on the crate. The voice was differently pitched, raspy, possibly from some throat injury since the man wore a thick scarf wrapped tightly around his neck, but the tempo and the words themselves became increasingly familiar. Old habits died hard.

Lucas pushed closer. He wanted to listen to a real master work the crowd.

Lucas was beholden to the Preacher for staking him when he first arrived in Denver, down to his last dime and in trouble with tinhorn gamblers for cutting into their action. The Preacher had gone through a saloon, preaching of the evils of gambling and illicit sex with the Cyprians working there. The owner had thrown him out, which suited the man just fine. He picked the saloon keeper's pocket and had given Lucas most of it to return to the gambling tables, where he had finally hit a winning streak. He had repaid the Preacher threefold but that hadn't been the only time Lucas had needed to call on the man for his questionable charity.

The man began his spiel, and Lucas found himself caught up in the power and rhythm of the words. He wasn't a religious man and he doubted the Preacher was either, but he had never asked. He might not like the answer.

The collection plate went around and most people added a few dollars to it. If nothing else, the Preacher gave them a fine show, castigating sinners even as he detailed their transgressions in graphic detail. Lucas dropped in five dollars and passed the plate on, watching how the men reacted. At the edge of the crowd he saw one man put in two bits as he palmed the five-dollar bill Lucas had contributed. The plate went on and the man, so tall he stood a full head above anyone else in the crowd, edged away, then turned and walked off briskly.

Lucas pushed his way through the crowd and followed. The tall man set a fast pace, long legs devouring the distance at twice the pace Lucas could comfortably maintain. Only the occasional flash of sunlight reflecting off the man's bald pate kept Lucas on the trail.

He stopped in front of the Merry Widow Saloon and peered into the dim interior. Again came the flash of light off the man's shaven head. Lucas pushed through the swinging doors and paused as he always did when entering a new saloon. A back storage room door was padlocked. A staircase went up to the cribs, but no soiled doves were in the saloon. It was too early for them to begin plying their trade. Only three customers drank. Two were at the bar, and the bald man dropped into the chair situated in the far corner of the room—where the bouncer posted himself.

Lucas walked to a spot directly in front of the seated man, ignoring shouts from the barkeep to order something or leave.

"We don't run a hospitable place," the man said, stretching out his long legs. Lucas gauged his height at six foot six. He appeared skinny but so much height concealed bulk. The man weighed more than two hundred. From the way he tucked his thumbs in the arms holes of his vest, he wasn't much bothered by anything Lucas might say or do.

"I noticed."

The man fished in a vest pocket, crumpled what he found, and tossed it to Lucas. He caught it with a quick downward swipe, rolled it about, and then produced the stolen unfolded five-dollar bill.

"I reckon this is my bill."

"Does it make a difference?"

"Only to the Preacher."

"He's not hurting much. Fact is, I never heard him in finer form. That story about the sweet little girl from a loving family who was lured into prostitution by the evil Fagin is worthy of Dickens himself."

Lucas considered shooting the bartender, who continued to shout at him for not ordering any whiskey. That made him wonder if the man intended to drug him and steal whatever he could.

"You always were a reader of things literary," Lucas said.

"And you weren't. You could learn a great deal reading Charles Dickens. *Oliver Twist* might be retitled *Lucas Stanton*, without much exaggeration."

"I don't like children."

"Neither did Fagin."

"What do you want, Otto? Stealing the greenback from the Preacher's collection plate got my attention."

The man laughed. He gestured for Lucas to move closer.

"You never learned the art of small talk. We should discuss Frank over there behind the bar and why he's so intent on getting you to drink."

"Drugs," Lucas said. "He's never seen me before, so he thinks I am easy pickings."

"That's why you don't need small talk. You size up people fast. Goes with being a gambler."

"Little Otto," he said, "never steals just to talk to me."

"I saw you in the crowd. You still working at the Emerald City?"

"I am." Lucas waited but Little Otto didn't expand on the question. Taking the bull by the horns, Lucas said, "I need information about a stolen dog."

If the request surprised Little Otto, he didn't show it. His blue eyes blazed, but with what emotion? Lucas found himself at a loss to describe it. Otto knew more about the underbelly of Denver thievery than anyone else. For a price he would deliver all Lucas needed to know, wrapped up in brown paper and tied with a pretty bow. But he was a passive source of such scurrilous knowledge. He never offered it for sale.

He wanted something only Lucas could give. The change in supply and demand put him on edge. Anything out of the ordinary with Little Otto always did.

"I can tell you some things but not much."

"What'll it cost me?"

Otto reached into his vest pocket, took out a small silver ball bearing, and using only thumb and forefinger, flicked it at Frank behind the bar. The man ducked in time to keep from getting a nasty bruise between his eyes. The ball bearing broke a bottle of whiskey.

"You keep quiet," Little Otto said in a voice low, level and utterly frightening with its promise of real destruction to follow if he wasn't obeyed. The barkeep grumbled and kicked the broken bottle out of his way. Otto turned back to Lucas. "An introduction, nothing more."

"You're proposing a swap? I need information about a missing dog and you want an introduction to . . ."

Lucas left the sentence hanging for Little Otto to supply the proper name.

"A missing dog? Is this important or are you joshing?"

"I'll give you a hundred dollars for real information."

"It's real, then," Otto said, stroking his beardless chin. He looked up. "I can ask. And will you provide the introduction I seek?"

"If I know the person well enough."

"You do. Introduce me to Carmela Thompson."

For a moment Lucas struggled for words. Nothing came as his brain jumbled everything. Then he tried to put Little Otto and Carmela into the same mental picture. Still nothing came. The combination was too absurd, and he almost said as much. The expression on Little Otto's face told him that would be a terrible mistake.

"She's scheduled to perform tonight at—"

"At the Emerald City," Otto finished for him. "I know. Her itinerary is etched in my brain, like words carved into stone."

Lucas tried to find a reason for the request other than one of pure adulation. Little Otto adoring anyone, even Carmela, struck him as wrong. It went against everything he knew of the man, which, granted, was not much. The only sane reason he could conjure up was that Carmela had information Little Otto could broker for something even more valuable.

"I'll do it," Lucas said, regretting it even as the words slipped free from his lips. "Here's all I know about the missing dog." He handed Little Otto the scrap of paper with Amanda's address and related what he could of the theft.

"It does seem that a person or persons stole away the dog. A wolfhound?"

"A puppy, she said."

"Even a wolfhound puppy is a large dog and to be feared. The thief might be familiar with the animal, or it with him. A battle involving snapping jaws and flowing blood would have occurred otherwise."

"Find what you can for me."

Little Otto nodded once. The far-off look in his eyes might have been the result of figuring out where to begin his hunt for the elusive dog and its kidnapper, or it might have been from something more carnal as his imagination swept him away.

Lucas had to believe the sappy look resulted from the promise of an introduction to Carmela. And what man wouldn't be smitten? Lucas certainly was. It would be amusing to see Carmela's reaction to the towering man with the shaved head. For all his book learning, Little Otto was a raw character and nothing like the chanteuse fancied. Somewhat self-consciously Lucas wiped away dirt from the front of his vest, knowing Carmela would immediately notice and wrinkle her nose in distaste.

Or maybe her disregard would be more sophisticated. A *bon mot*, a mocking laugh, and then disdain? Lucas looked forward to seeing the woman's response and then would come to her rescue. How Otto reacted to that would hardly matter since Lucas intended to have his information by then.

Little Otto blinked and his craggy face once more showed no emotion. Beads of sweat dotting his forehead glistened in the saloon's dim light. He made no move to remove the moisture.

"Who is the landlady?"

Lucas shook his head. He had no idea.

"If there wasn't any sign of forced entry and your Miss Baldridge had actually locked her door as she claimed, a key was used."

Lucas ran his finger over his collar and the two spring steel strips there. Keys were overrated.

"I remember now," Little Otto said. "She has a friend you might know. Amos Conklin."

"The gambler? I've been in a few games with him. He's not very good at his trade."

"You caught him cheating. Rather than calling him out, you began cheating him."

"Anyone watching could see how he palmed cards. I pushed two aces on him so he showed a hand with five." Lucas smiled at the memory. The cowboys in the game with them had not been amused. Conklin would have been strung up if the three from a Wyoming ranch had carried a rope. As it was, they whupped up on him. Lucas had divvied up the pot with the three men, keeping a fair amount for himself. The evening had been both profitable and entertaining.

Cheats irritated him. Clumsy cheats like Amos Conklin infuriated him because they never expended the effort to do it well.

"Tonight?"

"What's that?"

"You will introduce me to Miss Thompson tonight. After her debut?"

"If Conklin had anything to do with stealing the dog."

"I must find myself appropriate clothing," Otto said, already miles distant although he still sat in his chair.

Lucas grumbled and left the Merry Widow. At this time of day, Conklin would be hustling any cowboy he could find in any of a half dozen dives. He set out to check the gambling dens and found Conklin in the third one. Without drawing any attention to himself, he went to the bar and ordered a brandy, swirling it around in the glass when he was served by the taciturn barkeep. Positioning himself carefully, he got a better view of Conklin by looking into the cracked mirror behind the bar.

The man was arguing with two others over a poker hand. The pair got up and left. Lucas had to smile. Conklin ran off his marks rather than stringing them along. All the while he watched the man, he wondered why Conklin would steal Amanda's dog. More than this, what had he done with it?

Little Otto took too much pride in his information being accurate to send anyone on a wild-goose chase. More than this, he wanted the introduction to Carmela Thompson. If Lucas found he had been given punk information, that presentation to what amounted to Western royalty would be in jeopardy. Whatever sparked Little Otto to mention Conklin had some element of logic, if not truth, to it. But what?

Lucas sipped at the brandy and let it burn his tongue and throat before puddling warmly in his belly. He had drunk worse. The barkeep cut it with only a little nitric acid for kick and actually added a fresh peach for flavor and color. As he lifted the glass for another sip, Lucas froze. He put the glass down and turned.

Conklin had disappeared.

The gambler hadn't passed through the front door. Lucas found the back. The door stood partially open to let in a small breeze. He ran to the door and pushed it open with the toe of his boot. At the end of the alley, just off Colfax, two men poked at Conklin, pushing him back into a wall.

Conklin protested loudly, but Lucas couldn't hear any part of the argument, which ended abruptly with a gasp. Conklin bent over and grabbed his belly as one attacker drew back a bloody knife.

Lucas considered what to do. Talking his way out of being a witness to murder seemed unlikely when the second man nudged the first. They had seen him. He carried his Colt New Line, but both of them had six-shooters slung at their sides. In terms of firepower, they had him dead to rights.

"I say, where's the outhouse? The barkeep said it was back here, but I think he only wanted to get rid of me."

The men arrayed themselves on either side to cut off his escape in the alley. If he ducked back into the Merry Widow, he had a chance. Lucas tugged on the door, but it was stuck.

"You with him?" The one without the knife in his hand jerked a thumb over his shoulder in Conklin's direction. The man lay in a heap, not moving.

"I only want the dog back," Lucas said, thinking to shock the men. He wanted a reaction to see if Conklin had run afoul of disgruntled losers or had found even more desperate men in the dog napping.

Lucas expected a reaction. He got it. The one with the knife lunged. Lucas twisted sideways like a Spanish bull-fighter and let the blade slide past. In this position his punch to the man's cheek held little power, but it was enough to stagger him. Lucas had won a bet once going six rounds bareknuckle with a touring bruiser named John L. Sullivan.

He drew back and shot a second jab that took the man too high on the head. He had wanted to strike him in the temple for a possibly killing blow. Being off balance robbed this punch of real potential, and then he grappled with the second man, who caught him up in a bear hug and slammed him back against the door hard enough to rattle his teeth.

Using the impact, he snapped his head forward. His forehead smashed into the other man's head. The arms weakened. Lucas kicked out and caught the man in the knee. A second kick drove hard into his groin.

By this time the first man was recovering his senses. His eyes showed he was still groggy. Lucas feinted right, then drove a left hook into the man's ribs.

As he sat down heavily, the man grated out, "Gonna kill you if you don't back away. The dog's not for the like of you!"

Lucas hopped over the downed man, then hesitated. He needed to find out where Tovarich had been taken. More to satisfy his curiosity, he wanted to know why a puppy brought out a pair of killers. Finding who they worked for solved Amanda's problem and earned him more money.

Before he could kick the knife out of the man's hand or draw his own pistol, though threatening these two could backfire, he looked up. Not only didn't they look like the type to pony up information at the mere threat of being shot, but they were being joined by three more men intent on dragging out their pistols.

Lucas left them, ducked into a store, and waited for them to give up chasing him. Only then did he retrace his route to the laundry to get his cleaned coat. Little Otto had not steered him wrong. Conklin had something to do with

Tovarich's theft and stood at the front of the line as being the thief. Only he was now the dead thief. Did the men who had killed him know where the dog was, or was he now in a race to find the pup?

It began to look as if a hundred dollars wasn't adequate for the job. He needed to find out more from Amanda. But after he paid off his debt. Though the way the day had gone, Carmela might not even talk to him, much less be amenable to politely greeting Little Otto.

5

After a bath and shave, and a few hours sleep, Lucas Stanton felt like whipping his weight in wildcats. Or at least telling whoever would listen that he could. With the freshly cleaned and repaired coat once more gracing his broad shoulders, he strolled down Colfax warily looking for the men who had killed Amos Conklin. It came as no little relief that they had hightailed it after stabbing the man. To his disgust he saw that Conklin's body still lay where he had been killed. Both coat and vest were gone, as were his shoes. The city scavengers were as efficient as any buzzards circling above the plains waiting for something to die.

He went to a pair of policemen leaning against a lamppost, politely coughed to get their attention away from a ribald joke one was telling the other, and then pointed.

"What's botherin' you?" The short one closest to Lucas had pupils the size of pinpricks from chasing the dragon. The cloying odor of opium hung about his heavy wool uniform, as if his behavior and appearance were not enough to alert Lucas to the addiction. "Spit it out. Me and my partner ain't got all day."

"The man in the alley appears to be somewhat deceased," Lucas said. He held out his hands, palms toward the police. "I had nothing to do with it. I am simply pointing out that a corpse is unsightly along such a major street as this."

"Nobody else's complainin'. Why are you? You have somethin' to do with the killin'?"

The second officer was as large as his partner was small. He peered down at Lucas, tapping a slung shot against his left palm with meaty whacks. From the callus there, he habitually did this. If he intended to bully whomever he faced, he succeeded wildly. Lucas was sorry he had ever mentioned the body.

"The two men running down the alley in the other direction must have alerted the others to the body by now," Lucas said, edging away. As he backed off, he described the man with the knife, hoping this would deflect interest from him and direct it where it belonged.

"Mr. Dunbar's boys, you saw 'em snuff somebody?" The short one looked around as if the devils from hell were galloping down on him and he couldn't find a proper hiding place.

"Keep up the good work, men. I'll let Mr. Dunbar know you're doing a fine job." Lucas slapped the opium fiend on the shoulder, then thrust out his hand to shake with the larger copper. For a moment, the man couldn't decide what to do and finally tucked his slung shot under his left arm and shook. His hand engulfed Lucas's but was curiously feeble.

"You tell Mr. Dunbar we're on our toes. We'll get that body all hid so nobody'll ever find it."

Lucas touched the brim of his bowler and strode off. He

had done what he could for Conklin and, by doing so, had found yet another thread to follow. To the north in the Capitol Hill section lived the bluest of the blue bloods. A cute little puppy dog might be found there, though why a man as powerful as Jubal Dunbar would send out his thugs to kill for it posed something of a problem begging for an answer.

He dickered a few minutes with a pretty young girl selling apples, more to enjoy her company than for the apple itself or the extra nickel it cost him. When another customer came by, he paid and buffed off the red skin. He bit into the astringent fruit and almost spit it out. The taste matched that of a persimmon. He turned, judged distances, then heaved the apple at the two coppers with great accuracy. The big one whirled around, face livid. Lucas pointed down a side street, sending the policemen running away. Lucas took a moment's amusement at how the hopped-up officer had wobbled awkwardly and fallen off a curb into a mud puddle. It was small enough payment for them not going after Conklin's murderers.

His steps took him back past the Great West Detective Agency office, where the man and the woman paced back and forth, waiting for the owner to show up.

". . . the ad," finished the man.

"It's not a fake, and we're not leaving. We need this job."

"Dear, we can look elsewhere. In a town the size of Denver, there must be others who will hire us."

"After you were caught with the goat? I don't think so."

Lucas kept walking, never breaking stride although he wished he could get a more complete description of the affair of the goat and the man who looked so sheepish. Eventually the detective agency owner would return and the couple would beg him for whatever job had been advertised.

He wished he could be there to see not only what the owner looked like, without any of the disguises he apparently used in his work, but also to find if the persistent man and woman were hired. If it were left up to him, he would hire them to run the office.

If for nothing else, his curiosity about the goat ran wild.

He made his way through the maze of streets and finally stood in front of the Emerald City Dance Hall and Drinking Emporium. The green paint used on the front had begun to peel after a long winter of fierce blizzards and a summer of baking heat and little rain. The doors were propped open to let in what breeze could be found sneaking off the distant mountains as a steady rush of cigarette smoke and bad music came from inside.

A quick step avoided a drunken cowboy who found the double doors too narrow. As he entered, the cowboy fell face first into the watering trough with a loud splash. Lucas never looked back. He made his way to the bar. Lefty might as well have been a permanent fixture behind it. He never seemed to leave, making Lucas wonder if the man owned the saloon. All his dealings were with the one-armed man, and until now he had never wondered who the owner night be.

He chalked up the sudden interest to his hunt for Amanda's missing dog. Questions that went unanswered never troubled him as long as he sat across the table from a man with a big poke and a small hand.

"He's been here looking for you," Lefty said. "Blood in his eye. Him and *four* men with the look of gunslingers."

"The rancher?"

"I don't want trouble in here. If you can't take care of him, clear out."

"You know your revenue would drop through the floor if I left for another gaming parlor."

"Prying up the floorboards might expose gold dust and money these liquored-up sots have dropped over the years." Lefty scratched his chin, nodding to himself as he worked over the notion. In a voice almost too low to hear, he said, "That's not a bad idea. Gold dust in the dirt."

"Carmela getting ready for the show?"

"Hell, Lucas, I don't know if she's even in town. She might be. I'm not paying her to go onstage a minute before ten tonight."

Lucas glanced at his watch. Twelve hours until the light of his life made her grand entrance to a throng of cheering, jeering men.

"Deal some faro. Jenny's not up to it right now."

Lucas knew better than to ask why the woman had skipped work yet again. Lefty might tell him. The last time he had asked after a coworker, he had learned more than he ever wanted to about the effects of malaria on the human body and soul. Short of Rocky Mountain spotted fever, that had been the scariest description of symptoms he had ever heard.

"Usual split?"

"Whatever you can steal is yours, unless I catch you. It's a slow day, but I don't want to pass up a single sucker. Keep them in the saloon however you can for tonight's show." Lefty walked down the bar to serve another beer to a man dressed in tatters. As he went, he evaluated what he might find under the Emerald City's floor.

Lucas went to the faro table, pulled back a tablecloth covering it, and found a deck of cards wedged into a small compartment beneath. He shuffled, then began his spiel to draw the willing victims into his web. Faro was a simple enough game, or so the players thought. A pretty woman dealing, leaning forward over the table in a low-cut dress, gave them their money's worth even as their wallets were picked clean. Lucas's appeal had to be different to keep them pressed along the far side of the table as he worked.

A young cowboy came up and worked at building a cigarette. From his clumsy attempt, he'd either had little practice or he'd had a snootful of whiskey already. Lucas saw the man's yellowed teeth and realized the cowboy had likely pushed through the door first thing when Lefty opened that morning.

Such a guess gave him the way to hold the cowboy's interest.

"You're good enough with that smoke to do it on horseback," Lucas said.

"Have done it while stretched over a horse's back," the cowboy allowed.

"Then I'd better tell you how dangerous that might be," Lucas said. He motioned for the cowboy to lay down a bet. He took a deep breath and remembered what he had learned from the Preacher about spinning a web of words to keep his audience intrigued. Then he began telling his story to keep the cowboy distracted from the cards.

"My partner got consumption from smoking and upped and died on me last January. Don't think I'm prone to that." As if to put his words to the lie, he coughed, then spat, hitting a cuspidor at his feet with reasonable accuracy.

"Not what I mean. You ever hear of Glue Bottom Backus?"

"Can't say I have. That's a mighty odd name."

He lost another hand but wasn't budging. Lucas had him hooked.

"He came by it honestly. Glue Bottom could ride any horse, no matter how the son of a bitch bucked."

"Ain't never been a horse that can't be rode, and there ain't never a rider that can't be throwed."

"You're wrong about that," Lucas said. "Once old Glue Bottom plopped down on a saddled horse, no amount of sunfishing or quick spins ever unseated him. He was up in Wyoming on a ranch outside of Cheyenne when he about met his match, though."

"What I said. Any rider can be throwed."

"Glue Bottom set himself down on this maverick and was bounced about, jerked this way and that," Lucas said, all the while dealing faro and scooping up the coins the cowboy lost because he paid more attention to the story than his odds. "He thought he was a goner when the belly strap began to groan under the strain of the varmint's heaving. The leather stretched enough so daylight showed between saddle and the lathered up horse's back."

"Sure sign Glue Bottom's name got to change. He might stay with the saddle, but when the cinch loosens—"

The cowboy clapped his hands together loud enough to draw attention from the more serious gamblers and drinkers. Even Claudette looked up. Lucas shook his head. He didn't want her to break the spell he wove. Another quick move pulled in sorry bets. The cowboy put down more without even considering how he bet.

"That's so," Lucas said to string him along. "But the effort tuckered out the horse. That maverick settled down and Glue Bottom rode it out of the corral. I tell you, the other wranglers stared at him as if he was a bronco buster who'd go down in history as the best ever."

"Sounds like it," the cowboy said with more than a touch of skepticism.

"Of course, Glue Bottom got a mite arrogant about his skills when he rode that mustang out, thinking it was just another horse." Lucas lowered his voice for effect. "It wasn't anywhere near broken."

"Didn't think so."

Lucas saw that he had drawn a crowd as big as any Jenny could, and he didn't have her impressively displayed chest. The bets came fast and furious. Lucas paid out some winners, but the money mattered less than the tall tale he spun.

"Old Glue Bottom started to build himself a smoke, the reins draped over his left arm and not gripped properly. The horse knew and rocketed forward, straight over a cliff. Glue Bottom let out a yell as he and the horse plunged over the brink going straight down toward the river."

"If his body was swept away by the river, they wouldn't have to bury him," the cowboy said.

Lucas motioned for Claudette to start working the crowd and sell as much whiskey as she could. He worked his table, the cards flying so fast the faces blurred as they slapped down on the green felt. The speed of betting increased, and he finally continued the story.

"Yes, sir, his partners thought Glue Bottom had ridden his last trail. They fanned out along the base of the cliff, hunting for his body. They didn't find a danged thing."

"The river," the cowboy said. "A horse what leaps like that's gonna carry outwards quite a way."

"It wasn't the river where they found him. There was a huge cottonwood tree on the riverbank. One of his buddies looked up and there was Glue Bottom, still astride that horse. He held up his smoke and asked, 'Anybody got a light?'"

For a moment only silence greeted Lucas, then laughter rippled around.

"That there's a good story, gambler man."

This sentiment was echoed by others. They drifted away, but Lucas ran his knowing fingers over the stacks of coins won for the house. More than a hundred dollars had been bet and lost by the crowd as he spun his tale. Claudette winked broadly at him. Sale of whiskey had been good, too. He might not have Jenny's attributes, but he had other talents.

"I entertained you boys," Lucas said, "so now you can do me a favor. I'm looking for a puppy dog stolen a couple days ago."

"Is there a reward?"

"For the right dog, I'll pay . . . five dollars."

"I seen a dog out back 'fore I came in."

"Warn't no dog. That was a mangy coyote."

The argument between the men grew and took them away from the faro table. Claudette followed to capitalize on spilled liquor and emptied glasses. For a moment, Lucas found himself alone at the table, giving him a chance to catch his breath. He knew any number of ways of sweet-talking a crowd to keep them interested while they gambled, but it always sapped his energy.

He looked toward the back of the Emerald City, where the stage stretched empty, almost forlorn. The curtains billowed and moved, sometimes hinting at stagehands moving about to prepare the set for Carmela. He shifted in the direction of the stage but caught Lefty's eye. The barkeep sternly shook his head, then pointed at the faro table. Lucas shot him an insincere smile and went back to plying his trade.

More than a half hour passed. A cowboy walked away three dollars to the good, bragging on his luck. Lucas waited for the rush to the table when word got around that the cards favored the bettor. Luck meant everything to a dyed-in-the-wool gambler—and even more to a superstitious cowboy.

A loud yelp followed by fierce barking made him reach for his pistol. He paused when he saw a man as mangy as the dog he wrestled coming toward him.

"This here's yer dog, mister. Where's my money?"

"He's only got one eye and that back leg's all twisted around," Lucas said.

"So?"

"This isn't a puppy. It's five years old if it's a day." Lucas looked askance at the animal as it struggled, trying to escape the death grip the man had on it.

"You never said the dog you wanted wasn't all busted up."

"I said it was a puppy. I can't even tell what breed this is."

"What breed you want it to be? Looks like a bit of ever'thing's been mixed in."

"Get it out of here." Lucas edged back as the man tried to force the animal into his arms. He didn't want fleas when he intended to renew his acquaintance with Carmela Thompson.

"You ain't gonna pay me? You thinkin' on cheatin' me when I brung you yer dog?"

"Not mine," Lucas said. He realized now the error of even asking a drunken crowd in the Emerald City to find Tovarich.

A pair of high-stepping dancers came onstage, kicking their knees up high enough to give a quick glimpse of ankle, calf, and even higher. They danced without music; none was needed. A hush fell over the dance hall as their heels clicked on the stage and they exposed more and more. Flouncing about, they held the crowd in silent rapture. Then the piano player started. Lucas had to give him his due. He was not a bad player, but often he was too drunk to do more than bang on the keys.

Tonight his tinny piano sounded as if it had been moved into a grand concert hall and he were playing for the crowned heads of Europe. Lucas covered the faro table. No one would gamble now. He slid the stack of coins into his pocket. As they slipped between his fingers, he counted, stopped when he got to the usual percentage, then went to the bar and left the neat stack for Lefty. The barkeep had said he could keep everything until the crowd came in, but Lucas knew his credibility as an honest gambler would go up if he paid up. This was a good place to call home, and Lucas wanted to stay on good terms with the management.

In spite of the buildup for Carmela and the increasingly naughty dancers, Lefty came the length of the bar and counted the coins. He nodded, smiled in appreciation, pocketed the money, and left Lucas to his own devices.

Moving along the back of the crowd, Lucas found his special spot by a pillar. It took him a few seconds of fumbling, but he pulled out a two-by-two crate almost two feet high and stepped up onto it to give a view of the stage over the heads of the crowd. He wrapped his arms around the pillar and rested his cheek against the splintery wood.

It was his turn to be mesmerized. The two cancan dancers had disappeared behind the curtains as they slid open to reveal Carmela Thompson. He caught his breath. There were women who were more beautiful—women who had favorably viewed him as a fascinating partner—but never had he seen one who held his attention so effortlessly. She moved with liquid grace, her long blond hair and emerald eyes adding to a pale beauty at odds with most women he knew. And Carmela's voice! She opened her bow-shaped lips and let escape a single clear, pure note.

His heart began to beat faster at that single sound.

When she began singing, not a sound in the house interrupted her. Carmela sang opera and bawdy songs and Stephen Foster ditties and even hymns. All held him captive until the final dying note left him drained emotionally. Lucas shook himself and stepped down from his perch, carefully replacing it for future need. The entire while silence gripped the saloon, then a roar of approval exploded that showed real appreciation.

Carmela took a bow and gave an encore. By the time she finished, Lucas had made his way around the perimeter of the crowd and spoke briefly to a bouncer positioned to keep well-wishers at bay. Lucas slid past, letting the burly man shove back a cowboy immediately behind him.

The stage was familiar territory for him. Lucas frequently romanced the singers coming through Denver who performed here, but he had not gotten a bouquet for Carmela or even some small, expensive gift. Hunting for Tovarich had distracted him to the point that even retrieving his patched coat from the laundry had almost gone by the wayside.

He went to the dressing room where Carmela's name had been crudely painted on the door above a more permanent gold star. A few scrapes at the paint had finally convinced someone it was paint and not real gold. With a deep breath and a quick brush of dust from his coat, he knocked.

"Come in, Lucas!"

He hesitated, then went in, flustered. Carmela always seemed a half pace ahead of him. That robbed him of his normal suave demeanor.

"Who's the biggest star in Denver?" he asked. "After that performance, who can doubt it is a fascinating young chanteuse named Carmela Thompson?"

"No roses? I am at a loss for words, Lucas darling."

He went to her to plant a kiss on her lips. At the last instant, she turned so he hit a cheek instead. In true European fashion, he kissed her other cheek. This lacked the thrill of tasting her lips but kept him in the race, stealing a kiss she had not allowed him to bestow.

"Words, perhaps, but not lilting melodies. You held them all in thrall tonight, my dear."

"And you, Lucas? Were you also smitten?"

"By your beauty, by your wit, and certainly by your talent."

She turned from him to look into the mirror. The old, cracked one had been replaced with a newly silvered glass plate chased with delicate gold cobwebs.

A knock at the door irritated Lucas, but he left staring at Carmela long enough to see Claudette had a bottle of Grand Monopole and glasses. He blocked her entry and took them. She started to protest. Women as well as men wanted to hobnob with Carmela.

"Thanks for bringing the wine," he said. Before Claudette could protest, he kicked the door shut with his heel and held out the bottle and glasses.

"For me, Lucas?"

"The finest champagne in all Denver."

"How thoughtful."

"I am sure it is not up to your usual standards, but we are on the frontier. I wanted to get you only the finest—for the town, this is it." Lucas popped the cork and let the bubbles froth out before pouring the sparkling wine into the two glasses. He handed Carmela one and lifted the other in toast. "To the most beguiling songstress on either side of the Mississippi."

"What? On either side? Not on the river, too?" Carmela laughed easily, touched glasses, and sipped. Her nose wrinkled slightly. When Lucas tried his, he knew why.

"I have an entire evening of sumptuous feasting planned," he lied. "Oysters fresh from the Coast."

"Again? I so tire of them. Why not something different? Buffalo jerky or pemmican perhaps?"

Words failed him again. Then she laughed. The magical sound reminded him of her humor.

"I know of a tiny café where only the toughest meat is served with plenty of water to wash it down." He returned the joke but had to wonder as he saw her eyes change slightly. Before there had been mockery, but for that flash in her emerald eyes, there was something else. Respect? Surprise?

"I am so tired from my inaugural performance, Lucas. Another night."

The woman's tone shut him out entirely. Whatever her plans for the evening, he was not part of them. He brushed off a dog hair from his coat, remembering the cur presented to him as a wolfhound by the drunk.

"A pity, since I wanted to introduce you to a rather important man in Denver. He is quite an admirer."

"Important? How important?"

"Very," Lucas said. If he built Little Otto up enough and he disappointed her, that opened opportunities to woo Carmela after she shooed the shaved-headed giant away. "In town, few are held in such esteem."

"I am so worn out, dear Lucas, but as a favor to you, I will speak with this man. Is he here?" She perked up and looked past him toward the closed door.

Lucas had no idea but doubted Little Otto would allow anything short of Gabriel blowing the trump of doom—and maybe not even then—to keep him away from Carmela's opening performance. He had seen the man's expression, his determination, his willingness to make a deal.

"Let me see. If not, we can go somewhere for a bite to

eat and wait for him." Lucas saw this as a way to spend time with her while waiting for Otto to never arrive. His face fell when he opened the door and stared directly into the center of the man's chest.

Little Otto wore a tuxedo that barely fit him. That was to be expected, but Lucas had not believed diamond studs of such size could be used to hold a frilled dress shirt closed. The stones marched from the top of the vest all the way up to where a perfectly tied black silk bow tie circled Otto's thick neck.

"She wants to meet you," Lucas said in a choked voice. "She thinks you're a force in Denver."

Little Otto laughed.

"I *am* a force, not only in Denver but of nature."

"My, aren't you a tall one?" Carmela came to Otto, who took one hand and bent deeply to kiss it. "You are one of the true gentlemen, sir."

"I wish to perform a great service for you, miss," Otto said.

"What is that?"

"To order breakfast in bed for us."

Lucas was startled to see the calculating look on the woman's face.

"You are a bold one, sir."

"Not half as bold as you are beautiful."

Lucas backed to the door and slipped through it rather than listen to the banter between the two. That should have been him back there, not Little Otto. He had followed Carmela across the country, and they belonged together. They were of a kind, soul mates.

He left through the back door, followed by Carmela's delighted laughter. As the door closed behind him, a dog barked at him and jumped up, dirty paws on his pants.

"Get away," he said, pushing away the mutt that had been offered to him as Tovarich. Nothing had gone right tonight. "Oh, the hell with it." He bent and scratched the dog's ears. Somehow this wasn't quite the same as running his fingers through long, blond locks, but it had to do. For the time being.

6

"Dunbar."

Lucas Stanton stared at Little Otto, then shook his head. He ran his fingers around the brim of the glass until it made a squealing noise. In New Orleans he had listened to a glass harp symphony once. The maestro had dozens of water glasses filled to various levels. Dipping his finger in water and running it around the rims had produced strange and lovely music. Lucas never quite got the knack of producing any uniform sound, but right now he wanted to generate a screech that would pierce Otto's eardrums.

He kept his best poker face.

"I know that already. His boys tried to rough me up. They even warned me away from hunting for the dog. It was as if someone had told them my interest in the hound. Otherwise, they might have thought I was up to any number of other nefarious schemes."

"Jubal Dunbar is a dangerous man with many irons in the

political fire. He wanted to be Colorado's first governor but ended up at the bottom of a very long list. A man with his self-importance does not take such an affront lightly. He has worked himself into a political appointment, doing who knows what, but he is always on the lookout to move up."

"What did Dunbar want with Miss Baldridge's dog? More to the point, what did he do with the puppy?"

"He wants the dog but doesn't have it."

"He knows who does?" Lucas sucked at his gums, thinking hard. "How do I find who has the dog?"

Little Otto shrugged.

"This isn't much information in return for what I gave you." Lucas stood straighter when he saw the tiny smile come to the man's lips and the distant look.

"Breakfast was good."

Lucas opened his mouth to speak, then clamped it shut. He had nothing to say. The implication destroyed his own confidence. For more than two years he had connived to get closer to Carmela and had failed. A single glance on the part of this mountain of a man had been all it took for Carmela's resolve to melt away? He found that impossible to believe.

"Why does Dunbar want the dog?"

"That," Little Otto said, "is a matter of some dispute. I doubt companionship enters into it."

Lucas scratched at a bite on his belly and growled like a dog. The mongrel he had petted in the alley the night before had divested itself of a few fleas. The more he tried to do the right thing, the more he was punished for it. He should have kicked the dog instead of buying it a pound of ground meat at the butcher shop.

"Could it be that Dunbar wants to get the dog back to entice Miss Baldridge into a more intimate relationship?"

"Do you mean Dunbar or do you mean yourself?"

"I did you a favor. You owe me the information."

"You can't take back the favor," Otto said sensibly, "but I am beholden to you. Let me add one speck of gossip I have overheard. Dunbar is sorely pissed that he wasn't elected governor. He is willing to go to any lengths to gain that position."

John Long Routt was well enough liked and had been elected after serving as territorial governor appointed by U. S. Grant. Even if Routt met an unexpectedly abrupt end, Lafayette Head was capable of taking over. Lucas followed politics only as much as it benefited him through laws and loopholes, but neither Routt nor Head generated much opposition. If Dunbar attempted an assassination, he would never be the one chosen to succeed either man. Whatever he planned went beyond the Colorado state borders.

But a man with such soaring ambitions wanted more than to lure a lovely woman, even one as fetching as Amanda Baldridge, into his bed by stealing her dog.

"You find out more and tell me," Lucas said. He felt betrayed and angry now. Little Otto only laughed as he left the Emerald City.

Lucas ran his finger around the glass rim and produced a pure, clear note that cut through his ears and sliced up his brain.

"Now I do that." He snorted and shoved the empty glass away.

Lucas started to follow Little Otto when Lefty called out to him from the stage.

"Miss Thompson wants to see you. Lord knows why." The barkeep swung a beer keg around easily and balanced it on his left shoulder. "She said *now*."

Lucas had half a mind to keep walking. He wasn't a servant to be ordered around, yet the woman asked to see him.

Actually told Lefty she wanted to see him. Possibilities built like summer clouds over the Front Range. What had been pleasant for Little Otto might have been unendurable for Carmela. He had thought to rescue her from the big lout, and this was his chance.

He took the steps onto the stage two at a time and skipped across the boards to the singer's dressing room. The door stood ajar.

"Carmela? You hankering to see me?"

"Lucas darling, come in. Yes, I have a bone to pick with you."

"Introducing you to Otto?" His heart almost missed a beat. He pushed into the dressing room and his heart came close to exploding like a keg of Giant powder.

The singer was half-dressed, with expanses of delicious skin never seen by an audience exposed. He moved closer, but Carmela pulled up a thin muslin dressing gown and settled it about her creamy shoulders to steal away any additional view. Her hair was a blond mist around her lovely face, and she glowed with an inner light unlike anything he had ever seen. Or rarely seen.

"You should have introduced us so much sooner. I am disappointed in you. Never have I met a man like him. And I do mean *man*."

Lucas's spirits sank at such unexpected news. She and Otto had hit it off well, contrary to what he had expected.

"He's not the politically connected man he claims."

"What's that? He never said he was in politics. He's in investments." Carmela pouted a little. "I am not sure he meant money. He trades in information. What a curious concept, though if anyone can do it, Otto can."

"Information," Lucas repeated. That was exactly Little Otto's staple.

"So gentle for such a large man."

"I've seen him tear a man's arm off and beat him with it."

"Oh, Lucas dear, you exaggerate so. Otto is nothing like that. When he's with me, he's nothing like that at all."

Telling her he had seen Little Otto vent a bull-throated roar and do that very thing—it had been the man's left arm—did nothing to advance his own worth in her eyes. Even if he found the cheating gambler and paraded him past her, she wouldn't notice. Her infatuation with the shaved-headed giant was too great.

Otto had better deliver the promised information.

Carmela stood and whirled about gracefully, giving him a light peck on the cheek.

"You are such a dear friend. Could you see to having a bottle of wine sent? Some food, also. Breakfast seemed so long ago."

"I'm sure you were hungry soon after, too."

"Ah, yes, yes we were," she said, a dreamy look coming into her eyes that matched what Lucas had seen on Little Otto's face.

Lucas stepped back and gave the singer a long, longing look and then left, knowing his chance with her had passed. It was a waste of his time and honeyed words even to speak with Carmela until Little Otto had drifted out of her life, and he would. The worlds of each barely intersected, and he had been the one point of contact. Lucas doubted disappearing would be the reason the pair stopped seeing each other—he had served his role, but it had been one of contact, not one of renewing affection. Carmela would continue on her triumphant tour, and Otto would revert to his chair at the back of the Merry Widow, a spider in the center of a web, transmitting information from all over Denver to him.

"Lefty," he called on his way out. "She wants something to eat. Pigs knuckles or maybe the hard-boiled eggs."

"She asked for those?"

"Not the three-month-old eggs. Something fresher."

"There are some only a couple weeks old. For some reason, I can't get anyone at the bar to eat them."

Lucas almost stopped to tell Lefty to fetch real food for Carmela, then contented himself with a jaunty wave as he passed through the front doors out into the increasingly cool fall weather. If the songstress had her sights set on Little Otto, so be it. Amanda Baldridge was hardly an ugly hag. Finding her puppy dog would garner some respect in her bright eyes, not to mention the possibility of real admiration for his cleverness. That she had already paid him well elevated her mien in his eyes.

He worked through the streets, touching the brim of his hat to the ladies and feeling better by the minute. By the time he reached Capitol Hill, his outlook was bright and confident. Even the flea bite had stopped itching.

Lucas looked around as he walked among the politically powerful. Finding who had power and who did not proved too easy for him. The "I have power" attitude was never put into words, because actions dealing with those around them conveyed it like a king's crown tipped at a jaunty angle. Anyone seeing the crown knew the power of whoever wore it. It wasn't clothing, since some of those he saw wore threadbare coats and scuffed shoes as a badge of distinction. They told their voters they had not been consumed by the trappings of power, yet Lucas recognized two of those men as regulars in the Emerald City, where Lefty made sure they received royal treatment.

Clothes did not make the man—or his power. It was something more and always came down to the men wielding the power wanting to be recognized as being in command no matter what they wore.

He stopped on the steps of the Capitol Building, judging everyone going inside and finding most wanting. Realizing he had never seen Jubal Dunbar and had no idea what he looked like prompted him to enter the rotunda. Workers labored everywhere he looked, hammering, plastering, trying to fix up a building that fell down faster than they could repair it. For a new state, this was only a start. In a few years a larger, more impressive building would be constructed to hold the corridors of power. But now? Vast emptiness, unadorned by even portraits of the territorial governors. The sense of space and power did not impress him. The sight of two men flanking a short, well-dressed man did.

He stepped away to let the bodyguards who had roughed him up in the alley continue on their way, moving this way and that as they tracked their employer. Lucas had not seen Dunbar before. He had now.

After Dunbar and his guards left, Lucas went to a guard standing with arms crossed and looking as if he wanted to be somewhere—anywhere—else.

"As I live and breathe, it's . . . Samuels, isn't it?" Lucas thrust out his hand. The guard stared at him, confused. Lucas grabbed the guard's hand and pumped it. "I haven't seen you in the Emerald City in a long time. Lost your taste for poker?"

Lucas had no idea if the guard ever went into the saloon, but chances were good that he had at some time. Lefty often boasted how many of the rich and powerful came incognito into the dance hall, not always coming for either the lavish shows or the liquor. Lefty ran the best string of soiled doves in town, and the reputation for pretty waiter girls was unparalleled.

"That's not my name, and I ain't been there in a while. Do I know you?"

"Of course you do. I'll buy you a drink. Come by for Carmela Thompson's show. It's even more exciting than the last time she graced the stage there."

"A free drink?"

"On me. Guaranteed." Lucas hesitated, then asked, "Have you seen Mr. Dunbar? I was supposed to meet him but got here a bit late for the appointment."

"You just missed him. I heard him say he was headin' on home."

"His house on Humboldt? I'd better see if I can catch him there. This is important." Lucas gave a broad wink. He watched the man's face screw up in thought.

"He lives on York. Big white house, fancy garden with flowers in it along the street. Ain't never been in, but I escorted his missus home more 'n once."

"York, of course. I was thinking of something else. Remember, that drink's on me."

Lucas left quickly, intent on crossing York Street without actually going down it. He was glad for his caution. Not twenty paces to his right as he hurried along stood one of Dunbar's guards, arms crossed and chin down on his chest as he leaned against a fence post. The white house gleamed in the sunlight and contrasted vividly with the pure blue sky. If it had lifted off its foundations, it might have been mistaken for a cloud. The house had an airy, light appearance to it from the fine Italianate woodwork along the eaves. Hints of faces showed at the cornices, but Lucas allowed as to how that might only be his imagination and noonday shadows. He walked past to the next block, down it, and circled to come back at the far end of York.

From this angle he saw two more guards on the front porch. One paced restlessly while the other sat at a small table cleaning his pistol.

Bluffing his way past these men would prove dangerous. The one on the street had roughed him up. Lucas didn't recognize either of the others. Jubal Dunbar employed a small army to protect him. Unlike a real army with a competent commander, this one had left itself open to an attack from the rear. For all the guns pointed outward, the flagstone path to the back porch was unattended.

Lucas went up the path, wary of being seen from the second-story windows. Most had curtains or blinds drawn against the afternoon sun. As he stepped up to the kitchen door, a small black woman opened it. She hauled back and started to throw a pail of slop on him.

"I apologize! Are you the lady of the house?"

"Go on. What you sayin', mistuh? I'm not lady of this heah house." She lowered the bucket and set it at her feet. "I was fixin' to scrub the back porch. What you doin' out heah?"

"I was told there was work to be had and to inquire of the loveliest lady in all Denver. You're saying that's not you?"

In spite of her words, the woman warmed to him.

"You don't got no reason to be comin' round back heah. You go up to the front and announce yo'se'f all properlike. What job you lookin' for?"

"A small puppy requires training. I specialized in such tasks."

The maid scowled at him.

"We ain't got no dog heah."

"I must be mistaken. There isn't a puppy? A wolfhound."

"Not heah. The folks what live down the street, they got a bloodhound, but he's a cap'n in the police."

"I have been led astray. A prank played on me." Lucas hesitated. "Mr. Dunbar hasn't brought *any* dog home recently?"

He saw the woman's eyes widen and ducked, trying to avoid

what he knew was coming. The club crashed down on his shoulder rather than his head. That was all the fight he put up before a fist like a mallet drove into his gut, doubling him over. In the far distance he heard the maid complaining. The answer she received quieted her. Through tears of pain, Lucas saw the back door close. The roar of blood and the fierce hammering of his heart filled his ears.

He wished he had been totally deaf so he wouldn't have heard, "Kill him?"

Another blow, this time to the top of his head, left him stunned. He was aware of being dragged along the streets, then dropped on his face in the dirt. Strong hands grabbed his wrists and ankles and lifted him. He swung back and forth then sailed through the air to land in a sewage canal.

7

The sucking noise he made as he pulled himself free of the sewage sickened him almost as much as the stench. Denver had become a big town, pushing more than thirty thousand residents at the time of statehood a couple months back. Along with this came the civic duty of both town and state to provide sanitation. The solution had been the open ditches running away from the town. Where they drained, Lucas didn't care, nor, he suspected, did anyone else in Denver. All he knew was that his clothing had thoroughly absorbed both substance and smell.

He rolled over and sat up as the sluggish current moved past him. It took another minute to get his feet under him and slide over the earthen lip to drier land. He now was covered with shit, grass, and dirt. Lucas swiped at the drying filth in his eyes to get a better view around him. A trio of young boys came closer, whispering among themselves and laughing.

"Might I ask where I am?" Lucas called.

"You fell in and don't know where?" The boys snickered. "Who are you?"

"Your new schoolmaster," Lucas said, standing. Muck dripped off him as he struck a pose. "When I find out who you rapscallions are, you will clean the thunder mugs all year long."

This sent them running away, but not before one of them chucked a rock at him. Lucas caught it, weighed it, and then returned it with more skill than the boy, who rubbed his arm and garnered derision from his friends.

None of this made Lucas feel any better as he stripped off his coat, looked at it a moment, then gingerly dropped it back into the canal, where it caught the current and slowly worked its way to oblivion. After a careful search of his pockets, he removed what could be salvaged. A few greenbacks the men had not seen fit to steal. He hadn't put his Colt into a pocket so he had that waiting for him back at his room. His pocket watch and a soggy piece of paper with unreadable writing completed his inventory.

He stripped off his shirt and tossed that into the canal and would have added his pants but he already drew stares from people driving by on a narrow road paralleling the sewage ditch. He watched the looks from a few freighters, then chose one with an amused look. After flagging him down, Lucas got a ride back into the heart of town, where he had rented a room when he got to town several months ago.

Washing himself off the best he could, he sneaked up the back stairs to his room. The filthy remnants were quickly tossed out the window into the backyard. He wiped himself off and put on old clothing for a trip to the barbershop and a bath. Lucas paid the extra ten cents and got fresh water to go along with the lye soap. Even then he felt slimy and unclean.

The whole time he scrubbed his skin raw, he let thoughts tumble freely, trying to decide what to do. Finding Amanda and getting any further information he could seemed his best course of action, other than telling her he was going to chuck the hunt for her dog.

That rankled because he had promised—even sealing the deal with a wad of money failed to match him giving his word. But too many powerful people wanted the dog. If he couldn't find out why Dunbar sent out his bullyboys, breaking his word became a possibility no matter how much that offended his sense of honor.

"She hasn't told me everything," he said to himself as he walked toward the Emerald City.

"Mister, they never do," called a man sitting on the board-walk, his back against a wall. "You spare enough so's a man can get a square meal?"

Lucas fished out one of the bills that had taken the plunge with him into the sewage and passed it over. The man's nose wrinkled. A sharp look at Lucas almost amounted to the man's entire response. He mumbled "Thanks" as Lucas went on.

As he pushed into the saloon, he saw the man trying to get change from another passerby. Lucas decided that wasn't a bad idea. He bought a stack of chips and went to find himself a poker game. Lefty nodded at him from behind the bar, then inclined his head toward the stage. Sitting dead center of the front row, Little Otto stared at the closed curtain with an intensity that should have burned holes through the fabric.

Before getting down to serious gambling, Lucas went to sit beside the giant.

"The show doesn't start for another hour," he pointed out.

"I wanted a good seat."

"Why not watch from the wings? Carmela would invite you back." Lucas didn't say it, but he doubted any of the stagehands would try to stop Otto. They were not stupid, and the man was a force of nature. "Or would she?" Lucas tried to keep the hopeful note from his voice and knew he failed.

Little Otto turned to him and made a face.

"You stink."

"A poor choice of toilet water," he said.

"I prefer to watch her from the audience. The view is better."

"When she does the high kicks?"

"In all ways," Otto said.

His mood turned dourer, and Lucas realized he was poking fun at the man's behavior toward his paramour. He quickly changed the subject.

"I need to know more about why Dunbar wants the dog. He doesn't have it, but his men are inclined to go to great lengths to keep me from finding it."

"He doesn't have it. I hear rumors."

"What do they say?"

"You don't have anything to trade for that information."

"I introduced you to Carmela!" Lucas shot to his feet. "What more do you want from me?"

"That was a fair trade. You got what you wanted, I got what I wanted. Anything new is to be negotiated."

"I'll get you a copy of the new book from that writer you like. Mark Twain."

"You can get a copy of *Tom Sawyer*? How?" Little Otto turned from his vigilant watching for the slightest wrinkle in the curtain and focused completely upon Lucas. The dangled carrot worked.

"I don't ask where you get your information. Don't ask me how I can get books from literary luminaries."

Little Otto nodded and got a far-off look.

"I did enjoy *Roughing It*. He is a good speaker. I went to a lecture when he came through town a couple years ago."

"Who else is interested in the dog?"

"I know better than to give out information without payment first. Such facts are curious. Some are timeless, others evaporate when they're told. Still others are like a keg of blasting powder with a burning fuse attached. They blow up after a given amount of time."

"This is likely to blow up if you don't tell me," Lucas said.

"You miss my point. Whether I tell you or not, that information will blow up." Otto frowned until ridges formed halfway up to the top of his skull. "Gamblers. That's all I can tell you. Since you are a gambler, it ought to be easy enough for you to figure out who has the dog."

"Why would gamblers want a puppy dog?"

Otto no longer paid him any attention. He stood and started toward the green-felt-covered tables, where chips fell and cards whispered with the soft promise of wealth.

"Don't forget the book."

Lucas smiled wryly and never looked back. He found a table with a spare chair and soon enough fell into the ebb and flow of stud poker. A few players left when Carmela came onstage for the evening show but two remained. That provided Lucas the chance to make a few more dollars before the two, a tinker and a clerk at a mercantile over near Larimer Square, called it quits.

He leaned back and ran his fingers through his long brown hair. In spite of himself, he looked at his hands to be certain nothing else brown had come off. He had scrubbed furiously, but Otto was right about the stench remaining.

When he saw no takers for another hand because Carmela was swinging into the finale of her performance, he went outside into the crisp, cold air. Autumn's bite grew sharper. The Front Range was hidden by night and buildings towering up as many as four stories, but he knew clouds swirled about the highest peaks carrying a hint of snow that would come into town soon enough.

He had weathered the prior winter just fine in Denver, but drifting south might give a needed change of luck. Pretty señoritas in El Paso plying him with tequila could take his mind off Carmela being with Otto. He glanced back into the Emerald City. Dalliance with Claudette might be interesting, but a complete change of scenery revitalized a tired man's vanity. If anything, Claudette was too easy a conquest.

As a touch of wind kicked up, forcing him to pull his thin coat closer around his body, he wondered how grateful Amanda Baldridge would be if he returned her dog. She lived in a boardinghouse filled with transients. That meant she did not consider Denver home but only another stop along her travels to . . . where?

It would be interesting to find out.

Only he needed to retrieve her dog, unless he could console her grief at having lost Tovarich.

The sound of a scuffle came from around the side of the saloon. Lucas put his hand into his coat pocket. He had brought his Colt tonight, if Dunbar's men decided to press the matter of him remaining in town. Carefully stepping away from the building and standing in the middle of the alley leading toward the back, he saw the flash of a shining knife blade. He caught his breath. For an instant he thought the man clutching it had driven the tip into his victim's belly.

The guttural grunt convinced him the knife only nicked the man pinned against the wall and hadn't gutted him.

Such a showdown wasn't any of his business. Taking the pistol from his pocket and holding it at his side, down along his leg, he went to see what the fuss was about.

"You red ni—" The man used his free hand to grip the Indian's throat while keeping the knife jammed against his belly.

"Do you need help?"

The man said, "Ain't none of your business, but thank you kindly for the offer. I'm collectin' a debt from this thievin'—"

Lucas turned, lifted his pistol, and used it as a club as he swung in a wide arc that connected with the man's temple. He dropped to the ground as if he had been robbed of his leg bones. As he struggled to sit up, Lucas placed his boot squarely on the man's wrist and shifted his weight until he forced open the hand. He quickly kicked the dropped knife away.

The entire time the Indian stood against the wall, watching and not saying a word. Lucas had expected him to take off running. A quick look at the man's belly showed the knife slit in his shirt. It was too dark to tell if a drop of blood oozed out from a wound.

"What's the debt?" Lucas asked. He put his thumb on the Colt's hammer, ready to cock it. A .22-caliber was deadly at this range if he put the bullet into the man's eye. Even if he missed, a small caliber bullet tearing around an ear or forehead would put the fear of God into him.

"He owes me ten dollars."

"You'd kill him for ten dollars?"

"Damned straight I would. Ain't no Injun doin' me out of my money."

Keeping his Colt ready, Lucas rummaged about in a coat pocket and found two five-dollar bills. He tossed them down onto the supine man's chest.

"That square the debt?"

"Hell, don't much care who pays me as long as I get paid."
He crumpled up the two bills in his fist, edged away like an
upside-down crab, and reached for his knife.

"Leave it."

The man growled but obeyed. He lit out running and
disappeared into the night.

"You need money to tide you over?"

"No."

Lucas looked more closely at the man he had rescued.
From the complexion he was a half-breed, black and Indian.
The nose was thin but the skin was darker than midnight. His
hair had been pulled back and held with a beaded band.

"Creek?"

The man blinked, then nodded once.

"You're a long way from Indian Territory. You should
avoid thieves like that." Lucas pointed carelessly into the
night with his pistol.

"No thief. I owed him the money."

Such candor surprised Lucas. He had expected denials
and even anger at the thieving white man. He wasn't sure
which took him aback more: the admission of debt or the
fact that the man who'd fled had loaned money to an Indian.

"I can afford some charity. You sure you don't want a
few dollars?"

"No charity. I work for my money."

Lucas slipped his pistol into his pocket but kept his hand
on it. He studied the man more closely for any trace of fight,
of anger, of intent to steal the money that had been offered
freely to him.

"I will repay you."

"All right." He held out his hand to shake. For a moment,
the Creek hesitated, then shook.

"You will get your money back." He pulled his hand away. "There's no hurry."

The Indian grunted and left the alley, moving like a ghost. Lucas wondered if his feet even touched the ground. On impulse, he dropped to one knee and looked at the dirt. The smallest scuff marks showed where the Creek had walked. Tracking him would be hard, even if he had wanted to. Lucas didn't bother trying to find him out in the street. Chances were good he had simply vanished.

Not caring if he ever saw his ten dollars again, Lucas went back inside the saloon. *Cast your bread upon the water and it will return tenfold*, he thought as he made his way to a table. Carmela had finished her show, Little Otto was undoubtedly backstage with her, and serious drinkers were willing to try their luck at cards. Lucas found a table of men who looked as if they had no idea about odds and began playing.

A quick gesture to Claudette brought her by with a shot of whiskey, and all was good as the cards began running for him. Dogs and their lovely owners faded into the distance as his stack of chips grew.

8

Lucas began losing consistently when his thoughts drifted from the hand in front of him on the table to other gamblers. Little Otto had said a gambler was responsible for stealing Amanda's dog. That made no sense. How could anyone make a penny unless the intent was for a ransom? Since Amanda so easily forked over a hundred dollars to put him on the dog's track, any demand would have been met with immediate agreement.

"Damn, Stanton, you're trying to improve on a pair of treys? I want you doin' that all the livelong night." The black-smith sitting across from him dropped two pair onto the table and scooped up a considerable pot that Lucas had bet up for no good reason. "That wasn't even much of a bluff."

"I'm feeling sorry for you. Anything that'll get you away from the hard work of banging out a horseshoe has to improve your health."

"Suckin' in a lungful of this smoke's worse than the

fumes off my forge. I use good metallurgic coal that don't hardly smoke up the place."

It took Lucas a second to realize the talk had gone from cards to coal.

"From Wyoming?" he asked.

"Sure thing. For two cents, I'd close my smithy and go north to mine it. I can sell all that coal out of the Powder River Basin to other farriers."

"Good luck with that." Lucas pointed to the chips stacked in front of the blacksmith. "You can buy yourself two mines with that much."

"My luck's good. I want to make it three."

Lucas laughed and touched the brim of his new bowler hat, which he had bought to replace the one lost in the sewage. What clothing he had was adequate but lacking the grandeur of his former attire. He needed to make the rounds of several finer clothing stores to replenish his wardrobe, as befitting a gambler in the Emerald City Dance Hall and Drinking Emporium, where luminaries such as Carmela Thompson appeared. He waved to Lefty as he slipped into the night—or early morning. Faint fingers of dawn already stretched toward the top of the sky.

He yawned, realized he had been playing for almost ten hours without so much as stretching. Such was the life of a professional gambler. As he passed the mouth of the alley where he had buffaloed the man collecting his due, he slowed and tried to reconstruct the fight. It had faded into his memory already. There had been a half-breed. He remembered that and paying off the man's debt, only to be surprised when the Indian refused more money and even told him he would get his ten dollars back.

Lucas patted his coat pocket. He had to count it for an exact amount, but it might be as much as what he had received from Amanda to find her dog. His fortunes had ebbed and flowed. He snorted at that thought.

"Lucky at cards, unlucky in love," he muttered as he came to an intersection. He had plenty of money but had lost out to Little Otto with Carmela. How much longer that romance flourished was the stuff of a profitable bet. Then he remembered he would have bet that Carmela would want nothing more to do with Otto after the first date. That had been so wrong, he had better keep his money working on the pasteboard cards where he knew the odds and could read his opponents.

He realized he had dithered at the intersection longer than it ought to take to turn left and return to his room. He spun and went right, toward Capitol Hill and Amanda's boardinghouse. In spite of his run-ins with Dunbar's strong-arm guards, he was feeling on top of the world. A winning night at poker did that to him, better than any drug likely to be sold by the Celestials in Hop Town over on Wazee Street. The way things went this evening, he might even find Tovarich nosing through garbage along the way.

As he turned a final corner, he stopped, then edged toward the door leading into a bookstore. Not twenty feet away, Amanda was speaking with the two men who had dumped him into the sewage. His hand went to his pistol. At this range it wasn't accurate. He had to walk closer. The tiny bullet lacked stopping power, but a couple shots to the face always made the recipient pause and think about continuing any unpleasantness.

". . . you have to tell him I don't know," Amanda said.

"He ain't got it and wants it. You turn over the dog or—"

"Or what? What can Jubal do to me that will get either of us the dog? Punish me? Is that what he wants? He can do that without using the dog as an excuse."

"We're lookin'," the second man said. "You keep huntin', too."

"I've done what I can. I even hired a detective to track the dog."

Lucas tensed. The men exchanged glances, then laughed.

"We took care of him. Nobody told us he was workin' for you."

"Took *care* of him? You *killed* him?"

"Mighta drowned."

This produced deep-throated laughter on their part. Lucas clenched the rosewood handle on his Colt even tighter. He lifted it and considered a shot. At this range it was possible to miss, to hit the wrong target. That included Amanda, but he wasn't feeling too kindly toward her at the moment since she was in cahoots with Dunbar and hadn't mentioned that to him. He lowered the gun when she protested.

"If you've killed him, I'll turn you over to the police. The marshal won't care one whit you work for Jubal."

"We was joshin'. He ain't dead. If anything, he found all kinds of new friends since he was where he usually flops around."

They laughed again.

If he aimed low, he could hit them in the legs. If he missed and hit Amanda, it wouldn't be too serious since her thick skirts would devour the small slug. Lucas braced his hand against the door frame and started to squeeze off a round when the men moved away. As Amanda turned to follow them, she blocked a clear shot.

Lucas grumbled to himself. What was he doing? He wasn't a killer. He didn't shoot men from ambush, even if they deserved it. Besides, these two deserved something more than a bullet in their pea brains. A quick step took him back out into the street, then he saw his chance had passed.

Whatever retribution he would deliver to Dunbar's henchmen had to wait.

He wanted it to be more appropriate than an unseen killer gunning them down, even if he would take some satisfaction in pulling the trigger.

Another problem rose to push away his desire for vengeance. Amanda Baldridge had lied to him. The dog might have been in her possession, but it hardly sounded as if it was hers. That meant it belonged to someone else. She had hired him to possibly commit a crime, if stealing a dog was ever a crime. He knew men who ate their dogs and never had a second thought about it.

He tucked away his pistol and went after Amanda and the men, his steps allowing them to increase the distance so they weren't likely to notice him. Lucas had no clear idea what he intended until the trio ahead turned and started up York, going to Dunbar's house. Telling Amanda to her face he wasn't going to continue the hunt for her dog—or whoever's dog it was—looked more like a suicide mission by the minute. The three went to the front door, knocked, and were let inside.

Lucas found a stump across the street and sat on it, staring at the elegant house. He had taken her money and felt obligated to complete the job, but she had lied to him. Not once had she told him of her alliance with Jubal Dunbar or that the dog would be passed from her hand to the politician's once it was found.

Tovarich was better off scrounging through garbage than being in Dunbar's care.

It took some moral wrestling but Lucas finally decided the money he had received, or what was left of it after bribes and greasing information sources, had been earned in spite of not finding Tovarich. Amanda had forfeited his services.

The stench of sewage still clung to him in spite of fancy stinkum toilet water and hard scrubbing with lye soap. Spending Amanda's money, he would end up about even when he bought a new coat and replaced the rest of his clothing soiled in the dunking. This hardly evened the score with Dunbar's men, though.

A slow smile came as he thought that he was pretty much invisible to Amanda. She thought he worked for the Great West Detective Agency. Unless she happened to wander into the Emerald City, to see Carmela, he was safe from discovery.

He retraced his steps, but when he got to the intersection, he stopped. Ahead lay his rooming house and to his left the Emerald City. The hairs on the back of his neck rose, warning him he was being watched. Using a hitching post to lean against, he worked to build himself a cigarette, taking his time and looking around without seeming to do so. He caught his breath when sudden movement down a branching street caught his attention. Someone dodged out of his line of sight.

With his cigarette lit and a cloud of smoke rising around his face, he smoked for a couple minutes. He won the waiting game. The quick move of a head out and back showed that whoever was spying on him had kept up his vigil. Not hurrying, Lucas walked across the street toward a tannery, then spun and darted to the street in time to see his stalker running away. His fingers brushed over the butt of his Colt. Again the distance was too great and the reason for shooting nonexistent. He might be jumping at shadows.

He crushed out the cigarette and walked to the corner of the tannery, knelt, and looked at the tracks closest to the wall. All he could make out was a small footprint, possibly a woman's boot or that of a large boy. He sighed, then inhaled. As he did so, he caught a curious odor. He sucked in even more and tried to remember where he had encountered this before.

"Whatsa matter, mister, you havin' an attack? You a lunger?"

He looked up to a man wearing canvas pants and a red-and-black-checked shirt. His occupation fairly screamed out to Lucas, having sat across a poker table from others dressed similarly.

"Prospecting for gold," he said, sure he identified the man's profession.

"Ain't nuthin' in this town what ain't been extracted already. You got to get into the hills if you want to hit it rich. Oro City, Ouray. Them's where the blue dirt is, where you'll find color both gold and silver." The prospector fixed Lucas with a steely look, as if daring him to refute such logic.

"I'm not so sure I haven't hit pay dirt." Lucas stood and took a final sniff. The lingering scent was so familiar, but identifying it was just a tad beyond his ken.

"Don't ask me to stake you, mister. You dig there, you get nuthin' but tannic acid from all that leather. That will burn clean through your skin and ruin work gloves in a day. I know. I used to work in a tannery up in Missoula Mills."

"What do you make of that?" Lucas stepped around the prospector and watched a double column of men riding down the street in the direction taken by his skulker. They rode with military precision although none were in uniform. The man at the head of the column stared fixedly ahead as if he had all the bones in his neck frozen into place. The riders following him looked around them like hungry wolves.

The double column neither slowed nor sped up. As if he

counted cards, Lucas ticked off the riders one by one and reached a total of twenty.

"Don't make nuthin' of it, mister. They's ridin' through, that's all."

"They have the look of men sniffing after gold. You'd better watch your claim, old-timer."

The prospector moved on, cast a backward glance at Lucas before assuring himself the crazy man wasn't following.

Lucas watched until the dust settled behind the soldiers— he instinctively thought of them that way because of the man at the head of the column and the way they rode. And the way they looked. He had seen one company too many that looked like this as they rode through his hometown of Wolf Creek, Kansas, during the war.

Denver was getting to be an even more interesting place by the minute. Lucas decided it was time for him to find some new duds, catch a few winks, and get ready for the next evening at the Emerald City. With both Carmela and Amanda beyond his charms, he had to scout out new territory. Fortunately, with new clothes and a few dollars, that wouldn't be hard.

9

Claudette laughed joyously as Lucas swung her around to sit in his lap.

"You're my good luck charm," he said, trying to give her cheek a kiss. She avoided his lips by a fraction of an inch.

"You behave. I've got work to do." She looked toward the bar, where Lefty scowled at her. "Do you want another drink? If I don't bring something back, Lefty's not going to let me serve you anymore."

"Drinks for everyone at the table," Lucas said. "Bring a bottle."

Claudette pulled back and looked at him critically before saying in a soft voice, "You're not drunk, but you want the others to be?"

"You're a pretty girl and smart, too," he said, letting her climb free of his lap. He tried to swat her behind but she moved too fast for that. As she went to fetch the bottle, Lucas turned back to the cards. "Whose deal?"

The gambler to his left picked up the cards, fanned them out on the table, then scooped them up and began shuffling. Lucas saw how the man's dexterous control put the best cards on the bottom of the deck. When he put the deck onto the table for Lucas to cut, he grinned and winked. The gambler proposed an alliance, for this hand at least, which would bring a pile of money Lucas's way through dealing off the bottom of the deck. The intent was for Lucas to win and then split the take later.

There were few things Lucas valued more than his skill at cards. He had the skill to stack the deck and make any hand pop up that he wanted—but he refused to cheat in such a fashion. Or lose. He did it through skill of reading his opponents and judging the cards.

"My cut, eh?"

He was supposed to split the deck. The other gambler would simply move the cut back to the way it was, but doing so with a great flourish and a little deception returned the deck to the way it had been prior to the cut. Determined not to be a part of such cheating, Lucas split the deck into three sections, moved them around and then built it back before pushing it to the gambler. He had put the high-value cards originally on the bottom somewhere in the middle, out of reach for the card sharp.

He smiled as the gambler shot him a black look. The deal went down and Lucas folded. It didn't surprise him that the card cheat also folded what might otherwise have been a big pot for both of them. Lucas paid no attention as the gambler shoved his chair back and left. This only gave him a better view of the stage as Carmela finished her last performance of the night. Little Otto stood beside the stage, looking up at her. Lucas thought she might have given him a big, knowing wink but her act included come-ons for about everyone in her audience.

She turned, kicked up her skirts, and then dashed off-stage laughing.

"Why not admit she's not interested in you, not the way I am?" Claudette whispered in his ear, then followed the words with her darting tongue.

A thrill of expectation passed through Lucas. He needed to romance Claudette to restore some measure of his confidence, and it would be easy enough since she was already willing. But his mind kept wandering, not to Carmela but to Amanda Baldridge. The mystery of why she came to a detective agency to find the dog gnawed at him. She had continued the hunt herself, but was Dunbar part of the searchers she had enlisted? A man like Dunbar couldn't be used that easily, and somehow Lucas doubted Amanda had gone to him rather than the other way around. She was a lovely woman, and batting her long eyelashes certainly set a red-blooded man's heart racing a bit faster, but Jubal Dunbar valued power. Was he also a man who indulged in a woman's charms outside marriage?

"What do you know of Jubal Dunbar's wife?" Lucas looked back over his shoulder, his lips close to Claudette's.

"Who's that?"

Claudette's question was sharper than he'd expected.

"You fooling around with her because you can't get Carmela?"

"Nothing of the sort, my dear," he said. Claudette backed away from him. At the table the remaining players grew restive since he was interrupting their inexorable loss. "I wondered if he had a wife and cheated on her."

"You have business with him?" The pretty waiter girl looked at the others at the table. "Is he one of them?"

"No, not at all. Forget it. You're the light of my life and all that matters to me."

"Liar," she said, slapping him on the shoulder. "But I like it. Don't stop lying to me. Nobody else ever tries to sweet-talk me."

"Their loss, my gain."

"You gonna play? If not, let somebody else get into the chair."

Lucas turned to the players, nodded solemnly, then raked in his winnings. He had done what he could here. The gambler who left might return since the men remaining hadn't realized what had happened. Both professionals had lost, after all.

"May luck be with you, gentlemen." He stuffed the chips and greenbacks into his coat pocket and pushed back.

"I can't just go off with you now, Lucas," Claudette said. "Lefty keeps me here till the cows come home."

"He's sweet on you."

"Lefty? Don't joke, Lucas. He doesn't like anyone or anything but making money."

Pointing out the sour look the barkeep gave him wouldn't convince Claudette of such a romantic connection. He looked at the empty stage and wondered how the world worked in such a strange fashion. He had put Little Otto and Carmela together, even as he wanted the singer for himself. Claudette ignored Lefty's obvious glances while hanging on to Lucas's arm as they made their way through the crowded Emerald City. Everyone sought another's arms and ignored what was at hand. It made no sense.

And what of Amanda Baldridge? Did she share Dunbar's bed to find her dog? Only, from everything he heard, piecing together all that happened and Little Otto's snippets of rumor, the dog belonged to someone else. Amanda and Dunbar both sought Tovarich, but neither was the legitimate owner.

"Why would a puppy dog be worth so much?"

"You want a dog?" Claudette stared at him as if he had opened a new eye in the middle of his forehead. "I can give you something more to fill up your bed—all night long."

"But you certainly would want a bone, my dear."

"Damned right!"

From across the saloon, Lefty roared for her to get back to work. Claudette looked up at Lucas, then quickly, passionately kissed him before rushing back to work.

The taste of her lips on his was like a heady liquor. Her perfume was—not the scent he had noticed on whoever had tracked him earlier. The long cape hid the person's body, but the longer he thought about it, the more certain he was that it had hidden a woman. A woman using a perfume that was familiar, but one which he could not identify. He had encountered it before, but where danced just beyond his ability to remember.

He stepped into the cold night and felt as if he had been slapped. Only his lips remained warm from the aftermath of Claudette's kiss. He looked around. Denver was alive this night, and he felt the city's energy flowing through him. Coming to decisions helped. He had only a slim chance with Carmela and had moved on with his affections, though Claudette was a stopgap. Neither of them had real emotions in the mix as they sought a moment's respite from life.

His gambling had gone well, and he had more money in his pocket than at any time over the past year. Amanda's contribution to his poke helped make that bulge even larger. He began walking aimlessly, his mind slipping off the tracks and running wild. Lucas appreciated such times. At the poker table, his intensity sometimes annoyed the other players, but he always gave his complete attention to the game. This was a mental holiday for him and allowed new thoughts to poke up that he might otherwise never encounter.

Not realizing where his steps led, he stopped and stared at the front of the Great West Detective Agency office. It was as deserted as the first time he had blundered inside, getting away from the outraged rancher and his hired hands. He turned to walk on, then saw an envelope thrust between the door and frame. Lucas looked around. The people in the street were all intent on some destination and paid him no heed. With a quick move, he took the envelope and held it up.

The envelope carried no address, but it wasn't sealed. Moving under a gaslight, he pulled out the flap and peered inside at the letter inside. Again he looked around, but this time he hesitated and stared hard at a man and woman down the street, pressed together but not looking at each other. Their attention was focused on the plate glass window of a watch shop, closed at this time of night but perfect for watching those behind them without being too obvious.

Moving around the light, he saw that he could make out the couple's shadowy faces, meaning they could also watch him. His hand moved to his pocket, but he had to push aside a couple dozen high-value poker chips before getting to his pistol. He stared at the two, trying to make out more details. They might be the man and the woman he had seen before in front of the detective agency office, but he didn't think so, although the woman did most of the talking and the man only listened. The man was taller, as was the woman. Then they both walked away without so much as a backward glance in his direction.

Lucas pushed aside what was becoming a growing nervousness on his part. If he hadn't gotten involved with Amanda Baldridge, he wouldn't jump at every shadow or be suspicious of anyone even looking in his direction. That would teach him to fall under a lovely woman's spell—and to take her considerable amount of money offered for an improbable job.

He held up the letter written in a crabbed, perfect hand. Every letter looked as if it had been drawn painstakingly. A quick scan of the page told of a telegram offering a job, a question of where the Great West Detective Agency staff was, and finally a resolution to persevere until personal contact had been made. The letter had been signed by Raymond and Felicia Northcott.

From running his finger over the cheap paper, he suspected this had been supplied by a lesser hotel. The ink had been smeared in places, showing the author lacked a roller blotter to prevent ink smudges. He pressed his finger into a word, then looked. Dry. The letter had been written sometime earlier. With deft moves, he replaced the letter in the envelope and the envelope in the door.

Trying to remain nonchalant, he went to the rear of the building and tried the back door. It remained locked, the way he'd left it when he had first sought refuge inside. Lucas dropped to his knees, fished out the slender picks, and quickly opened the door again. He stepped into the small storage room, then closed and locked the door behind him.

The office seemed mustier from being closed. This spurred him on, knowing he wasn't going to be surprised by the detective agency's owner. He stepped into the main office and hesitated, taking a deep whiff. The elusive scent he had detected when the mysterious woman had been spying on him matched that in the office. It was faint, more than a distant shout from over the horizon, but his sense of smell hadn't been completely ruined by long nights in saloons filled with cigar smoke, the stench of spilled beer, and vomit mixed in with sawdust.

Somehow the Great West Detective Agency tied in with a woman spying on him.

He settled into the desk chair and began working on the locked desk drawers, hoping to find—what? Lucas had no good idea, but curiosity drove him to paw through files painstakingly compiled and with detailed reports. From what he could tell, one man had written all the reports. The owner of the agency worked alone. The volume of reports, though, suggested a reason why the Northcotts had been solicited. The agency was bursting with work, and the owner needed help running the office while he was in the field.

Lucas leaned back and considered that. In the field meant far afield or the office would have been opened in the past few days. He touched the pocket bulging with money. It hadn't been that long ago he had taken money from Amanda to find her puppy—or someone's puppy. He continued rooting around in the files, holding some sheets up to catch a slant of pale yellow illumination coming from the gaslight out in the street.

He let out a whoop when he discovered the owner's signature on a report.

"So I am poaching business from Jacoby Runyon, agency operative." Lucas chuckled to himself at the discovery, then sobered when he found a biography of the man. He had become expert listening to men's tales and deciphering the lies from the truths. Those who spoke the loudest about their lives invented the most. This seemed truest of the war veterans, either of the Civil War or any of the innumerable Indian wars. The true participants had their voices muffled due to grave memories.

Lucas saw more missing from Runyon's biography that hinted at a dire road to this Denver office, meandering through death and larceny of great proportion. He shoved the pages back into a file drawer as he wondered if Runyon would have taken Amanda's money for what might have been a trivial chore. How long would it have taken a real detective to find the political connection with Jubal Dunbar? Lucas doubted even an expert detective like Runyon would have navigated through the turbid waters around Amanda any better than he had already.

He idly leafed through another file in the top right desk drawer, then read it more carefully. The railroad down in Durango had been shut down due to recurring robberies with track blown up and railroad crews slaughtered, and Runyon had been hired to bring the criminals to justice. The huge amount of money already received showed that the railroad owners were willing to go to any length. That gave Lucas new insight into Jacoby Runyon. The man wasn't to be crossed. Dunbar might have thugs working for him, but Runyon had the spine—and hard fists—to oppose them.

Lucas held up his own fist and smiled. He wasn't a slouch when it came to bare knuckle fighting either. He had gone a few rounds with the best for a bet and had won. Relaxing his fist, he ran his sensitive fingers over his left cheek. The hard knot where a cheekbone had been broken and mended improperly was immediately obvious. Lucas knew it didn't mar his good looks with an unsightly knob on his face, but more than one woman had stroked over his cheek and commented on it.

He had won a thousand dollars betting on himself by going six rounds with an up-and-coming fighter named John Sullivan. Sullivan had knocked him down five times, but he had always answered the bell for the next round. Lucas was glad the bet hadn't required him to go a sixth or the bare knuckles fighter would have killed him. He touched the poorly mended cheekbone again as a reminder of his own limits.

Lucas closed the desk drawers and relocked them. The excursion into the office once more had satisfied his curiosity. Now he could keep Amanda's money with a clear conscience. He wasn't taking bread from a poor detective's mouth. If anything, Jacoby Runyon was better heeled than most of the merchants in Denver, taking money from the richest men in America for dangerous commissions no one else could tackle.

He stood, sampled the air again, but no longer detected the scent. On impulse, Lucas went to the file cabinet and searched it as much for the source of the odor as anything else. He found a bank bag—empty—and not much else but dust and an all-pervading smell of old paper and ink.

Lucas considered leaving through the front door, then decided to retreat out the way he had come. The Northcotts' letter wouldn't be disturbed any more if he did that. He wished them luck getting the job Runyon had advertised with the agency. Neither of them struck him as detectives. Runyon needed office help, and the married couple would provide it, especially the woman.

At the back door, he hesitated. A tiny sound in the alley alerted him that something was wrong. It might be nothing more than cat-sized rats dining on garbage or a hungry coyote come to town to dine on those same giant rats. He slipped his pistol from his pocket and cocked it before opening the door.

A dark form slammed hard against the door and sent Lucas stumbling back. He fired point-blank and hit his target. But he didn't stop a snarling, biting dog trying to rip out his throat. His second shot directly into the gaping, fang-filled mouth blew the top off the dog's head and sent it reeling to die.

Lucas scrambled to his feet and found himself facing another large dog, sleek and slender and measured in hands high rather than inches. Two more shots crippled the dog. A big jump carried him over the snapping, crippled dog. He started to run and realized there were more than the two dogs he had shot.

A pack of gigantic wolfhounds coursed from the far end of the alley, intent on ripping him to shreds. His pistol carried seven rounds and he had expended four. Lucas jerked as sharp teeth snapped at his leg, sending him careening off balance out into the street and his death.

10

Lucas hit the ground, rolled onto his back, and kicked hard. Teeth sank into his ankle just above his boot top. He winced as pain knifed into his leg. He jerked back on the pistol's blue-colored trigger and sent a round into the wolfhound's head. To his surprise and panic, the bullet glanced off, leaving a bloody streak in the dog's fur. It didn't kill him or slow him down. It only infuriated him. Lips drawn back to show pearly white teeth, the dog leaped for Lucas's throat in retaliation.

Another round fired without the man realizing it. And then he prepared to die with the dog's jaws clamped firmly on his throat. He felt hot liquid running down his neck, and the smell of dog and fear and blood made his nostrils flare.

Heavy weight pinned him to the ground—but it was dead weight. Kicking, feeling his injured calf protest even this small movement, Lucas heaved the dog off his chest and sat up, waving his small pistol around. He vowed to swap it for a Colt Peacemaker. If .45-calibers of heavy lead didn't stop a dog dead in its track when he shot it, nothing this side of a Sharps buffalo rifle would.

"Dead?" The word slipped from his lips. He tasted blood. As he ran his tongue over his lips, he realized he had bitten down hard on his own flesh. He spat, then stared at the dead dog. It had a deer horn–handled knife protruding from its side. The blade had sunk deeply through both lungs and maybe the heart, killing the dog instantly. He yanked the knife free, knowing he was down to a single round. Or had he fired all seven? Everything jumbled in his head.

He saw a half dozen wolfhounds snarling and snapping at the mouth of the alley, fighting over some prey. As the pack shifted position, he saw they fought for a large haunch of meat. It might have been beef or lamb. Whatever it was, the hounds thought it gave them more food than his trembling body would.

A light touch plucked the knife from his hand. He twisted about, his pistol coming to bear. Only a powerful hand pushed it out of line. He looked up into the middle of the man's chest, then even farther up to a dark, impassive face. Tight braids of black hair flopped on either of the man's shoulders.

Lucas struggled for words. A strong hand grabbed his arm and lifted him to his feet. By now he recognized his savior.

"Reckon we're even," he told the Indian he had saved a couple nights earlier.

"Still owe you ten dollars," the man said. He shoved hard and sent Lucas stumbling along. With his bad leg, the gambler found running difficult, but he summoned up the stamina and ignored the pain.

Their hasty retreat drew unwanted attention along the

slowly filling street. It was still a half hour until dawn, but the businesses had to prepare for their customers at the first light of day. Lucas heard a squishy sound as he hobbled along, looked back, and saw he was leaving bloody tracks. He slowed and began to fumble to pull off his boot, but his rescuer slipped an arm around his shoulder and lifted him off his feet as if he weighed only a few ounces.

"No time to stop."

Lucas did his best to keep up with the quick pace set but quickly became light-headed. Before he fell, he was gently placed into a chair in front of a boarded-up store.

"Nobody'll notice us here. Nobody'll come to work," he said. The dizziness robbed him of his usual facile thought. Everything that had happened in the past few minutes worked to confuse him.

"Do not take off boot. Your foot will swell."

"And I won't get it back on." Lucas nodded. It felt as if something had come loose inside him. He cradled his head in his hands as he leaned forward. This cleared his mind after a few seconds and he sat upright. "My name's Lucas Stanton."

"I know."

"That's not the proper response," Lucas said. "You're supposed to answer 'My name is,' then you tell me what you're called."

"Good."

"I'm happy it pleases you. What's your name?" His anger further sharpened his senses. The pain in his left turned to a dull throb.

"Good."

"You pulled my fat out of the fire. Thanks. You didn't have to do it." Lucas scowled. "You knew I was going to run afoul of the dogs, didn't you?"

Fathomless dark eyes stared at him.

"Unless you carry a leg of some dead animal around with you all the time, you wouldn't have been able to entice them away." He saw no hint of emotion on the man's broad face. Playing poker with him would be a pisser.

"Good."

"What are you saying 'good' to now?"

"That is my name. Good."

"Just Good?"

"Why do I need more?"

Lucas laughed at the logic. Why did any man need more than one name?

"It might keep you from getting confused with everyone else named Good."

"No one else is Good."

"Now that, sir, is something I will not dispute."

The Indian looked at him curiously now.

"Why do you call me 'sir'?"

"You deserve it. You are obviously better than I am at some things, such as keeping me alive." Lucas used both hands to pull his leg around. The trouser leg had plastered itself to his flesh, but the blood had stopped oozing out. "It's clotted. The wound's not too serious, then, unless the dog had hydrophobia."

"Dogs were all well tended, well trained."

"Russian wolfhounds," Lucas said, finally remembering enough of the attack to wonder how it was connected with Amanda's lost puppy.

Good nodded once, then bent and used the tip of his sharp knife to cut through the cloth and expose Lucas's bite. He poked about with the knife tip for a moment more, then sheathed it at his waist and drew out an Apache hoddentin bag. He opened it, took out a pinch of brown powder, and sprinkled it on the dog bite.

Lucas recoiled in pain.

"The dog didn't kill me. Are you trying to finish the job?"

Hot lances ran up to his knee, through his hip, and into his groin until he was sure he was going to explode. Then the pain subsided. Good put away his medicine bag made from cured deer hide.

Lucas frowned. He recognized the medicine bag but had thought the man belonged to one of the Five Civilized Tribes. He was seldom wrong, but why would a Creek carry an Apache shaman's fetish?

"Are you Apache? That's an Apache medicine man's symbol on the bag of—"

"Tule." Good settled his belt, moved his knife around to where he could whip it out in a hurry, then pressed his hand over the medicine bag. "I killed the Apache. He was Lipan. I do not like Lipan. I am Creek."

"Eastern Oklahoma?" Lucas heaved a sigh of relief that he wasn't wrong. Good might hail from somewhere close to his own hometown in Kansas. For some reason Lucas couldn't immediately identify, this made him more comfortable with the man. Trust never came easily, and he warned himself to be wary or something of his might go into the dead Apache's medicine bag dangling from Good's belt.

Good simply stared.

Before the war, the Creek had been slave owners but not in the way white Southerners tended theirs. The Creek slaves had been a part of an extended family, but they had been chattel nonetheless. After the war, many of them and their offspring had left Indian Territory. It wasn't out of the question to find a black Creek in Denver seeking his fortune.

Lucas was damned lucky Good had been there.

"Did you take that knife off the dead Apache?" He pointed to the horn-handled knife that had gutted the wolf-hound so intent on ripping out his throat.

"You take your coat off a circus clown?"

Lucas was taken aback, then laughed. It wasn't his place to interrogate the man.

"You've been watching over me, haven't you? Did you see the woman who was following me the other day?"

Good nodded slightly, then ran his finger under his nose.

"She wears a strong perfume," Lucas said. "Spikenard. That's what it's called. It's made from some plant found only in the Himalayas."

"I know of those," Good said. "Tall mountains on the other side of the world."

"You do get around," Lucas said, standing. His leg felt strong enough for him to walk. "Thanks for the help." He started back toward the detective agency. Good fell into step beside him.

"You go after them?"

"No pack of dogs is going to chew me up and spit me out without paying for it."

"Dogs were killed. That is enough."

Lucas wasn't going to explain to the Creek what he felt. He had been attacked, but more than this, he thought this was the only chance he had of finding Amanda's dog. A wolfhound puppy had to come from a wolfhound sire and bitch.

"Not for me. I'm going to find the pack—and the woman siccing it on me."

Good started to speak. He shook his head no, then stared straight ahead as they returned to the detective agency office. The dead dogs had already been removed from the street and the back room. From the footprints left in the dogs' blood on the floor, a woman had come in and taken the carcass. Lucas went to the far end of the alley and saw deep ruts left by wagon wheels. Of the dogs, woman, or wagon, he saw nothing.

"I need to get a horse."

"You cannot go alone."

"I won't say a word against it if you're offering to come with me. Sitting in a chair all day long is more my style than astride a horse."

"Then stay. I will follow them."

Lucas tried to figure out the reason for this strange offer. Good had been ready for the dogs' attack. He wanted to ask how that came about, but the offer to ride after the pack by himself gave Lucas more reason to wonder.

"I owe you," Good said, as if trying to answer the question before it was asked.

"Don't get me wrong. I'm mighty appreciative of what you've done. If you think you need to do any more to pay back the ten dollars, consider the debt paid. My life's worth about that much." He grinned crookedly. "And the magic dust you used on my leg is worth even more."

"You will go after the dogs?"

Lucas used the Indian's method of answering. He nodded once. Good sagged a little, as if in resignation, then straightened.

"I will get horses."

Lucas stayed at the alley while Good fetched horses for them. He spent the time staring into the distance at the Front Range. The wagon had rattled off in that direction. If they rode hard, they would overtake the dogs and driver before noon.

That had seemed a reasonable estimate, though Lucas had overestimated his own endurance in the saddle. Parts of him hurt that he didn't even know existed, and the places he knew about blistered after an hour on the trail. For reasons known only to him, Good said nothing. If Lucas could read the man's thoughts, he was happy for the delay. That made no sense, but Good was always ready to continue when Lucas forced down his pain enough to hit the trail again.

"There," Good said as the sun dipped behind the tall Rockies.

Lucas shielded his eyes and tried to make out the wagon tracks. Good proved himself a far superior tracker. All Lucas saw were scrapes on rock. Left to his own devices, he would have never chosen this route.

"Camp on far side of hill. We can look from the crest." Good indicated a game trail going up a steep knoll.

"How do you know there's a camp anywhere nearby?"

Good snapped his reins and worked his pony up the trail without replying. Lucas took a deep breath and thought he caught a hint of wood smoke. That might have been all the hint the Creek needed, but Lucas thought it was chancy to bet on a camp on the far side of the hill.

Twilight held the land when they topped the rise. Lucas caught his breath as he looked down into a gentle, grassy bowl.

"I bow to your expertise. That's a good-sized camp."

"Four wagons," Good said. "Ten men."

The baying of the wolfhounds added to the count below. How Good came to his tally on the men was another tribute to his skill—a skill Lucas did not possess. He kicked his leg back, winced as skin stretched over burning muscles, then he dropped to the ground.

"What do we do now?" Good remained astride his pony.

Lucas damned Good for asking the question before he could. Now he had to find an answer rather than see what the Creek came up with. He had no chance of finding Tovarich in Denver. Locating the source of the puppy gave him a new thread to track back so he could find the wayward canine.

"First, hold the reins." Lucas passed them up to the Indian. "If I get into trouble, come get me."

"No!" Good's cry fell on deaf ears.

Lucas stumbled and slid down the far side of the hill, going directly for the camp below. He reached the grassy bowl and walked with more confidence than he felt, the nearest campfire his destination. Dark forms rose and he felt eyes fixed on him as he came within a few yards of the easternmost wagon.

He worried about the men throwing down on him. Death came from a direction he should have anticipated.

11

His hand went to his pocket with the loaded Colt, but the onslaught from the dog would make a shot impossible. Lucas was a good marksman, but it was past twilight and all he saw were fleeting shadows and chimeras dancing about as the wolfhound thundered toward him. He heard its paws smashing into the ground as it gathered speed and saw the fangs in its huge mouth. One quick snap on his throat would kill him. Waiting until the dog came close enough for a decent shot would mean his death.

He had been lucky back in Denver, killing two and injuring another. The power and ferocity of the attack would overwhelm him.

The wolfhound jumped. Lucas dropped to one knee and jerked hard to the side. Once a four-legged animal launched, it couldn't change its direction. There couldn't be any fancy footwork as it launched either. Straight on. That was it. The dog plunged past, twisting its head and snapping its jaws in an attempt to catch him. The wolfhound landed hard and skidded in the dirt, its momentum carrying it away from him.

"Stop!"

He had half drawn his pistol. His only chance was to shoot the wolfhound before it recovered its balance and brought the attack back to him. The sharp command froze him. To his surprise it also caused the dog to hunker down on its haunches. It still pulled back its lips and snarled, but it had stopped its attack.

The woman walking up would have been prettier if she hadn't worn a mask of black fury.

"I should let Sasha kill you."

"Why not?" Lucas got to his feet, warily turning to face her. The dog at his back presented a constant threat. "You loosed your dogs on me in Denver."

"Is that why you followed me? Because of that?"

"One dog ripped my pant leg." Lucas held out his injured leg. It throbbed dully now as Good's medicine wore off. "You owe me a new pair of pants."

She stood with her mouth agape, her confusion obvious. Lucas decided she was prettier confused than angry. Her brunette hair had been pulled back and held in place with an intricate silver band. Her wide-set eyes and sallow appearance made him wonder if she was part Celestial. Her skin was tanned but might carry a hint of a xanthous hue. The closer he looked, the more he imagined epicanthic folds around those eyes, giving her an exotic look. She was shorter than he by a few inches, but her real height was something for him to determine later since she wore glossy, high-heeled leather riding boots that added a few inches to her. What intrigued him most was her clothing.

It was gaudy to the point of being funny, but he didn't laugh. At her waist, tucked into a broad black leather belt snugged about her, she carried no fewer than three knives. Those blades took away the circus mien to her tight riding britches and flaring embroidered jacket that looked like a confused rainbow with its reds and yellows vying for attention from the bright greens and cobalt blues.

Most fascinating of all was her perfume. He inhaled deeply.

"Spikenard," he said.

She stared at him, her confusion growing. Then she understood what he had said.

"How do you know this? It is a spice that grows only in the Himalayas. You have not been there." She spoke with contempt.

"Unlike you, I wasn't born there," he said. "But I fancy myself a connoisseur of fragrances, especially those used by such a lovely lady."

Behind him the dog growled so loudly he fancied he could feel it shaking the ground. He knew how to run a bluff. Looking nervous now wasn't the way to stay alive. Expecting Good to pull his fat from the fire wasn't a strategy he wanted to rely on.

"You know a great deal about me," the woman said.

"There is much about you that is still a mystery shrouded in secrecy," he said. Keeping her talking kept him alive for another few seconds. The longer she listened and responded, the better his chance was that the dog wouldn't dine on him.

"My business is my own."

"I referred to your name."

"Why do you want to know it?" Her suspicion told Lucas a great deal.

"I do not intend turning you over to the authorities." From her reaction, he had hit the bull's-eye. She and her gang were on the run from the law. "I expect a lovely woman such as yourself to have a lovely name. Katarina? Alexandra?"

"Vera," she said. "Vera Zasulich."

Lucas bowed deeply, doffing his bowler and sweeping it in a grand arc. He regretted the movement because the dog barked and edged closer.

Vera snapped her fingers and said something in Russian. The wolfhound settled down, but it had crept a foot closer. Lucas held his hat in his hand but hid his Colt inside the bowler, just in case. The small pistol wouldn't slow the dog, but a shot in Vera Zasulich's direction might produce more results—if necessary.

"You already know me."

"I don't," she said, surprising him. "You go about town asking questions. That is all I know."

Lucas introduced himself but said nothing about the Great West Detective Agency. He moved to better see her face, the wrinkles, the grins, the movement of her eyes, the tension, all the small signs he studied while playing poker. The cards only meant riches or ruin for him, with the exception of the rancher who had lost the deed to his ranch. Somehow, Lucas thought Vera's reaction would prove more dangerous if she turned on him.

"A gambler? I can see that. What is your purpose coming into our camp without introduction? You followed us from town."

"Your dogs almost killed me."

"Three died." Vera's tone turned steely. "You were responsible?"

"Having one of your dogs trying to rip out my throat made the fight simple enough. The dog or me."

"I would have preferred to have the dog live."

"I'm sure," he said. "Those are magnificent animals. Do you have any small ones? Puppies?" There had to be more of a connection between Vera Zasulich and Amanda than the shared perfume. The obvious one was the breed of dog. Tovarich might only be a puppy but Amanda had said he was a Russian wolfhound like these.

"You are not the type to care about dogs," she said. "Why are you here?"

"You know why." He watched her closely for any hint of what to do next. If he hadn't stared so intently, he would have missed a curious movement of her hands, fingers moving in a quick pattern.

Lucas wondered if he had blundered into a Freemasons' meeting with secret symbols and passwords, but he duplicated the woman's sign. Her eyes widened and she started to speak but no words came out.

"Yes," he said. "We share more than meets the eye." He refrained from invoking the secret hand signal again. That might have been too much. One of his acknowledged faults in poker was overplaying good hands, spooking his opponents and causing them to fold before he'd milked the most from them.

Vera Zasulich had to fill in all the missing pieces and then Lucas had to ease the truth from her to find out what was going on.

"This country never ceases to amaze me," she said. "Revolutionaries in Mother Russia do not dress as you or look as you."

"I'm sure they cannot be as handsome," Lucas said, bowing slightly. He moved his hat around so he could slip his pistol back into his coat pocket. With both hands he settled the bowler on his head at a jaunty angle and gave her the biggest smile he could muster.

She seemed immune to his charm, so he changed tactics.

"Feed me to the dog or let's talk business."

Vera called out something more in Russian. Two of the men near cooking fires came over, rifles held in the crooks of their arms. They dressed in a manner similar to the woman, in a style Lucas struggled to identify. He had seen gypsies leaving New Orleans in a small caravan. These wagons were of similar construction. The clothing differed, though it had some details in common.

"Cossacks," he said in a low voice.

The woman snapped at the men, who backed away. She circled Lucas and took hold of the dog's thick leather collar. A quick tug got the dog to its feet. With a few whispered words, she let the dog go free. It trotted past Lucas, but the way it sized him up for dinner made him put his hand back in his pocket. His fingers stroked over the varnished rosewood butt of his pistol, but the dog gave a yelp, then raced off.

"Many of us are Cossacks. We have no love for the czar, but you knew that."

"The smell of your brewing tea reminds me how thirsty I am. Could you spare a cup?"

She gestured for him to precede her. Lucas worried that she would use one of those knives when he turned his back, then realized the number of times she had already passed up to kill him if she wanted. He settled down on a smooth rock near the fire, where a pot of boiling water hung over the flames.

Vera called to one of the men to bring her cups and a samovar. The boiling water was carefully decanted into the samovar, which she put on the ground between them before adding a few fragrant tea leaves.

"The big pot is too cumbersome. The samovar is more convenient."

"And traditional," Lucas added. He watched the vapor

curl from the spout and be spirited away by the growing breeze. "Very fine odor." He sniffed deeply and caught not only the brewing tea but the woman's perfume.

This set off a confusing series of thoughts of Amanda and Tovarich and the pack of hounds Vera commanded so expertly. He forced them all away. Being in such a dangerous position required all his wit. Charm hadn't played well with the woman, so he had to rely on other ways to find out what he needed to know.

"We are revolutionaries. Tradition means little." Vera poured the tea into a cup and handed it to Lucas. She poured for herself and raised the enameled cup in salute. "Death to the czar!"

"Death to all tyrants." Lucas sipped the tea, expecting it to be undrinkable. To his surprise, it was nothing like the tea a British companion had forced on him as they idled away the time one winter in Kansas City. "Very good."

"It comes from Nepal. The Shah Dynasty allows very little to leave the country, but I have friends there."

"Your home?"

"My grandfather's. I am Russian!"

"How long before you overthrow the czar?"

Her eyes narrowed as she studied him. She used the teacup as a way of hiding her mouth in an attempt to keep her reaction away from him. That turned him cautious.

"Not that it matters to me one way or the other," he added. "Our concerns only overlap on other matters."

This eased her suspicion. Tribes always had strong bonds. The Russians were every bit as loyal to their tribe as any Indian, and any outsider pretending to believe as they did was just that, an outsider.

"It is good belonging to a group you are loyal to and that

is loyal to you." He heaved a sigh. "I am something of a loner."

"You are loyal to no political philosophy? How strange. That is even alien to me, but you Americans are loyal to money."

"Gold is good." Again he was surprised by her reaction. She accepted him more now, thinking he sought only money rather than ideology. Who were her allies?

She poured him more tea.

"Mr. Dunbar would appreciate this tea. It is that good."

"Dunbar?"

"I thought you knew him. Jubal Dunbar."

He became even more curious about the Russians and their mission when he realized her ignorance was not feigned. He had thought Tovarich was the thread binding Vera with Amanda and Dunbar.

"What is your role?"

"To bring nothing but success to the venture," he said. "I hadn't been told that my job was going to be so pleasant dealing with a lovely lady such as yourself." He saw a flash of irritation pass as Vera looked at him more closely. Charm still had a place in keeping him alive.

"I am sorry I sent the dogs against you in Denver. You should have gotten to us."

"I had another job to deal with. Bankers and the like," he said vaguely.

"Bankers, pah! They are in league with those in power."

"Tell me how you would deal with them."

Lucas found the woman sitting beside him, her leg pressing into his. Her perfume was thicker but not overpowering. Or not as overpowering as Vera's sheer presence. She was a strong, vital woman, and he had not realized how the gypsy—or Cossack?—dress suited her by emphasizing her hidden curves. She moved so she half faced him. Her lips parted slightly, and her eyes closed as if she wanted him to kiss her. He bent forward, only to check himself as she rocked back and pulled a book from her jacket.

"It is all here," she said breathlessly, waving the book around. "Only by taking the land from the czar and giving it to the serfs can Mother Russia prosper. Under the thumb of Czar Alexander, we will suffer and eventually perish. In here, in *Catechism of a Revolutionary*, is our plan."

Lucas glanced at the book in Russian. It could have been a book on dog breeding for all he knew, but the pages were dog-eared and the lettering on the cover had worn off from being studied so intently.

"That's something you wrote?"

"No, no, I am not a political theorist," she said, moving closer to thrust the book into his hands. "Mikhail Bukanin is a genius, a master, and the one we of the Narodniki look to for inspiration. The czar has failed to make agrarian reform and continues to enslave the serfs. We will seize the farmland from him and put it into the hands of all citizens."

"Not the farmers?"

"Everyone will own the land. They will work the land for the good of all, not for only the nobility. The power of the state will be crushed, and we will all live in harmony without the tax collectors stealing from us."

"That's a mighty lofty goal. Of course, you need money for it."

"The gold will spark the revolution. We will not fail!"

Lucas took the book thrust into his hands although he could never read it, even if he wanted to.

"Do you have any other books? In English?"

Vera laughed. It started out as a robust laugh but built into something almost loco.

"I have many such books by your cleverest writers. *The Innocents Abroad* tells me much of your country and how you think." Her lip curled into a sneer. "We will free Russia of the imperial yoke, then do the same with yours."

"It'll take more gold than either of us have got," he said, trying to ease out a bit more information about the gold. That sounded promising, but he still saw no connection between Vera and Amanda. Asking outright if Amanda had stolen one of the hound mistress's dogs felt wrong. He still edged along a brink of a very deep abyss. Vera Zasulich might easily nudge him over the edge at any instant as she went from rational to crazy.

"There is plenty to go around, but you know that."

"Do you have that Twain book you mentioned?"

"In my wagon." She looked at him like the wolfhound had earlier, and he wondered what he had gotten himself into. He trailed her to the central wagon. She stepped up and pulled the door open wide. "Is this what you wanted to see?"

He shifted his gaze from the book in her hand to her. She had contrived to open the neck of her blouse.

"I'll trade you."

"What do you want to trade?"

"This book for the one in your hand."

He stepped closer. Her scent filled his nostrils and proved almost as intoxicating as the tarantula juice Lefty served at the Emerald City. Their bodies touched lightly, but for Lucas it was electric. Vera was wild and sometimes insane, and he couldn't help wondering if that carried over to more amorous activities.

She plucked the book from his hand and tossed it into the wagon. Her arms circled his neck and pulled him forward so his face was buried in the open neck of her blouse. His lips pressed against warm flesh. Before he could take advantage of this artificial height difference, the pounding of horses' hooves sounded. She shoved him to one side, forcing him to sit heavily on the step.

"Take the book. Do it." She vaulted over him and walked briskly, head high and shoulders back, toward the fire.

Lucas picked up the book she had dropped and looked at it.

"I'll be damned," he said. "What are the odds?" He tucked the book into a pocket already crowded with poker chips and money, settled his Colt New Line to come to his grip quicker without rummaging through everything, and then got his feet under him.

"Is he the one?" The question boomed, deep and bass, across the camp.

Vera and the newcomer exchanged increasingly shrill words in Russian. Lucas considered his chances of walking away to be slim now as the other men poked their heads from their wagons. Every one of them hefted a rifle or a six-shooter, and all looked from the man arguing with Vera to Lucas.

Boldness had gotten him this far. He walked to where the woman stood a little behind the tall, broad-shouldered man. Lucas sized up their relationship immediately. It wouldn't do to boast that he was with Vera.

"Good evening," Lucas said. For good measure he made the secret sign. If Vera was a revolutionary and a member of a secret anarchist group, this had to be the leader. If nothing else, the sign had to pour oil on the turbulent water swirling around now.

The man looked to Vera and fired off a chain of more Russian. Lucas didn't have to speak the language to know that little of it was complimentary.

"He is one of us, Dmitri," she replied in English for Lucas's benefit. "He is here to help us find the treasure trove."

Lucas fought to keep his face a mask at those words. He had intended to slip away as quickly as he could, but this verified what he had suspected. The Russians were hunting for hidden gold, and Vera wasn't the starry-eyed sort to go looking for fool's gold. The scars on Dmitri's face, crisscrossing like poorly harrowed farmland, showed he wasn't likely to fall for any tall tale. So many Americans back East bought a treasure map thinking it would give them untold wealth. All it did was open the door for a lot of misery and an empty pocket. Dmitri, Vera, and the others lacked the trust required to buy such a fraudulent map. They were here in Colorado because the chances of finding gold—lots of it to finance their revolution—were good.

"I have never seen you before," Dmitri said.

"I've never seen you either. That doesn't mean we're not after the same thing."

"You work for *him*."

Lucas hesitated, not knowing if he should deny it. He had no idea to whom Dmitri referred.

That pause brought the others moving in. Lucas found himself at the center of a circle of guns pointed at him.

"Look," he said, desperation growing.

Sweat beaded on his forehead, forcing him to choose between wiping it away or going for his pistol. He did neither. One would have betrayed his bluff. The other would have brought a dozen ounces of lead ripping through his body.

"We're both hunting for the same thing," Lucas went on. "Tovarich—"

He had not expected the reaction he got. Dmitri reached out and took him by the throat, massive hands squeezing down hard and forcing Lucas to his knees. He fumbled for his pistol, but the world turned blacker by the instant as the life was choked out of him.

12

"Dmitri, stop! Don't kill him!"

The words came through a gathering fog, but the pressure on his throat lessened. Lucas struggled to wrap his finger around the trigger of his pistol, though in some distant part of his brain he wondered if firing while the Colt was still in his pocket wouldn't put him more at risk than Dmitri.

A rapid burst of Russian produced a complete slackening around his neck. He gasped, choked, and rolled away to get free. Vera put her arm around him and brought him to a sitting position on the ground. He looked up at the hulking Dmitri. All he could see was the man's fierce black beard, the blazing eyes, the set to his mouth.

"He did not mean to kill you."

"Thanks for saving me," Lucas said. He got to his feet and sucked in a deep breath to steady himself. "Why'd you choke me?"

"You stole Tovarich!"

The Russian's roar forced Lucas back a step. He wanted to go for his gun, then knew that was suicidal. Not only would the bullet not slow Dmitri if he charged like the bull that he was, but the others around held their weapons ready to cut him down. Only Vera showed him any charity.

"Where is the dog?" Vera spoke softly, almost seductively, but her fingers cut into his shoulder like a bear's claw. "The bitch took our dog. Tovarich should be with his litter mates."

"What are you talking about?"

Feigning ignorance gave him time to recover, but it did nothing to get him out of his predicament. He looked past the circle of Russian anarchists hoping to see Good charging down on them. The rescue didn't happen. He couldn't blame the Creek, but that didn't make him feel any better.

"You know the dog's name. You know what happened to the dog. Who are you?"

Lucas flashed her the secret sign again, but she backed away and spoke to Dmitri. Lucas tried to understand the argument between the two of them and came to the sorry conclusion they were at odds on how to kill him. Dmitri clenched his fists and waved them about while Vera refused to look back at him, as if she felt guilty about allowing him to be ripped apart.

"Vera, I want nothing less than you do. I don't know where the dog is, and I don't know who stole it, but I will find out if you give me more to go on."

She pushed Dmitri away, then came to Lucas, smiling insincerely. His years at the poker table and working confidence schemes made her intent obvious. Try as she might, she wasn't going to fool him. So he had to fool her.

"Who is he?" Dmitri tried to push past Vera, but she brushed him off. Lucas wondered who was in charge in this camp. The huge man could crush her without even noticing, yet she held some sway.

"Beauty and brains," Lucas said softly. "Beauty and brains against muscles and stupidity."

"Come with me." Vera steered him away. "Do not let Dmitri hear such things."

"That I think you are both beautiful and smart? You're the leader, aren't you?"

"Dmitri is. I am what you might call a political operative."

"What's that?" Lucas had no real curiosity. He only wanted to keep breathing another minute or two.

"I teach the others our philosophy and keep them focused on our task."

"If you want to teach me, I'll be happy to learn."

She shot him a cold look. Trying to romance her would get him nowhere. He seemed to be having great luck with cards and none with women. Carmela had taken up with Little Otto, and Amanda was always just beyond his reach and likely in bed with Jubal Dunbar, in more ways than one.

"Into my wagon," she said, pushing him ahead of her.

He went willingly because it got him away from Dmitri's angry stare. Dmitri and Vera were a team in all ways. She philosophized and he acted. Brains and brawn. That combination kept tumbling like a rock going downhill as he stepped up into the wagon. Vera pulled the door shut behind her.

"Why do you hunt for the dog?" Her demand was punctuated by a tapping foot and arms crossed over her chest.

"You know why," Lucas said, playing for time. "How did you lose the dog?"

"I never had it. It was stolen from Gregor before he arrived in Denver."

"What's he got to say for himself?"

"Nothing!" Vera stepped toward him, her fists as menacing as Dmitri's. "He was killed for the dog."

"Where was he coming from?"

"You know nothing of this, but you know the dog's name. How is that?"

"I only want to help the cause. You must get the dog back to overthrow the czar." He saw this did nothing to soothe her mounting rage at him. "What was Gregor to you?"

"My brother. Of all men, I trusted him most. Dmitri found him dead on the road from Cheyenne. How do you know of Tovarich?"

"Do you trust Dmitri not to have killed your brother?"

"Dmitri is a simple soul. He does not think so deeply, and he knows better than to double-cross me in this. His entire family was murdered by Czar Alexander. Without the dog, without the uprising, the nobles will continue grinding the serfs under their heel!"

Lucas didn't care for the polemic he received, but it kept Vera from returning to the question she so persistently asked. If he told her of his connection with Amanda—whom Vera was likely referring to as "the bitch"—he doubted he would see the dawn. No matter how he turned everything over in his head, all that made sense was Amanda killing Gregor to steal the puppy. Then she had somehow lost the dog and had thrown in with Dunbar to regain it. But the Russians sought the dog, too.

Who had it? And why was Tovarich so important? The mention of vast quantities of gold kept him interested, but not to the extent that he would risk his life.

Lucas grunted as Vera punched him in the belly. He hadn't expected the blow and took a step back. He caught his heel and sat down heavily on the narrow bed. From here he looked up into her brown eyes. Brown eyes were supposed to be chocolate and soft and all the things that he loved most in a woman. All he saw were tombstones in this woman's eyes. He couldn't read the name on those grave markers but it had to be his.

"I am good with a knife. Once, a tax collector for the czar took three days to die. He screamed in pain until his voice became too hoarse. He choked to death on his own blood when he bit his tongue."

"We can work together to get the dog. Whoever killed Gregor stole it. Tell me about what was found around the body."

"You sound like a detective."

"I . . . you caught me coming out of the Great West Detective Agency back in Denver. I was just leaving the office."

"You are a detective?"

"What was the condition of your brother's body?"

"He was almost naked. His clothing had been cut off and shredded. No strip was longer than a few inches. All his belongings had been rummaged."

"How was he killed? Was he shot?"

"His throat was slashed. Twice." She ran her thumb from left to right on her own throat, then worked back across more slowly.

Lucas tried to imagine small, lovely Amanda Baldridge using a knife to savagely open a new mouth across a Russian throat. She might have been lying to him about ownership of the dog, but murdering anyone in such a fashion seemed unlikely. If he had to guess, she would use poison or perhaps even put a bullet into the back of a man's head, but to slit a man's throat made no sense. Amanda would want information, and a man drowning in his own blood wasn't going to utter more than a gurgle or two before dying.

Killer, possibly, but Amanda was above all else pragmatic. When she hadn't been able to locate Tovarich on her own, she had sought disinterested help. A Denver detective knew nothing about the dog's history or importance—or that men were dying to recover it. Lucas wondered how many others she had out searching for Tovarich.

The question boiled up and escaped his lips before he could stop himself.

"How is Tovarich the key to finding the gold? Can he sniff it out?"

Vera puffed up like an angry alley cat's tail and reached for one of the knives at her belt.

"You don't know?"

Lucas saw no reason to deny it. He shook his head, not daring to say another word. She was as edgy as a rotted tooth, and anything he did only made the matter worse.

Before she could whip out a knife and force Lucas to defend himself, the thunder of hooves coming from the direction of Denver caused Dmitri to bellow a warning in Russian. Vera looked from Lucas to a Cossack at the wagon door. The rapid, staccato exchange caused the woman to hop down the steps. Outside, she looked into the wagon at Lucas.

"You will stay here until I return." She slammed the door. He heard a lock hasp clicking into place.

Lucas didn't bother testing the door or the lock imprisoning him. A quick survey of the wagon's interior convinced him that was the sturdiest part of the wagon. He ran his fingers over the back wall until he found a crack. It afforded him a limited view of the area around the campfire. Two mounted men were in view talking to Dmitri. Vera joined him, her hand resting on a knife. The exchange between them was in English, but Lucas couldn't make out much more than the fact that a tenuous truce existed between the riders and the Russians.

A tapping on the wagon floor caused him to leave his peephole. He located another crack in the floorboard and found himself staring into a dark eye. Good rapped again, then whispered, "Leave now. Bad men have come to camp."

"You're just figuring that out?" Lucas sat back and wondered what Good considered "bad." If the Russians didn't provoke him to such a description, the newcomers had to be extraordinary.

Extraordinary and known to the Creek.

"Help me break open the flooring," Lucas said. The sounds of the men outside sent a thrill of fear up his spine. They were arguing. He knew if his presence ever got tossed into the pot, both sides would have a common enemy to unite against, and he would be dead the instant the lock on the door opened.

He caught the edge of one plank and peeled back the old wood. Good lay on his back and used his feet to shove up against adjoining planks. Between the two of them working to demolish the wagon, a hole large enough to slip through finally gaped. Lucas wasted no time wiggling down beside Good.

"Who rode up?"

"No time to talk. Come. Now!"

With a lithe twist, Good rolled onto his belly and scampered away like some desert creature. Lucas was slower to follow. He hesitated, peering past the wagon wheel to where a half dozen mounted riders stood guard behind two men arguing face-to-face with Dmitri and Vera. The tenor told Lucas the dispute might erupt into gunfire. With less agility but not a whit less speed, he trailed Good into the brush.

He collapsed to his belly when a Russian guard came by,

alert for anyone trying to sneak into camp. Lucas waited for the sentry to hurry past. The Russians worried about the newcomers ambushing them. Exploiting this mutual suspicion entered Lucas's mind, but he didn't want to be in a position where he had to try. The guard disappeared into the dark, letting Lucas flop into the ravine where Good crouched, hand on his knife. Seeing Lucas, he motioned for him to follow.

In less than ten minutes, they circled the hill where they had first spied on the Russians and mounted their horses.

Lucas felt about ready to bust with questions.

"Who were they?"

"Old soldiers."

"Federals? Rebs?"

"What is the difference?" Good pulled even with Lucas and finally said, "They lost."

"So they're Confederates," Lucas said. "How do you know them?"

"I watched them rob a stagecoach and kill the driver and two passengers." Good turned even more somber. "I buried the three after they rode off." Good brightened a little and added, "I took the horses."

"You stole the horses after that gang robbed and murdered the passengers?"

Good shrugged. "Horses would die on plains. I saved them."

Lucas considered the matter from the Indian's standpoint. Turning in white men for robbing a stagecoach and killing three people held little promise of success. Most marshals would accuse the messenger of the crime because he was Indian—and in Good's case, a half-breed black Creek. That was a double reason to toss him in jail for the murders. And

Good was right about the horses dying. The way stations were far enough apart and the station masters slothful enough not to scout out an overdue stage so that the yoked horses had no chance of survival. In that light, Good had performed a humanitarian act that saved a team of horses.

Good didn't simply release them, he suspected. Selling them to men able to feed and use them produced enough money to live off.

"Why do you think those men are Confederates?"

"What they said. The stagecoach driver was black."

Lucas had no idea how a band of former CSA road agents had found themselves allied with Russian anarchists, but the single common interest was one he shared. Gold. Vera Zasulich had said Tovarich could lead them to hidden gold. He reconstructed what the woman had actually said and knew he was adding his own take to their conversation, but it was all that made sense. The Russians wanted the puppy because it could sniff out the gold. How anyone could train a dog, much less a puppy, to do this posed a great mystery to him, but if Vera believed it, he had to also.

She might be fanatical about overthrowing the government in her country, but she wasn't crazy when it came to knowing gold made that possible. It wasn't out of the question that she, Dmitri, and the others had come to Colorado to use the puppy dog to capture the gold for their cause. But the stew pot contained more than the Russians and the road agents. Amanda had come into the drama, along with Jubal Dunbar. It didn't take a dog's sensitive nose to sniff out the promise of gold. Any ambitious, greedy human could come to that point, too.

Lucas found himself with a twitching nose along with all the others. How much gold was at stake? Enough to allow

Amanda to buy the services of a detective, enough for Vera to believe it paid for a revolution, enough to get road agents and corrupt politicians on the trail of hidden treasure.

"Ride faster." The Creek snapped his reins and brought his horse to a canter, leaving Lucas behind.

"Why?" His question bounced unheeded off Good's back. He put heels to his horse's flanks to overtake his companion to repeat the question.

Lucas looked around. The clouds high on the mountaintops to their back showed no hint of a storm that would wash them all the way back to Denver. The night was quiet to the point of being worthy of a graveyard. The road stretched straight and abandoned in front of them. With a bit of imagination, he thought he saw the gaslight glow from Denver far ahead, but nowhere did he see a reason to risk having his horse step in an unseen prairie dog hole and break a leg.

"Hounds," was all Good said.

"You mean the Russians will loose the pack of dogs when they find I'm gone?"

Good sped up.

Lucas bent over and brought his horse to a gallop. He hadn't spent all his life astride a horse as the Creek likely had, but he was a decent enough horseman to know the animal would die under him if he pushed it too hard. Galloping for a couple miles actually helped a horse. The horses left to their own devices in a pasture made up their own races, winners and losers. But carrying a human drove it into the ground fast.

He began to draw rein and slacken the headlong pace when he heard distant baying. Lucas twisted about in the saddle. Dogs. From behind. From the direction of the Russian camp. He remembered the wolfhounds and how the one had attacked him in the camp. Only luck had saved him back in Denver. Those dogs had scented his blood and had to remember him. He might have left behind something with his scent on it to get the dogs on his trail.

"Giddayup." His horse flagged but kept running.

It took Lucas another mile toward Denver before he realized he rode along by himself. Good had disappeared.

He wished the dogs had, too. The yelping came closer. Were only the Russians with the pack or did the road agents join them in tracking him down? It wasn't something he wanted to find out.

Lucas reluctantly slowed to a quick walk to rest his horse before leaving the road and cutting across the prairie in the hope of confusing the dogs' sensitive noses. Without water anywhere to be found on the dry prairie, he had little chance of that. But he had to try. To fail was to be torn apart by the fierce dogs.

13

Lucas slid from the saddle. His legs caved for a moment. It had been a while since he'd ridden so long, but he strode off, pulling the reluctant horse behind him through a prairie dog town. The starlight gave enough illumination for him to walk without breaking his own ankle. Guiding the horse took more effort since it tried to bolt and run often.

He didn't blame the animal one bit. The sound of barking dogs neared, but they were still along the road. He cut off at an angle, found an arroyo, and led the horse down a place where the wall had collapsed. The bottom of the dried bed was rocky and made riding difficult, but he urged the horse on until they found another break in the sandy bank. Another prairie dog town would cover the scent well. If the wolfhounds blundered into it, the smell from the small rodents would mask any passage and might even rouse some of the sleeping prairie dogs to pop up and give voice to warnings. That would further confuse the wolfhounds.

By the stars, Lucas read that he rode more northeast. This took him to the north of Denver. Only when he had successfully avoided the howling pack of slavering dogs and the quiet of the rocky plains settled around him to soothe his agitation did he turn to the town. It was well past dawn when he hitched the horse to the iron ring mounted on the wall of the Emerald City and he dragged himself in.

"Do you live here?" Lucas asked the barkeep. He collapsed into a chair and hiked his feet up to a table top as Lefty stared at him.

"You look like you was drug through a knothole backwards."

"Give me a shot of whiskey, will you?" Lucas began emptying his pockets. He had lost some of the chips he had won, but the greenbacks were all there from the game where he had walked away thinking he was sitting on top of the world.

"Good that you can pay for it. Your deadbeat friends all try to stiff me."

"I don't have any friends."

Lefty snorted and dropped a half bottle in front of Lucas, then pointed.

"What about him?"

Lucas craned around and saw Little Otto coming down the steps at the side of the stage. Nothing had gone well for Lucas, being abandoned by Good somewhere out on the road to town while chased by a pack of vicious dogs, and now he had to give mute witness to Otto's continued happiness.

"Are you sleeping here now?" Lucas continued to rummage through his pockets. He touched the book he had taken from Vera Zasulich and dropped it onto the table.

"I'm not sleeping," Little Otto said. He started to walk past, then slowed and stared at the book. "You remembered."

"I want information," Lucas said. "You wanted a copy of *Tom Sawyer.*"

"Where did you get it? No book dealer in town has a copy."

"You don't tell me where you get your information."

Little Otto pursed his lips, ran his fingers around the tattered edge of the book, then pulled back reluctantly.

"It's yours if you can tell me something about a gang of road agents. They held up a stagecoach, killed the black driver and two passengers."

"Your requests are eclectic."

"What's that mean?"

Little Otto scooped up the book, riffled through the pages, then tucked it away in a coat pocket. He settled down in a chair, put his hands on his knees, and leaned forward. His voice was so low Lucas missed what he said at first.

"Why are you whispering? There's no one to overhear."

Little Otto glanced in Lefty's direction, scooted his chair closer, and continued to talk in the same hoarse whisper. That he didn't trust Lefty made Lucas wonder what trouble there might have been between them. It had to do with Carmela, he reckoned. In spite of himself, a small spark of hope blazed. If Lefty chased Little Otto off, that would mean that Carmela . . .

"Go talk to Gallatin. He can tell you what you want for the price of a drink." His eyes darted to the bottle and back. "Maybe more than one drink."

Lucas raked in the chips and bills he had spread across the table. He saw no reason to advertise how much money he had, especially if he tracked down Lester Gallatin. When he had been learning how to work the crowds for the Preacher, Gallatin had been an old hand. Away from the booze, there wasn't a swindler with a more engaging line or heartrending story of tragedy. But that had been a year ago. Gallatin had taken to the bottle and never bothered to sober up. What pain afflicted him lay beyond Lucas's understanding, and dealing with him now only added to the confusion.

"How did he come by this information?"

"He rode with unsavory men during the war." Little Otto stood, smoothed his rumpled clothing, patted the pocket where he had placed the Twain book, and left. His gait was a trifle unsteady.

Lucas spat. Otto hadn't been drinking. His nocturnal activity with Carmela had left him sore, if not stiff.

"It won't last," Lefty called to him. "It never does. She's off to a month-long engagement in San Francisco at the Palace in another week."

"Why doesn't that make me feel any better?" Lucas stuffed the greenbacks into his pocket, then stacked the chips on the bar. "Take care of those for me, will you?"

Lefty swept them off the bar into a cigar box.

"It'll go against your bill."

"I'm even with you."

"For now. You'll hit a stretch of bad luck soon enough. All gamblers do."

Lucas grumbled as he left, the whiskey bottle tucked under his arm. It would be the ultimate insult if Lady Luck abandoned him at the poker table. He had lost out to Little Otto, been attacked by ferocious dogs, lied to by Amanda Baldridge, and was being pursued by Dunbar's thugs. He had plenty of money and had considered dropping the hunt for Tovarich until he had the carrot of hidden gold dangled in front of him.

For so many people to be on the trail of that gold, it had to be real. Treasure maps were sold back East all the time to suckers. When he worked with the Preacher, he had been responsible for more than one himself, so he knew the tricks and come-ons, what enticed otherwise sensible people to uncontrollable greed, and what it took to get away before they realized how they had been swindled.

Lucas mounted and walked his tired horse through the morning streets until he got to the livery stable a few blocks from his boardinghouse. A disheveled man came out, squinted, one eye swelled shut from a losing fistfight, and asked, "You want me to give the horse a good cleaning?"

"Hello, Lester." Lucas dismounted and handed over the reins.

"Ain't seen you in a spell, Lucas." Gallatin wiped his mouth with the back of his hand. "You stayin' out of trouble?"

"Never. You work here very long?"

"Since last Sunday. Not sure I like muckin' stables and curryin' horses all that much. Nowhere near as much fun as workin' the crowds like we used to. People's got class. Not like the ornery horses folks stable here. One of them bastards kicked me a couple days ago." He rubbed his thigh. "That's why I'm limpin'."

Lucas had a different explanation for the man's uneven gait and bloodshot eye, but he didn't say anything. Little Otto claimed the information he wanted could be wrested from Gallatin. Upsetting him with the truth would get him nowhere.

"I might be able to contribute a bit toward getting some medicine," Lucas said, flashing a dollar bill. "In addition to whatever it costs for you to feed and curry my horse."

Gallatin bent a little closer to the bill, turning his body into a question mark, as if unsure he saw it. For the man, money was a mirage disappearing in an alcoholic haze rather than a desert-induced heat. Lucas moved the dollar bill around. Gallatin followed it like a cat bobbing about to attack a bird. He finally took pity on his old companion and handed over the bill. A shaky hand snared it and made it vanish. Lucas saw that Gallatin's quickness remained from his pickpocketing days.

"You're doin' an ole friend a boon."

"And that old friend can return the favor by telling me what you know about a stagecoach robbery. Driver and two passengers were killed by a gang of road agents."

"I heard tell of such a thing," Gallatin said cautiously. The change in how he stood alerted Lucas that getting the information he wanted might be more difficult. Gallatin's face reflected a fear out of place for a man working as a stable hand.

"Let's go sit and talk about it." Lucas fetched the whiskey from his saddlebags and pulled the cork. He took a long pull, then passed the bottle to Gallatin. That was likely his last taste of the whiskey since the stable hand clutched the bottle with a feverish grip almost impossible to break. If it got him his information, fine. A half bottle of whiskey was a small enough price to pay for a clue as to where a mountain of gold was hidden.

They sat on overturned crates to the side of the stable door. Inside, restless horses kicked at their stalls. Lucas's horse pawed the ground, as if begging to be placed in one of those stalls, fed and watered, and left to sleep. He ignored the horse and concentrated on Gallatin.

"Good liquor." Gallatin sipped at it, as if pacing himself. The second pull he took was longer. The third drained almost a quarter of the bottle as his willpower weakened. He belched, wiped his lips, and then held the bottle in both hands. The shakes Lucas had noticed vanished as if they had never existed. In spite of downing several shots of potent liquor, Gallatin approached normal.

"Who robbed the stage?"

"Are you a deputy now, Lucas? Never thought of you as a lawman, not after all we been through."

"Those were the days," Lucas said. "The Preacher's still working the yokels over around Larimer Square."

"Heard tell that he was. Me and him, we had a falling-out six months back. He got all uppity and said things nobody ought to say to me. I took it personal." Gallatin sucked at the bottle again, further lowering the level. He made no move to pass it back. After seeing how few teeth Gallatin had remaining, Lucas wasn't inclined to ask for more of the popskull.

"He has his way of working. It's kept him and the law far apart, except for that one time when he tried to swindle a federal deputy's wife."

"The cookbook swindle," Gallatin said. "I remember that. Promise of all them recipes."

"From his grandma," Lucas cut in.

"Yeah, handed down from his granny in the old country, but only the first page had a recipe. The rest of the book was blank pages. Nuthin' but foolscap all bound up real neat."

"It took him a whale of an effort to get free of those charges. That deputy had it in for him since his woman was such a terrible cook and she had wanted to please him with something decent."

"Those were the days," Gallatin said, nodding in remembrance.

"How bad are the men who robbed the stage?"

"The worst. Leftover soldiers from the war."

"Confederates," Lucas said. "I know that much."

"Well, sir, you ain't understandin' the half of it. Them's

a guerrilla band that's been together since Second Manassas. They moved west of the Mississippi and kept raidin', callin' themselves soldiers but they wasn't no more than thieves and killers. The war ended. They kept on, only movin' farther west to keep ahead of wanted posters on their heads."

"You have a name for any of them?"

"The leader was Thoreau's right-hand man."

Lucas had heard that name but details slithered away just beyond true remembering. He said so.

"Judge Thoreau from Lawrence, Kansas."

"I remember him now. A Reconstruction judge who got himself filled with lead down San Antonio way."

"He hired Dennis Clifford and his bully boys as enforcers. Talk about odd fellows gettin' together, a Yankee judge and Southern guerrillas. They tore up the land for close to a year 'fore he got shot down. Nobody ever found who did the deed, but some think it was Clifford because he was bein' cheated out of most of the spoils. Others say the local folks finally got a bellyful of Thoreau. Whoever cut him down made it too hot for Clifford and his boys, so they drifted north, robbin' and killin' as they came."

Lucas tried to figure out how Clifford and his guerrillas had come across Vera and her revolutionaries—and where the gold fit into the puzzle.

"Have Clifford and his boys ever robbed a train? Scored a lot of gold?"

"Not that I ever heard, though they was always huntin' for just a few cents more." Gallatin drained the bottle and belched. "I knew 'em over around Palo Duro, Adobe Walls, that area. Always steered way clear of them. Nasty fellows, the lot of them, always pretendin' to be soldiers still, and Clifford talkin' 'bout how he was gonna be king of some country or other."

"You mean he was putting together a filibuster, like Walker down in Nicaragua back in '52?" Lucas snorted in contempt. Invading a foreign country with only a handful of soldiers and no money to back the attempt was sheer folly. "No money," he said aloud.

"What's that? Naw, I ain't got much, but thanks for the dollar, Lucas. You're a good man, no matter what ever'one says about you."

"Do you think Clifford would launch a filibuster if he had enough gold to buy supplies and raise a real army?"

"Don't see why not. He was only a captain in the cavalry but was always goin' on 'bout how he shoulda been the president of the Confederacy." Gallatin laughed ruefully. "Toward the end, Jeff Davis woulda gave him the presidency if 'n he'd asked."

Lucas stared down the street, not seeing anything as he thought hard. Dennis Clifford and Vera Zasulich. A soldier and a revolutionary. Their paths led them to violent overthrow. The gold notwithstanding, the two might have joined forces to whip up a filibuster aimed at Saint Petersburg and the czar rather than the more usual Latin American targets. Taking over an entire country was a huge undertaking, requiring men and materiel, weapons and financing. For Clifford to have any hope of success, he had to transport an army halfway around the world, establish a foothold, and fight an army that had repelled Napoleon eighty years earlier.

"How crazy is Clifford?"

"Crazy like a fox, I'd say." Gallatin rolled the bottle around, hunting for any amber drop remaining. In that he was disappointed. He swung the empty bottle around carelessly. "Him and the men with him's all aimed like a shootin' show I seen up in Cincinnati. Baughman and Butler, it was.

That lil girl, Annie Oakley, was only fifteen. Couldn't have been a day older. She had a shootin' match and she beat this fella name of Butler. Why, I never seen such shootin' in all my born days." Gallatin picked up the bottle and heaved it into the air, where it caught the sun and reflected brightly as it spun. "Bang, she went with her rifle. Butler missed after twenty-five and I left 'fore she missed. Don't remember how many targets she'd busted but it was more 'n a hunnerd."

Gallatin jumped a foot when the bottle slipped from his numbed fingers, crashed to the street, hit a rock, and broke into a thousand pieces.

"Lester," Lucas said gently, putting his hand on the man's arm. "Settle down now. You're saying none of Clifford's gang is loco enough to go along with a filibuster?"

"Ain't sayin' that at all. Not a man amongst 'em would pass up the chance to go to battle again. But crazy like you mean?" He shook his head. "Stone killers, the lot of 'em. They don't go 'round talkin' to cactus or wantin' to marry their horses."

"They would try to overthrow another country," Lucas said. He leaned back against the splintery wall and considered everything Gallatin had said in light of what he had seen at the Russian camp.

"Has Clifford ever mentioned a dog?"

Gallatin looked at him as if he had been in the sun too long.

"The only business he'd have with a dog would be to kick it. Might be wrong, though, since I avoid him and his boys like they have the pox. Safer all around."

"Where can I find Clifford? Does he hang out at your watering hole?"

"I left off goin' to the Seventh Saloon 'cuz he'd took up there. I go to—"

"Thanks, Lester." Lucas peeled off another dollar bill and handed it to the man. With the other already in hand, this would buy a bottle of whiskey and hold the pain at bay for another day.

"You're a prince among men, Lucas. You are. I'll take real good care of your horse. I promise."

Lucas slapped him on the shoulder, then set out for his boardinghouse. He tried to decide whether food or sleep mattered more to him. Instead of deciding, his thoughts jumbled up as he tried to make sense of the anarchists and filibusters joining forces. The two gangs had already left a sizable number of bodies behind them. Gregor had been killed and Tovarich stolen, and Clifford's gang had robbed and murdered everyone on a stagecoach. Lucas came to the conclusion these were only the tip of the knife and others had died along the way.

He slowed when he reached his boardinghouse, then spun and retreated. He recognized the man lounging under a tree across the street as one of Dunbar's men. Rather than trying to sneak in the back way, Lucas chose to let the henchman boil in the sun. Another of Dunbar's guards undoubtedly stood sentry at the rear of the house.

Being hunted like this told Lucas a couple things. Dunbar hadn't found the dog. And he considered it a possibility that Lucas had. While the politician might be pissed at being bothered by someone poking around his home and talking to his hired help, he wasn't the kind to waste manpower unless there was a payoff for him. Staying away from Dunbar should have been enough to gain invisibility. That it hadn't proved to Lucas that Dunbar still sought the puppy.

His route took him back toward the Great West Detective Agency office. Another idea came to him. Amanda might be stirring up Dunbar.

Lucas walked past the empty office several times, attentive to anyone staking out the building. Business outside appeared normal. Around in the alley, he saw patches of blood where the dogs had bled after attacking him. A few quick jabs with his lock picks opened the door. He slipped into the storeroom. The damp bloodstain on the floor reminded him how close he had come to dying there.

After he'd closed and locked the door behind him, he hunted for a blanket or something to provide a pallet so he could stretch out and sleep. After he was rested, dealing with Dunbar's henchmen could follow.

Finding nothing, he went into the main office. He saw a blanket tossed into one corner and went for it but froze when he realized he was being watched. Hand going to the pistol in his coat pocket, he slowly turned and stared out the front door.

Amanda Baldridge stood there, motioning for him to open up.

14

Amanda pressed closer and waved to him, then knocked. When Lucas didn't move to open the door, she looked over her shoulder and rapped harder. Her consternation finally prompted him to go to the door and work it open. He needed to make a set of keys for the office if he intended to keep squatting on Jacoby Runyon's property.

"Miss Baldridge, I hadn't expected to see you."

She shoved past him, closed the door, and tried to grab the string on the blinds to pull them down. She wasn't tall enough to succeed, but Lucas got a nice view of her figure as she strained.

"Please, Lucas, we can't be seen together. Lower the blinds."

He did so, then asked, "Are you afraid of what Jubal Dunbar would say if he knew you were here?"

"Jubal? I—" She clamped her mouth shut and turned a touch whiter, causing the rouge on her cheeks to appear as tiny fires against porcelain. "You know Dunbar and I have been talking over business matters?"

"I'm a detective. Of course I know," he said, taking some small pleasure in the words. He had pieced together a large picture beyond a stolen dog and had revealed the real mission. An entire country's fate hung in the balance.

"Then you know."

"I know a great deal." He pointed to a chair. She settled into it, hands in her lap, looking even paler than ever. "Are you faint?"

"Faint? I, no, not at all. It's just that emotion overwhelms me."

He stared at her, not sure what to say. Her presence played on him. She was a lovely woman and one who wrapped men around her little finger like a string. With a deep breath, he again scented her perfume.

"Did you get the perfume from Vera?"

"Vera? Who's that?"

She was a good actress, but Lucas saw real confusion on her face. Then the mask lowered and her eyes went emotionless.

"I am not here to discuss my perfume, as fascinating as you find it, Lucas." She smiled insincerely. "What are you going to do about Tovarich?"

"Have you discussed this matter with Dunbar?"

"Why do you keep mentioning him? He's not involved in this."

Lucas looked up, then craned around to stare at the brilliant blue sky outside. Only a few white clouds moved in the direction of the mountains.

"What are you searching for?"

"A storm cloud. I wouldn't want lightning to strike you dead for lying."

"How dare you!" She shot to her feet. Now the color in her cheeks came from a blush of anger, not artificial rouge.

"You wanted Dunbar to find the dog, too, and you never told me. His bully boys have beaten me up a couple times." Lucas sniffed delicately as he remembered being thrown into the sewage canal. "They have also ruined my favorite coat."

"I know nothing of this. He never mentioned you to me. If he had, I'd have warned him off."

"He's not looking for Tovarich?"

"I . . . I won't lie to you. Yes, he wants the dog because he thinks to win my favor. My *sexual* favor. He must consider you a rival for my affections." She fanned herself as she slowly sank back into the chair. Her blue eyes glinted with emotion now.

"Am I?"

"Are you what?"

"A rival for your affections. You are a lovely woman with far-reaching interests, ones that extend to foreign countries."

"I don't understand. Are you saying that because Tovarich is a Russian wolfhound? It is only the dog's safety that interests me, Lucas. Truly." She smiled winningly. "When can you return him to me?"

"I have to find him first. Although I have examined a number of leads, all have been dead ends."

"But you said—" Again Amanda appeared flustered, but he wasn't sure how much of this was an act. Then it was his turn to be left without anything to say. "I found Tovarich."

"You found the dog?" He felt his throat tighten. "You came here to tell me my services aren't needed any longer? That is decent of you."

"You sounded as if you had found Tovarich, too. You'd know that I can't get him back without help. Your help." She fumbled in her purse and passed over another hundred dollars. "Here is the balance of your payment since you'll need it."

"To buy the dog back for you?"

"If possible, though I fear my poor little puppy will need to be stolen back. A very bad man by the name of Makepeace has him."

Lucas recoiled at the name. Benjamin Makepeace operated at the other end of the social scale, gambling on blood sport rather than the turn of the card. He acted as bookmaker on bear fights, dogs against bears, dogs against rats, dogs against dogs, even, it was rumored, dogs against men to the death. The biggest event in Denver the prior year had been a match Makepeace sponsored of an elk against a bear. The ursine beast had won, though the victory had been short lived. Makepeace had then sold bullets to the onlookers and bet on which round finished off the bear.

"You know him?"

Lucas swallowed, considering giving back the money he had already received from the woman.

"I'll need some help."

"Oh, you're so clever and strong," she said, reaching out. Her fingers touched his wrist and sent thrills up his arm. "I can go along and do what I can to take care of Tovarich."

"How'd you find out that Makepeace had the dog? You aren't the kind to travel in his social circle. Neither is Dunbar."

"I put out a reward for any news of Tovarich. A woman of ill repute collected the money." Amanda looked aggrieved. "She was in such sorry shape. My heart went out to her. I gave her an extra few dollars reward, though I fear she might spend it on some hideous addiction."

Her hand tightened around his wrist, keeping him from pulling away—from running like hell.

"Is Makepeace at his gaming pit?" The words caught in his throat. "He might not start his matches until after sundown."

"We can steal Tovarich away from him before he starts!" She looked at him with wide, innocent eyes. "What is he likely to do with the poor little dog?"

Lucas chalked it up to lack of sleep and food. He stood, Amanda's hand not leaving his now. She clenched his fingers tightly. He touched the pocket where his Colt rested. Seven shots might not be enough, but if he got close enough to Makepeace, he could combine threatening to fill the gambler with lead and bribing him to return the dog. What it took to overwhelm his need for sheer cruelty to both animal and human was a question that had to be answered, and Lucas was afraid it might be answered in blood.

His.

The old barn looked like a fortress. From the hayloft door poked a rifle barrel. As Lucas moved around, he caught sight of not only the man holding that rifle but two others, both armed and looking fierce. The main door into the barn was even better guarded. Both outside and in were four men who looked like winners from bear-wrestling contests. Past them, inside around a deep pit in the floor, crowded a dozen men, clutching money in their hands and cheering. Their attention was focused entirely on the bottom of the pit.

From over the men's cheers came snarls and snaps. The crunches and death chitters warned Lucas a dog was in the pit killing rats while the men bet on a score of different fates.

Few bet against the dog. Most were betting on the number of rats killed in a minute or five or whether the dog finished off all the rats before they swarmed over it.

A shower of blood rose up and misted down. For a heart-stopping moment, utter silence prevailed. Then the crowd went wild, cheering and slapping each other on the back.

"A big bet went against the house," Lucas said. "You'd better stay outside. This isn't the kind of place for a lady."

"You're so polite, even in a crowd like this," Amanda said. She pressed close and rubbed against him, more like a cat greeting a human than a woman on the way to recovering her dog. "I'll be safe if I stay close to you, Lucas."

"Stay outside," he said more sharply as he pulled free of her grip. "People might die."

"Oh, bother. How bad can this be?"

"Makepeace is bad enough to steal a puppy."

He went to the outer guards and passed over a dollar, then went inside to repeat the bribe to the remaining man blocking his way.

"Where's Makepeace?" He looked around, trying to spot the gambler. He had never seen the man and knew him only by his sordid reputation.

"Don't matter. Go bet or get out."

"Have a nice day," Lucas said, touching the brim of his bowler, smiling, and pushing past the mountain of gristle and ugly.

He hardly left behind unpleasantness. The bettors stank to high heaven, and the rank stench from the pit told its history of blood and death. Lucas edged closer to the edge of the pit and looked down. A bulldog strained at a chain at the bottom of the pit. Two men lowered cages of large black rats on the far side of the pit.

"Put down yer bets, gents. How long 'til the rats eat the dog?"

Lucas saw that the bulldog wasn't going to be unchained. A half dozen other cages of ferocious rats had been stacked on the far side of the pit, ready to be lowered if the dog bested the first wave of rodents. His belly tried to turn over end for end when the cages were opened using strings that ran up to the lip of the pit. A half dozen poured from each cage and went straight for the snarling dog.

While the men bet, Lucas backed away and circled to a small, seedy-looking man covered in chalk dust as he scribbled odds on a schoolhouse blackboard propped up on a chair. Two men moved constantly through the crowd gathering bets and bringing them back. The man snatched away the bets and thrust them into an iron box between recalculating and posting odds.

Lucas glanced up to the hayloft and saw two of the men who had been at the upper door watching carefully for any sign of robbery. From their elevated vantage, they could fill any imprudent thief with bullets before he could even touch the money-laden iron box. Lucas made a point of keeping his distance. The guards had the look of men who would err on the side of caution.

"Are you Makepeace?" Lucas had to shout to make himself heard over the din of cheers and death.

The small man stared up at him with dull eyes. He looked more like a rat thrown into the pit than he did a dog. His nose was long, and a bristly mustache twitched as his upper lip twisted about. Prominent buckteeth and a narrow face added to the look, but the final touch was the man's skin. It had a poorly tanned look to it, almost dried leather but not quite.

"You lookin' for a job? Come back after midnight. Got

a full card runnin' all day long." He gave Lucas a once-over, then dismissed him.

"I want to buy one of your dogs."

"Not for sale. All my fighters are top of the line. They'll make me more fighting than they ever could bein' put up for sale."

"A wolfhound," Lucas said. "I'll give you more for him than he could ever earn."

This caught Makepeace's attention. He carefully placed the chalk on a ledge, wiped his hands on his thighs, and looked up at Lucas curiously.

"Why do you say that?"

"He's just a puppy. Such a small dog can't stand up for more than a few seconds to a cage of rats."

"I only got one wolfhound, and he ain't shy." Makepeace jerked his thumb over his shoulder in the direction of the pit.

Lucas missed the yelping dog being tossed into the pit but not the four cages filled with rats. They were dumped squealing and snapping. Not realizing he did so, Lucas drew his pistol and spun to the edge of the pit to protect Tovarich.

He stared at the large Russian wolfhound in the pit, lunging, snapping, and killing with a cold methodical fury that put the other dogs to shame.

"Tovarich?" The name escaped without him realizing it.

"Best ratter I've seen in a month," chortled a bettor. "I made twenty dollars on him so far. Never seen a mutt that vicious."

"Tovarich?"

"Don't know if he has a name. Makepeace don't put names to 'em."

Lucas stood with the pistol drawn, then realized how the

guards were coming for him. He lifted the .22 and fired into the pit. He was a crack marksman and his first three shots each dropped a large rat. The dog, if it was Tovarich, looked up as if thanking him, then went back to its bloody task.

"Stop him. He's ruinin' the odds," complained a man halfway around the pit.

Lucas looked up and saw Amanda frantically shoving men out of the way. All she saw was the dog in the pit. The jeers and cries of protest drowned out her voice, but Lucas read her lips.

"Tovarich!"

Then he was bowled over, hands reaching for his pistol. He fired again and was rewarded with a grunt. The slug had found its way into a guard's chest. Lucas kicked out and sent another man tumbling into the pit. This produced pandemonium in the barn. Fights broke out on either side. Another guard swinging an axe handle came for him. With a hand far steadier than it had any right to be, Lucas leveled his Colt and thumbed off two more rounds. Both struck the guard in the face. One cut a deep groove in his cheek. The other creased his scalp and snapped his head back.

Jerking about, Lucas got to his feet. In time to duck under a roundhouse swung by a drunk bettor. He grunted, lowered his shoulder, and drove forward. Both he and the drunk tumbled into the pit. Lucas landed on top of the man and knocked the air from his lungs. When he looked up, he saw a fierce red eye. A rat. He fired and killed the rat. This drew the unwanted attention of the other rats.

Lucas scrambled to sit up and get his back against the dirt wall to restrict the directions of attack. He found himself with an unlikely ally. The wolfhound snarled and snapped— at the rats. Lucas fired until his pistol came up empty, then relied on Tovarich to keep the rats at bay as he reloaded. He began firing with deadly accuracy. Seven shots, five dead rats.

He winced as one fastened its teeth into his leg. He used the butt to hammer at the rat's head until it released its grip. If it hadn't been for the wolfhound, he would have been overwhelmed. Lucas fumbled to reload one final time. He hadn't brought that many spare cartridges with him.

He looked up and saw the guards in the hayloft trying to draw a bead on him. Resting his right hand on his left forearm, he took careful aim and fired. The Colt New Line made a tiny *chuff!* sound. The guard in the loft let out a scream as the slug tore along his right arm, and he dropped his rifle.

"Lucas, hoist Tovarich up to me. Hurry!"

He looked directly above and saw that Amanda had dropped to her stomach and reached down with both hands.

"This is the 'puppy'?"

"Yes, yes, that's Tovarich!"

Her idea of a puppy was very different from his. He tucked his pistol back into his pocket, stamped on a couple remaining rats, then got both arms under the dog's belly and heaved. Lucas almost lost his balance. The full-grown wolfhound weighed more than he could lift. He braced himself and fought the dog's struggles. Amanda tried to calm the dog but all she did was further confuse the animal.

Getting his feet braced, Lucas strained and got the dog's front paws lifted so Amanda could grab them. She tugged and got half the dog over the lip of the pit. Looking up at the dog's rear, Lucas placed his hands as best he could and shoved hard. The sudden release of weight caused him to smash his face against the dirt wall. Amanda had drawn the dog up and out of the pit.

Lucas got back to his feet and called up, "Give me a hand. Help me out of here!"

All he saw was the ebb and flow of fighting bettors. Amanda and the wolfhound had disappeared in the crowd. Lucas stepped back to catch the woman's attention—to find her in the crush.

A man came flying down, flapping his arms as if he could fly. Lucas swiftly jerked aside and let the man land hard on the dirt floor.

"You," the man grated out. He spat dirt from his mouth. "You ruined the fight. I was winnin' twenty dollars!"

Lucas judged distances, the man's fury, and then jumped. His right foot caught the man in the chest. His left foot rested on the man's shoulder and then he launched himself into the air. Flailing about, Lucas caught the edge of the pit and heaved up and out of it. He knocked over two men swinging wildly at each other and found himself on the receiving end of more than one hard fist. Instinctively blocking, he prevented the blows from connecting with his face until he climbed to his feet and returned a punch with scientific precision. The man's nose broke. As he tried to flee, he collided with the other fighter, giving Lucas the chance to get out of the barn.

Gunshots sounded above the din, warning him that Makepeace wasn't going to take the dog theft lightly—or the huge loss of revenue from the gambling. Ducking low, Lucas bounced from side to side and found the door.

He looked out in time to see Amanda running away, Tovarich loping along at her side. He started after her, only to find Makepeace blocking his way.

"You owe me. You owe me big time for all this." The small man loosed a left jab that caught Lucas on the ribs and sent him reeling back. "Come on. I want to thrash you good. Then I'll see how long you last in the pit against a pack of dogs."

Lucas widened his stance and waited for the gambler to come for him.

15

Lucas dug his left heel down into the soft dirt, reached into his pockets with both hands, then watched as Makepeace came forward. The man moved like a prize-fighter. The broken nose hinted at more than one match lost—or perhaps won—after a furious exchange of blows. Lucas had done his share of bare knuckle fighting and was decent, but his head spun from lack of sleep and food, as well as all that had happened in the pit. His legs hurt, and any fight with Makepeace would be short lived.

As the ratter moved forward with murder on his face, Lucas yanked both hands out. One strewed greenbacks into the air, startling Makepeace. The man's eyes widened, and he instinctively grabbed for the fluttering bills. Lucas pulled his pistol from his other pocket and swung it with all his strength. The barrel collided with an exposed temple. Lucas felt bone break and saw Makepeace's eyes roll up into his head. As the ratter staggered, Lucas kicked hard. He aimed for the man's knee but hit higher and to greater effect.

On his way to full unconsciousness, Makepeace writhed about on the ground like a snake with its head cut off. He grasped his groin until the last vestiges of awareness left him.

"Didn't even have to wait till sundown for that snake to die," Lucas said, gasping for breath.

He looked over his shoulder and saw two guards coming for him. He pointed his pistol, made a show of cocking it, and then kicked some of the greenbacks in their direction. Having to choose between snatching up the money or helping their boss wasn't a long debate for either man. They fell to their knees and grabbed wildly for the bills, giving Lucas the chance to hightail it.

By the time he was far enough away from the barn to be out of breath, he looked around for Amanda. She and Tovarich were nowhere to be seen. He checked his Colt, worried that smashing it into Makepeace's head had knocked the cylinder out of true, but not seeing any way to find out short of firing it or having a gunsmith dismantle it, he made a beeline for the detective agency office. Lucas tried to decide if he was surprised that Amanda and the dog, which was certainly no puppy, were not there or if this was the obvious conclusion to a dangerous hunt.

He worked at the back door and jimmied it open, pulled the blanket from the corner of the main office into the back room, and stretched out. As tired as he was, sleep eluded him. Amanda had paid him well, in spite of being beaten up, shot at, bitten by a dog, and almost fed to famished rats. He should simply walk away now, with the money he had in his pocket.

Lucas pulled out the remaining greenbacks and counted them on the floor. He had carried Amanda's fee along with the money he had won at Emerald City the night—two nights?—before and only had a few dollars more than thirty left. It had been necessary to divert Makepeace and his men. Lucas considered that money well spent, but so little left for all he had been through seemed increasingly unfair.

He lay back, the bills clutched in his hand as he stared up at the ceiling. A crack extended from one side of the storeroom to the other, somewhat larger in the middle and showing signs that the roof leaked during rainstorms. That ought to be fixed. If he intended to keep intruding on Jacoby Runyon's office so cavalierly, he ought to make a key for the back door. His mind seemed to slip to more interesting things as sleep sucked up his consciousness. A smile came to his lips. Amanda. They would make such a good couple. And gold. There was a huge treasure trove out there that both Vera and Clifford sought.

Revolutionary. Filibuster. Dogs.

He finally slept with dreams of Russian wolfhounds burdened with burlap bags stuffed with brightly shining gold filling his night.

He lost another hand and hardly noticed, but Lefty did. The barkeep waved him to the bar from the faro table, put a shot of whiskey in front of him, and said, "You're costing me money."

"You've got a stack of my chips in a box behind the bar. Take it out of that." Lucas knocked back the whiskey, tasted the gunpowder and rusty nails Lefty used to give it kick and flavor, then put the empty glass back on the bar.

"I don't care about them," Lefty said. "You're not doing your job. If you keep losing at a game like faro that favors the house, I'll have to boot you out."

"You don't have any other dealers."

"The way Claudette watches you, I could put her there. If she pulled down her bodice and did that little wiggle with her ass that she does whenever you come into the saloon, she'd triple your take on your best night."

"Things aren't setting well with me right now." Lucas almost bit his lip as the words slipped out. He wasn't the kind to make excuses for his own failures. What Lefty said about Claudette didn't worry him much. There were dozens of women faro dealers in Denver and their appeal was physical. He was a gambler, and he made more money for the house because the cowboys were systematically fleeced in a hurry. They left feeling like Lady Luck hadn't been with them rather than angry that Claudette—or any female dealer—wasn't interested in them after they lost all their money. After all, they shoved that money across the faro table to impress, not to gamble.

"You ought to take a day or two off. She's going to be on her way by then."

"She?" Lucas frowned, wondering how Lefty knew anything of Amanda. Then he realized that wasn't who the barkeep meant. "What Carmela and Little Otto do isn't much interest to me."

"You're the only one sayin' that. I've heard customers betting on what it's like to roll around in her bed all night long." Lefty chuckled. "There's even a pool building up to damned near twenty dollars on whether you get your chance with her before she's out of Denver and off on her tour."

"I ought to join in. I know which way I'd bet."

"See? That's not the old Lucas Stanton I'm familiar with. You'd be taking the good side of the bet and winning both girl and money."

Lucas wasn't going to tell the barkeep about the Russians or Clifford's men and especially was not going to mention a mountain of gold out there somewhere that only Tovarich could sniff out. That worried him as much as beating the anarchists and filibusters to the hidden treasure. How was the dog going to find the gold? Had Amanda already given the dog its head and found the gold? Dogs had an incredible sense of smell, but why was Tovarich better than any of the others in Vera's pack?

"You're getting that far-off look again. Your mind's not on gambling, Lucas. That's costin' me a mountain of money."

"It's not," he admitted. "I've been dabbling in politics. What do you know about Jubal Dunbar?" Lucas surprised himself with the question. Amanda had no reason to take the dog to the crooked politician, yet their relationship remained something of a mystery.

He hadn't slept at his own boardinghouse in days since Dunbar's men remained across the street. What they would do if they spotted him was another of those mysteries he didn't want to discover. If he waited long enough, the dust would settle. He just wished he could find Amanda.

He wished he could find Tovarich to take him to the gold.

"Get you anything, Lucas?" Claudette sidled up and pressed herself warmly against him.

"Go deal faro. He's taking the night off."

"You're getting the night off?" Claudette looked at Lefty in disbelief. "You're not firing him! I won't let you."

"Not cannin' his ass like I should. But I will yours if you don't get to the faro table and start dealin'."

"You're not fired?" Claudette's soft brown eyes fixed on him. "That's good. If he fired you, I'd quit, too."

"Why do I bother with this place?" Lefty said, throwing up his one good arm in resignation. "It's not because I make any money from it."

"It's because you love us all," Lucas said. He turned and found himself pressing fully into Claudette. The feeling was nice but not what he wanted now.

The customers roared and made a dash for the stage. Carmela's show was beginning, and they all wanted a front row seat. Not a one of them dared try to remove Little Otto from his in the middle of the row, but that didn't stop them from crowding on either side of the shaved-headed giant.

"I'll check back later and see how you're doing," Lucas said, not sure if he spoke to Claudette or Lefty. Claudette answered.

"There's a big dance going on at the Palace. When Lefty finally lets me go, we could—"

"Work!" The barkeep bellowed again at the other pretty waiter girls to work the audience and sell more whiskey.

Lucas bent and gave Claudette a quick peck on the cheek. She grabbed him by the ears and pulled his face down firmly for a more passionate kiss. When she released him, his ears burned. Her face was flushed, and her eyes remained closed for a moment. She slowly lifted the lids and looked at him in her sexiest manner.

"It won't matter if the dance is still going on. Come for me when the Emerald City closes. Lefty won't let me go an instant before then."

"I know," he said.

He put his hands on her trim waist, lifted her easily, and sat her on the bar. A touch to the brim of his bowler in Lefty's direction told the barkeep he wasn't competition for

Claudette's affections. And yet he was, not wanting to be. If Carmela said frog, he'd jump, asking how high on the way up. For all that, Amanda intrigued him in spite of the trouble she had caused for him and the hints that she and Dunbar were more than acquaintances. Even the fiery Russian revolutionary with her pack of dogs interested Lucas more as a romantic partner.

The ones he wanted were all out to humiliate or kill him, and the one who wanted him was too . . . easy. There had to be an element of challenge to make the conquest perfect. Lucas found himself whistling as he stepped out into the cool night, happier than he had been in a few days. Everything came together for him. Gold, women, dogs. It all made sense now.

He hurried to the livery stable and took a quick glance around before opening the door. From the rear came heavy snoring sounds that drowned out the occasional horse's nicker or idle kick at a stall wall. Lucas pulled the door shut behind him.

"Lester, wake up. I've got a job for you."

"Wha?" The sleeping stable hand rolled off the planks he had balanced between two sawhorses and fell into the hay on the floor. He scrambled and got to his feet, rubbing his eyes. "You said it was fine if I slept, Mr. Justin. I remember you sayin' that if 'n I warn't tendin' the horses, I could sleep and I ain't and—"

"It's all right, Lester. Settle down. It's me, Lucas Stanton."

"Lucas? You scared me somethin' fierce. I was havin' a dream and thought you was the owner and—"

"I want you to do a job for me."

"I got one. Here, muckin' stalls and feedin' other people's horses."

"You knew of Dennis Clifford. Do you *know* him?"

"The filibuster fellow?" He settled back onto his plank bed and worked to arrange the blanket again. "He's a powerful lot of trouble. You don't want anythin' to do with the likes of him."

"The man's in town for a reason. I think he's forming a new expedition to overthrow a foreign government. I want you to join up with him."

"I don't want to overthrow no furrin government. Muckin' stalls ain't great work but it's safe, 'less you get kicked in the head. Even that's better 'n tanglin' with Clifford. He's a bloodthirsty killer."

"All I want is for you to pretend to join his army. Find out what he's up to. What country he's planning to invade, if he has allies, that kind of intelligence."

"Intelligence?"

"That's what the soldiers call it. You'll be a spy, getting intelligence from Clifford and his men about what they're up to."

"I don't know, Lucas. Like I said, they don't kid around. They think I'm spyin' on them, gettin' intellygence, they'd kill me. And it wouldn't be too pretty."

"All you have to do is listen to them. Men like them will talk freely if you get them liquored up." Lucas pulled out twenty dollars and stared at it. This reduced what he had made working for Amanda even more, but the reward would be immense. Gold. Lots of gold. Gold enough to finance a revolution in Russia. "Here, take this. I'll have another twenty for you when you get the information."

"Well," Gallatin said, weakening. His shaky hand touched the bill, then snatched it away as if Lucas would retract the offer. "I don't make no promises."

"I know some of what they're up to. I need to check it. Make sure it all matches."

"You would know if 'n I was I makin' up whatever I told you?"

Lucas said nothing. He knew some, but if Gallatin reported that Clifford was trying to invade Canada, he would know it was his attempt to take the money without risking his dirty neck.

"You got my word, Lucas. I ain't much of a human bein', but my word's as good as gold."

"Gold," Lucas said, the image of an entire mountain of the shiny metal in his eyes.

"When you want me to go?"

"As soon as you can. I'll talk to Mr. Justin for you if you like so you won't lose your job."

"You always was a sweet talker," Gallatin said. "Talk the clothes off any woman, talk the—"

"If you know where Clifford is camped, head on out now. You might want to pick up a couple bottles of whiskey for sitting around the campfire with his men." Lucas knew one bottle would be drained before Gallatin ever reached the camp.

"It's a ways off, from what I heard tell. Might be better to wait till tomorrow afternoon. That way I kin talk to Mr. Justin myself. If I got trouble with him, I'll let you know."

"That's good, Lester, that's real good," Lucas said, but his mind was drifting far away, back into the foothills of the Front Range and Vera Zasulich's camp. Without knowing it, he did a quick dance step, spinning around as he thought of her.

"You headin' over to the dance?"

Lucas stopped and looked at Gallatin, not really seeing him. His reverie died, and he returned to reality.

"What dance is that?"

"The Palace? Not sure but I heard folks who stabled their

horses this afternoon soundin' real sad they wasn't invited. Big affair. You're always gussied up like you're headin' out on the town."

"I'm not sure. What do you know of it?"

Gallatin shrugged. "All I know's I'd rather be hobnobbin' with the likes of the governor and Jubal Dunbar and their ladies than pumpin' Clifford's boys for information."

"We each play a role." Lucas settled his bowler at a jauntier angle and went to find the dance. If the governor was there and Jubal Dunbar was there, then Amanda Baldridge might be there, too. That suited him just fine.

He might even ask if he could have a dance with Tovarich, but the dog would have to let him lead.

16

Lester Gallatin was wrong. Lucas wasn't dressed for this soiree. He stood across the street from the Palace Ballroom, watching carriages pull up and elegantly dressed women step out. The sight of so much jewelry sparkling in the gaslight ignited his avarice. Trying to go straight, or as straight as a professional gambler working at the Emerald City could be, was something new for him. His days of working confidence schemes with the Preacher, Little Otto, and others out on the street weren't that far behind him.

Glittering diamonds delighted him, but the colored stones drew him like a moth to flame. Rubies, emeralds, star sapphires. Their crystalline depths stirred him in ways he hardly understood. Possessing them was a worthwhile pursuit, but the women wearing them proved an impediment. Almost as much an impediment as the men whose arms they held. More than one of the men had come through the Emerald City to see the shows, but seldom did any of them gamble. Their games were more private, more exclusive. Lucas doubted he had played even one hand with as high a limit as these men would demand to feel alive, to make the slip of playing cards across a table worthwhile.

He knew the mentality. These men were rich and powerful. They wanted others to cater to them, kowtow as the Celestials in Hop Town might say. Whether they lost or won fabulous sums mattered less than their surroundings and how the game was conducted. They had their private clubs with fancy imported champagne to drink and ladies whose beauty put even Carmela's to shame.

Lucas swallowed hard as the thought hit him that Amanda fit well into the milieu of the politically connected, wealthy sons of bitches. He could easily picture her serving these men drinks, pouring champagne, and making witty comments with just a touch of biting wit that those she served—serviced?—overlooked or simply didn't understand. Perhaps a woman offering rebellion would excite them since they need only snap their fingers to have any woman in Denver they wanted.

He caught his breath when the governor and his wife arrived. A flock of well-wishers rushed forward and swallowed him in the press of tuxedos and gowns made prominent with flouncy crinoline until discreet bouncers moved to separate the parasites from their host. His wife sported a necklace with a diamond as large as a goose egg. Even from a dozen yards away, that stone pulled at Lucas as if it were a magnificent magnet and he were a helpless iron penny nail.

He took an involuntary step and then halted in the middle of the street. He wore an expensive coat and his pants held knife-edged creases. His shoes needed shining but were passable, but that was the problem. He was richly dressed— for the Emerald City. For a gala like this, he looked like a vagabond. Even if he still owned the coat ruined by Dunbar's thugs when they threw him in the sewage canal, he would have seemed like a poor country cousin. This was what happened when a territory became a state. Limitless money flowed in and was put to use by the men inside the ballroom.

At the point of considering a way of sneaking in through the servants' entrance, he heard a lilting laugh and a voice he remembered well. He stepped back and used the gaslight to partially hide him as Jubal Dunbar climbed from a four-wheeled carriage, then helped Amanda to solid ground. Dunbar thought nothing of leaving his wife at home with the hired help, it seemed.

Walking quickly, Lucas crossed the street and peered into the carriage as it rattled away. It was foolish to believe she had brought Tovarich with her, but it cost Lucas nothing to sneak a quick look. As far as he could tell, there wasn't even a strand of wolfhound hair on either of the plushly cushioned seats. He stepped back to keep from getting his toes run over by the wheels.

He was never quite certain how the plan formed. His days with the Preacher returned, complete with all the skills he had been taught.

Another carriage pulled up. A gruff man, huffing and puffing, helped his matronly wife down. There was no one to help what had to be their daughter, so Lucas stepped forward and extended his arm.

"May I, miss?"

She looked at him in surprise, then grinned. Her teeth were crooked and her acne rivaled a bad case of smallpox. The former went untended but her face and bare shoulders had been powdered over until every step she took caused a chalk-like dust to rise. Too much rouge on her cheeks made her look like a circus clown. Mascara around her eyes changed that aspect to more like that of a raccoon. She might have been pretty enough without the inexpertly applied cosmetics, but Lucas guessed she had done it all herself to spite her mother and father. If she was much more than fifteen, it would have surprised him since she moved with the gawky, coltish gait of a tomboy not yet inducted into the society of boys seeking to do more than dip her pigtails in a school desk inkwell.

Lucas held out his arm. The girl looked at it, then up at her mother on her father's arm, and realized what was necessary. She let Lucas help her down. As if he belonged, he turned and walked slowly down the carpet toward the door.

"Who're you?"

"I am your escort for the evening, miss."

"Papa didn't say anything about this. He specifically forbade Phillip from accompanying me tonight."

"Your beau?"

She blushed, even under the plastered-on makeup, and averted her eyes. She giggled just a little.

"Yes. He's a nice boy, but Papa won't even let him into the house. He says he's not good enough for me."

"Your father is a wise man." She jerked away, but Lucas held her on his arm with his right hand clamping firmly on hers. "What boy could possibly be good enough? Please allow me, wretched replacement though I am, to substitute for your Phillip."

"You think I'm pretty?"

Lucas divided his attention between fielding the girl fishing for compliments and the two gatekeepers keeping riffraff from the ball. Her parents had already passed through, not bothering to even show an invitation. Whoever her pa was, he was a powerful, well-known man.

"Your invitation, sir." The strong hand on his shoulder bit down just enough to warn him how a fight would go.

"We're with them," Lucas said, pointing to the couple now melting into the throng within the main ballroom.

"No invitation, no entrance. Sorry, sir."

"Well, my dear, this means that you must take your leave of me and perhaps spend the evening with Phillip."

The girl squealed in joy at the prospect. Her joy halted her father, who looked back. He scowled, then impatiently motioned her forward.

"Don't keep us waiting, Hannah. Come along now. Right away."

"I'd rather be with Phillip."

Lucas gently told her that her father wanted them inside, then watched the reaction of the two guards. As much as he wanted to make a sarcastic remark, he knew that silence worked to eat out their resistance.

"Hannah!" This time her mother called.

"Enjoy the cotillion," said the man on Lucas's right. His tone relayed how his cotillion would be perfect if he could tear off the arms and legs of those trying to get in without the proper fancy printed invitation.

Lucas bowed slightly to the man, appreciated the feeling of power and triumph for a brief instant, held up his arm for Hannah, and forced himself to walk slowly although he wanted to run inside to get away from the two guards. He felt their eyes boring into him, but as with holding back his sarcasm, he knew better than to look. To do so would have alerted them to an intruder. Pretending he belonged, in spite of his relatively shabby clothing, mattered more than anything else.

The swirl and gaiety around him caught at his senses and carried him to a world he barely knew existed. The perfumes mingled with sweat from overweight men struggling to dance with their wives or, in some cases, Lucas suspected, their much younger mistresses. He sought out Dunbar and Amanda, but the throng provided a curtain of gems, silk, and whirling couples he could not penetrate.

"Would you care to dance?"

Hannah sounded scared when she agreed.

He spun her about and stepped out into the waltz. To his surprise, the girl followed his lead with the quickness of youth and the assurance of a woman much older.

"You dance well," he complimented. "How often do you practice?"

"The dance master comes once a week, but I have been taking lessons for almost a year. He says I am a clumsy oaf and sticking one foot in a bucket would only improve my dancing."

Lucas laughed easily. He whirled her about and got a better look around the dance floor. Nowhere did he see Amanda or Dunbar, though he caught sight of the governor dancing with a woman half his age. That it caused no furor told him this was part of the governor's dance card, making the wives and daughters of important men see his way—and influencing husbands, lovers, and fathers that way.

"He is not much of an instructor. Look around. What do you see?"

"I don't want to see anything but . . . you," she said shyly.

"Up with the chin, back with the head." He spun her about furiously so her hair came a little undone and formed a fine brown mist around her head. Here and there sparkled a pearl, but compared with the other women, Hannah wore no jewels at all. That, if nothing else, made her stand out.

But he exaggerated the waltz step, sweeping a path through until the girl finally noticed a gaggle of swains watching her every step.

Lucas circled the floor once more and timed the end of the dance so they stopped directly in front of the four young men. From the cut of their tuxedos, they all came from money. And all had noticed her for the first time.

"Miss, thank you for being so gracious to dance with an old man." He bowed and stepped back. It took only a few seconds for all four to block him from Hannah, each vying for her attention. She might have been an ugly duckling before but the figure she cut on the dance floor drew the unattached boys like flies to honey.

Lucas quickly moved away from being the center of attention. He had gotten strange stares because of his clothing. He doffed his bowler and tucked it under his arm as he made his way around the fringe of the crowd. He saw that bouncers moving restlessly through the dancers, whether looking for him or simply intending to keep out the riffraff, whoever it might be, hardly mattered. The men had worn top hats; he wore a bowler. They had tuxedos. He had a fine brocade coat far gaudier by their standards than any peacock. His one advantage now that he had abandoned Hannah to her new suitors lay in not going to the food table or asking for a drink. Either would identify him as an interloper wanting only to live off the generosity of others. As thirsty and hungry as he was, he would make a spectacle of himself.

He edged along a wall, found a staircase, and slowly ascended until he had a better view of the dancers. It took a few minutes of patient watchfulness, but he finally spotted Amanda. Like Hannah, she had quite a coterie of admirers, but Jubal Dunbar was nowhere to be seen. To speak to her would require him shouldering his way through men likely to take offense. If nothing else, there would be a disturbance that would draw the wards to evict him.

If he was lucky, that would be all that happened. Being tossed into the street was nothing new for him, but the level of political power and wealth represented in this room told him he was likely to be interrogated. That meant the same thing as being squeezed dry, then discarded. This time he wouldn't be alive when tossed into the sewage canal.

He reluctantly took a few steps down to go speak with Amanda, no matter what the attention it caused, when he heard a familiar voice booming up the stairs.

Lucas dared not face Jubal Dunbar or the half dozen men with him. They were arguing about something and would only hasten his death if they found him. Making his way to the head of the staircase allowed him a better view of the dance floor. Amanda spun out with a handsome young buck. A knot formed in his throat. She was a splendid dancer, and the couple looked as if they belonged together, every move liquid and perfect.

Dunbar and the men with him trooped up the stairs. Lucas darted for heavy hangings behind a table, almost knocking over a piece of statuary. He steadied it and ducked out of sight as the men walked past.

". . . it *can* be done. All we need to do is be *men*, dammit!"

"Speak of that in the room where we can have some privacy, Jubal. For God's sake, man. You'll have us all on the gallows if you aren't more careful."

Dunbar snapped back. Most of his words became too muffled as they went down a corridor and found their meeting room. Lucas slipped back out, gripped the polished mahogany railing, and saw Amanda accepting a flute of champagne from her dancing partner. For an instant Lucas caught his breath. She looked straight at him and seemed to lift her glass in silent salute. But she touched glasses with her partner and allowed him to put an arm around her waist and guide her to chairs at the edge of the dance floor. Lucas swiped at his forehead. The mere thought that she had acknowledged his presence had caused him to break out in a sweat.

He knew going back to the ground floor and leaving while he was still in one piece and relatively free of bruises from a beating was the smartest thing to do. Instead, he cautiously went down the corridor, pressing his ear to each heavily paneled door in turn until he found one vibrating from the argument raging inside. The wood prevented coherent words from escaping. Opening the door a crack would allow him to spy on those inside. It would also put him at jeopardy of being seen.

Lucas went to the next room and warily opened the door. The smartly appointed room stood empty. He scooped up a wineglass from a table and went to the wall separating this room from the one where Dunbar conducted his clandestine meeting.

Placing the rim against a bare spot on the wall and pressing his ear into the base amplified the sounds. The words came to him muffled but clearer than before. With a little imagination he worked out what Dunbar said and the objections the others presented.

". . . this is the best time," Dunbar said.

"Jubal, please, we are a state now. What you suggest is nothing less than treason. Do you think generals like Sheridan and Sherman would allow us to secede?"

"They are always on the lookout to go back to war," chimed in another man. "They would relish the chance to put down a rebellion."

"All the more reason for us to act swiftly," Dunbar said. "The longer Colorado remains a state, the better organized the Federals will be. We must strike quickly, pry their grasping fingers from our throats, and form our new country!"

"It takes more than a handful of men to overthrow a government, even one that hasn't been in power more than a few months. You forget that Routt was territorial governor before becoming state governor. There is no chance of a crack in his power, no miscue in the handoff from territory to state. His staff remains as loyal now as before."

"John Routt is a dedicated man but he lacks ambition and vision," Dunbar said.

"And you have both."

Lucas wasn't able to tell if that response was sardonic or supportive.

"We have the army necessary to seize key forts. We take Routt captive. Then we present Washington with a reality they cannot fight. I have the promise of recognition of two foreign governments."

"Two? Which?"

"Russia and Nicaragua," he said without hesitation.

Lucas pulled away to rub circulation back into his ear. He hadn't realized how hard he'd pressed against the wineglass to hear. Vera Zasulich had promised recognition of Dunbar's break-off country, and from the sound of it, Dennis Clifford had made a similar promise.

How much gold was there to finance not only Vera's and Clifford's but also Dunbar's revolts?

He put the glass to the wall once more. He'd pressed so

hard it had cut a ring in the plaster. Lucas moved to a different spot but heard only indistinct sounds of chairs and gruff voices still arguing the merit of Dunbar's revolt. As he drew back, he felt a draft of air across his neck.

The door had opened.

He was caught!

17

Lucas sucked in his breath and lifted the empty wineglass to his lips as if draining the dregs. He took a staggering step and caught himself on a chair so his fingers curled around the back. If he heaved hard enough, he could bowl over the man in the doorway using the chair as a battering ram.

"Sorry, old chap, didn't know the room was occupied."

The man wore a brilliant red British Army uniform festooned with decorations that clanked as he moved and reflected golden light off the medals. Behind him a plain-looking woman with mussed blond hair and a flushed face wobbled about, as drunk as Lucas had pretended to be. These two sought a room for an assignation.

"Quite all right, G-General. Was j-just l-leaving." Lucas kept up the charade of being soused. He bowed deeply to the woman and said, "Do enjoy yourself, madame. It looks to be a fine night for a British invasion of hitherto unoccupied territory."

"What's he mean by that, Georgie?"

"Nothing, my dear, nothing. Let's find some of that wine he was imbibing."

Lucas closed the door as he left and heaved a sigh. He hadn't seen any wine in the room. While they might think he had already drunk it all, he worried more that the British officer would come hunting for an adequate amount to complete the woman's inebriation and his conquest. He had to be long gone when that happened. Answering questions would only put him in peril of being discovered by the men assigned to keep his like from this dance.

He reached the head of the stairs and glanced down, checking to be certain Dunbar and his coconspirators in rebellion had melted back into the crowd. Lucas froze when he saw two well-dressed men at the foot of the stairs. The bully boys who had dumped him in the canal both looked up and spotted him at the same time. He had to admire their coordination. Without a word passing between them, the pair hit the stairs and took them three at a time in perfect step like an infantry company passing in review, racing to reach him.

If it had been any other guards, he might have talked his way out by claiming to be with Hannah. These two recognized him for who he was. He sprinted down the hall, considering enlisting the colonel's help. The quick passage past the door told him how unlikely that was since the officer was no longer in uniform and undoubtedly pressing his advantage to advance. With a sudden turn, he found a branching corridor lined with more private rooms. Lucas dashed past the first, opening the door a fraction before going to the next and ducking inside. The two chasing him would hesitate seeing the open door and have to search that room. It bought him precious seconds.

He hunted for a place to hide, then saw this room opened onto a balcony overlooking the dance floor. The band was almost immediately below him. Looking down he saw the tops of their heads and how they played their instruments with both gusto and expertise. Even with the sounds of classical music rising, he heard the bulls in the china shop next door. Dunbar's men made no effort at finesse.

It was only a matter of seconds before they entered.

Lucas hopped onto the railing, balanced for a moment, then turned and fell. His fingers caught the bottom of the railing, letting him dangle for a moment. With a powerful kick, he sent himself sailing out and onto the dance floor, where he crashed and lay flat on his back for a moment, stunned.

"Lucas?"

He looked up to see Amanda standing over him, her dance partner confused.

"Why, yes, thank you, I would love this dance." He got to his feet, bowed slightly to her spurned partner, and whirled away. The empty circle around them collapsed and once more the dancers waltzed. Such interruptions, while unusual, were to be expected when too much of the fine wine was consumed.

"You certainly know how to make an entrance."

He pulled her closer. Her body fit nicely against his. She leaned back as they whirled around. He guided her toward the far side of the floor, then held her as a shield between the men on the balcony looking down and his own all too obvious fancy coat. He stood out amid the men in their black like a ladybug on a daisy.

"For you, my dear, walking on air is only the beginning."

"You can be quite a charmer."

"Where's Tovarich?"

"And also irritatingly blunt." Amanda pressed her face to his chest to keep her expression from being seen. He took this to mean whatever she said would be a lie. "I don't know."

"Where did you and the dog go after you got away from the rat pit?"

"Must we speak of such ugly things? This is a fancy dress ball." She reared back and looked at his clothing. "However did you get inside wearing such rags?"

"Who's being irritatingly blunt now? I lack a patron such as the one you have corralled."

"Patron? You cannot mean Jubal. He isn't a patron, he's more of my prison warden. When I left that terrible place with Tovarich, we ran away, but Jubal's men—the ones you are so intent on fleeing and who have finally gone in search of you elsewhere—caught me. Tovarich ran off before I could catch him."

Lucas spun about and saw she was right about Dunbar's men; they had disappeared. He knew that even if they searched the entire second floor of the building, they would be back downstairs in a few minutes. He couldn't dance all night to avoid them. His feet would give out before then, even if they weren't intent on frog marching him outside.

"How did you come by the dog?"

"Oh, Lucas, that's such a boring story. I fell in love with the little mutt the instant I laid eyes on him. He was being abused. I had to take care of him." She looked up and batted her long lashes. "I would certainly enjoy taking care of you tonight."

"I'm not sure I would enjoy that."

She tried to jerk free, but he held her securely. Amanda gave up and once more molded her body to his as they moved to the music.

"I know things that would definitely give you memories of the night for the rest of your life."

"Why did Dunbar bring you here tonight? People will gossip. You're not his wife."

"Well, sir, I am *not* his mistress." She tensed again. He pulled her closer. Both of Dunbar's bodyguards had returned to the first floor and studied every couple passing them. Whatever he did had to be quick. The last strains of the music were fading and the dance was over. He and Amanda would be left alone on the floor since the conductor was signaling his orchestra to take a break.

"Come with me. We can get away from Dunbar."

Her reaction confused him. She didn't tense as she had before, showing how she considered his offer. But Amanda didn't make a move to leave, either. Staring up at him, her bright blue eyes questioning, she shook her head.

"I can't. Not the way you mean."

Lucas had no time to argue. Both bodyguards were crossing the increasingly depopulated dance floor, intent on him. He judged distances, then whirled Amanda about and sent her staggering into the men's arms.

"I don't mind if you cut in," he said.

As the two tried to keep Amanda from falling, and he thought she flailed about far more than necessary to give him the time he needed, Lucas headed for the far side of the ballroom, away from the front doors where four men moved in to see what was causing the disturbance.

"Hannah," he said, passing by the gangly girl. "Have a good evening."

"Why, uh, yes, thank you, Mr.—"

He left her with a youngster who glared at even this minor intrusion. He ducked behind a pillar, considered his escape route, then dropped to hands and knees and slid under a table, pulling down the tablecloth as he sat, hand on his Colt, waiting to see if Dunbar's men ferreted him out. He saw feet going back and forth, and the four he took to be those of the guards stopped within reach. Lucas barely breathed as they shifted about, obviously scanning the room and not finding him. When they walked away, he chanced a quick look under the edge of the cloth.

The men fell in behind Dunbar and Amanda as they left in a rush.

Lucas sat under the table considering all that he could do next. Amanda befuddled him. She lied consistently about Tovarich and her involvement with Dunbar, yet a small current of truth ran though much of what she said. What bothered him most was being unable to decide what was truth and what amounted to huge lies. He had learned the technique from the Preacher. Tell a series of improbable truths, let the mark find out how accurate all the small statements had been, then the big lie delivered the payoff. Whether Amanda did this on purpose with him or if it simply came naturally was something he wanted to find out.

Either way, she was an intriguing woman.

He moved from under the table, heading for the kitchen and the servants' entrance. Walking fast, he got around to the front of the building in time to see Dunbar handing Amanda up into the carriage. They rattled off with the two bodyguards remaining behind. They argued for a moment, then went back inside. Lucas suspected they had been dispatched to find and kill him.

He smiled. He would show them. He wouldn't be inside. Stride long, he headed across Denver toward Dunbar's house. The would-be revolutionary might not take Amanda there, but this was his best guess.

Lucas was panting with exertion by the time he stopped

in front of Dunbar's house. A single lamp in the upstairs window gave the only hint that the house was occupied. He leaned against the gas streetlight and stared at the window. He caught his breath when a woman moved across the window, then returned to close the curtains. Whoever it was, he had not found Amanda. This woman's bulk was easily twice that of the slender Amanda Baldridge.

"Dunbar's wife," he said softly. He went around to the back door, thinking to work his way inside past the maid and any other servant to search the house for Amanda.

He stopped when he came around to the carriage house. If that was Dunbar's wife, Amanda would be elsewhere. Noise from inside the carriage house caused him to find shadows and fade into them. Hand on his pistol, he waited as the door opened. Inside stood the carriage he had seen outside the dance hall. Dunbar held the door, his voice muffled. Then he turned and Lucas heard him clearly.

"She's safely tucked away for the night. Don't worry about that."

"You're playing with fire, Mr. Dunbar." The words came out in a slow Southern drawl. "Why don't you let me and the boys find what she knows?"

"She'll talk soon enough. If you took her, you'd likely skin her to find the dog."

Lucas perked up. There was no question Dunbar spoke of Amanda.

Stepping out to light a match and apply it to a cigar, the hidden man's identity was revealed.

Lucas etched the man's face in his mind. This wasn't one of Dunbar's lackeys. In spite of the deference, the voice carried arrogance and even superiority.

"You make us out to be barbarians, Mr. Dunbar. You and I, sir, are pragmatists."

"I won't have you harming the young lady."

"No reason to, if she'll tell us what we need. I must question your dedication to the cause."

"Colorado will secede and form a new country." Dunbar slammed the carriage house door. "You have no reason to question my determination in this matter. I understand the penalty for failure."

"Do you now, Mr. Dunbar? I wonder."

Without another word, Jubal Dunbar stalked off. Lucas took an involuntary step to follow. Dunbar had imprisoned Amanda somewhere, and it wasn't likely in the house with his wife in the upstairs bedroom. He caught himself before he gave away his presence. The other man puffed on his cigar a couple times, then ground it out. Lucas followed him with all the skill he possessed.

The man doubled back twice, almost catching Lucas trailing him. Then Lucas began to look on it as a game and found it easier with every step to remain hidden as the man worked his way south to a run-down house a half mile from Dunbar's mansion. Two men came out to greet the man from the carriage house. In the cold, still night their words carried to where Lucas crouched behind a ruined wagon lacking two rear wheels.

"You find where she is?"

"No, the stupid son of a bitch wouldn't tell me. He has no idea what's at stake."

"An entire country."

"Nicaragua," the first man said. He took out another cigar, lit it, and puffed furiously. "Dunbar's a fool thinking he can pry away a new state after all the political infighting it took to gain admittance." He expelled a smoke ring that rose in the night until it caught the faint moonlight and turned to wavering silver. "If he doesn't find where the gold is soon, we'll have to be more resolute."

"Can't supply an army with promises," one man said.

"Even with a million dollars, it'll be hard. Clifford's good at outfitting an expedition, but nobody wins when it's rocks against rifles."

With that the trio went into the house.

Lucas stared at the spot where the men had been, his heart racing. A million dollars in gold. Amanda's life would be forfeit if she didn't tell them where the dog was and how Tovarich could locate the treasure trove. A cold lump formed in his belly when he realized her life was over the instant she did tell them.

There wasn't any good way out of her predicament, not dealing with the likes of Dunbar—and Clifford.

18

Lucas paced anxiously, waiting for Lester Gallatin to return to the stables. The horses grew increasingly restive because of his constant movement, his occasional tapping of his fingers against whichever stall was closest, and his outbursts of cursing because of his helplessness. Finding Amanda demanded his full attention. If Dunbar wouldn't do it, Clifford would torture her to find what had happened to the Russian wolfhound.

The woman's insincere answer as to what had happened to Tovarich worried him. Lucas felt they'd had some bond while on the dance floor, moving smoothly to the music and responding to each other's slightest motion. She had even faltered when it came to her incessant lying, or so he believed. His life depended on reading others, though his true expertise lay in seeing what drunken cowboys and crafty clerks and others who thought they held good hands really had been dealt. Bluffers were easy to spot. Those who honestly believed proved more difficult and required other skills to read. Whatever it took, Lucas played and won more than he lost.

With women, the stakes were different, but he had won more than he'd lost there, too. His recent streak of bad luck with Carmela, and perhaps with Amanda, worried him. In Amanda's case, her life might be forfeit. She thought making him believe her tall tales got her off the hook. Dealing with ruthless men like Dunbar and Clifford upped the stakes. She knew where the dog was. He hadn't bought her lie for an instant, and neither would Clifford. Dunbar might be smitten with her charms, but the filibuster had greater goals than slipping between the sheets. Dunbar might want Colorado to secede, but his level of mercilessness failed to reach that of Clifford. For all Lucas knew, it might not even match that of the Russian anarchists. Vera Zasulich showed the fire of the fanatic and had lost a brother.

Lucas went for his pistol when the livery stable's door creaked open.

"For God's sake, where have you been?"

"Lucas? Been doin' what you asked of me." Gallatin staggered in, canted his head to one side, and squinted through one eye to keep the world in focus. Even at a distance of yards, he reeked of booze. "It might not be safe if you keep comin' on by here. They don't really trust me. Think one followed me here. They see us together and we're both dead men."

Lucas went to the door and peered out into the street. The few pedestrians out at this time of night walked briskly on their way. A solitary rider never glanced in his direction, and a clattering carriage drove in the wrong direction. Even as he watched, it turned a corner down by a gaslight and disappeared toward the center of town. Shadows and silence reigned once more.

"I don't see anyone on your trail."

"Them's cagey men. Shadows, ghosts! Animals, I swear. Not a one of 'em's got a human feeling in his breast. All they talk of is killin', past, present, and future. Them boastin' on the number of soldiers they are gonna kill when they invade Nicaragua bothers me most. The others might be lies. But the looks on their faces when they get to talkin' of cuttin' down men when they get to Nicaragua—"

"Lester, forget that for now. I know Clifford wants to overthrow the Nicaraguan government. He needs financial backing to do that. Did they talk about that?"

"Heard a hint of some gold comin' their way real soon. Never figgered what they meant, though. Them boys are cheap. Made me buy 'em a round and never returned the favor. Had to buy my own tarantula juice."

"Where are they holed up?"

"Can't say for certain sure, Lucas, but I think they got an old house south of Colfax, away from all them rich folks' houses. They mighta been lyin' to mislead me, but I don't think so. No reason, and I never asked. I was just listenin' real hard."

"Don't worry about that. What are Clifford's plans?" Lucas had little hope that the mercenaries had dropped any hint about the gold in front of a recruit who couldn't hold his liquor.

"Like they was sayin', he's expectin' to come into a mountain of gold. That's what one of 'em said. 'The general's gonna find a mountain of gold.' That was his precise utterance. I asked what he meant, but they clammed up and wouldn't say another word. I thought that was kinda suspect, but askin' too many questions might've got my throat cut."

"You did fine, Lester."

Lucas despaired of finding Amanda now. He already

knew where the filibusters made their headquarters after trailing Clifford there. An overheard comment about a million dollars whetted his own appetite but he was building fantasies of how grateful Amanda would be when he came riding up and saved her. Lacking either a white charger or shining armor became an increasing problem, especially when his only ally was the drunken Lester Gallatin.

"You wanted me to listen on any secrets about a dog. I heard one, though it don't amount to a hill of beans."

Lucas knew that Clifford still hunted for the dog, so his men hardly knew where the animal could be found. That was the purpose of torturing the information from Amanda.

"Anything you heard would help," he said, not expecting real details.

"They said that Dunbar had the bitch buried, so they might as well make that her grave. Don't know what it means."

"The bitch?"

"Gotta mean a dog since none of them's a woman. I can't imagine why they'd say a thing like that about Mrs. Dunbar. From all I heard, she's kinda sickly and never leaves her bedroom."

"The bitch," Lucas said, smiling a little. "Could they have meant Amanda Baldridge?"

Gallatin shrugged. The act of shaking his head caused things to come loose inside. He moaned and clutched his temples with both hands.

"I think I'm gonna be sick. That was awful firewater they served up."

"Take care of yourself." Lucas stepped away as Gallatin began retching out the contents of his tormented belly. The smell turned his own stomach, so he hurried out into the night.

Dawn would be on the way in less than an hour, but Gallatin had given him a clue. The filibusters might have been spewing nonsense, but it made sense. Dunbar hadn't had long to stash Amanda far from his house, not given the brief time between his carriage reaching his home and Lucas arriving. Dunbar wouldn't lock up Amanda inside the house—and the real clue lay in "grave."

Feeling that time worked against him, Lucas ran back to Dunbar's house, reaching there just as the sun poked above the plains and sent rays racing to warm the Front Range. The servants in the house began their chores, but he ignored them and went straight for the carriage house. The door creaked open to let in the new day's light.

He froze when he heard nails tearing out of wood, followed by hard hammering as if someone knocked on a door. Toward the rear of the carriage house he saw a trapdoor rise a few inches and then collapse. Nails pulling from wood sounded louder and then the trapdoor slammed open with a loud crash that caused him to jump. A mop of dark hair poked up, paused, then rose.

Lucas moved to hide behind the carriage as Amanda forced her way through the small opening to a root cellar. Underneath the carriage he saw her torn dress and filthy shoes. The sight of a well-turned ankle almost made him go to her aid. Instead, he moved toward the rear of the carriage house as she went to the door and stood silhouetted by the rising sun. She looked like she had been rode hard and put away wet. Her hair rivaled any bird's nest, the underclothing she still wore was ripped and dirty, and she rubbed at minor cuts and scratches on her arms.

After the brief hesitation, she darted away. Lucas counted to ten and went after her. He had misjudged how fast she could run, and run she did. She was all the way down the street before she made a quick turn and vanished from view. In spite of being bone tired, Lucas lit out after her, running as hard as he could. His legs ached and the wind came in fiery stabs through his lungs. Having the stamina to play poker for thirty-six hours straight did not properly speak to real physical endurance. He had walked all over Denver that night, danced away from Dunbar's thugs and with the lovely Amanda, and now had to chase the woman running for her life.

He put his head down and doggedly kept loping along until she came into view again. She dodged down another street. This time he slowed and caught his breath since the street stretched far to the west. All too soon, she cut south again, heading down toward the old settlement along Cherry Creek where the first Denver pioneers had huddled against fierce blizzards and occasional Arapaho attacks.

Another twenty minutes of increasingly circuitous roads that were hardly more than ruts brought him to a shack that would fall down when the first winter winds blew against it. He suspected the walls were sturdier than they appeared—this building had withstood the rigors of weather for a long time and would still be standing long after newer structures in Denver had tumbled.

Lucas tore out running when Amanda screamed. He skidded to a halt and pressed his back against the weathered planking. The Colt came to his hand easily. He waited for another sound to give him a hint as to what he was bulling his way into, but all he heard were low, muffled curses. Then came the sound of flesh striking something hard. Twisting about, he pressed his face against the wall and peered through a crack.

The darkness almost defeated his spying. His eye gradually adapted to the interior light. Amanda pounded her fist against the only furniture in the room, a table that trembled with every blow. She spun about and grabbed for her head as if she was hurt, but Lucas had seen this gesture before. She was furious.

Another loud, unladylike curse cut through the air. He moved around to find a better view, then spotted two men coming down the path for the shack. Not even realizing it, he lifted his pistol and triggered a round. For a .22, the range was extreme, but it served its purpose. The slug whined past Dunbar's henchmen. They dived in different directions, throwing themselves flat on the ground.

He got off another shot, which accomplished nothing but relieved the tension he felt. Lucas looked through a knothole into the shack and saw the door swing open. For an instant Amanda stood there, then ran off. He called to her but his warning was drowned out by the thunder of a pair of .45s. Both of Dunbar's men had unlimbered their side arms and fired steadily into the cabin.

Lucas crouched, braced his wrist against the corner of the shack, and waited for the perfect shot. He might not have the killing power of either of those attacking, but a small piece of lead rattling around in a belly or taking off a kneecap worked as well for his purpose as killing them.

He never got the chance to fire. Both men scrambled up and crossed the path, using the shack to hide themselves. Waiting for them to come around, one on either side, heightened Lucas's senses. Every sound, every odor, every flash of light keyed him up that much more.

They never came after him.

He duck walked around and saw that they had seen Amanda and gone after her. Chances were good they thought she had fired on them. Standing slowly, he saw that it was impossible to overtake them. Amanda ran for her life and gave the men the chase of their lives. The best he could do was shoot them in the back, but he doubted he could ever catch up or even narrow the distance enough for another shot.

Pistol tucked back into his pocket, he started to leave, then pivoted and went into the shack. Amanda had come here for a reason. His nose wrinkled at the smell coming from a pile of dog excrement in the corner of the room. If that hadn't been proof enough that Amanda had chained Tovarich here, the chewed leather leash told the true story. The dog had gnawed his way free. That was the reason for her anger. She had rescued the wolfhound from the ratter, only to lose him again.

Lucas coughed and gasped. As he sucked in a breath, he recognized the strange perfume Amanda used. The same that she shared with Vera Zasulich. If he wanted to find the dog and learn where a million dollars in gold was hidden, he had to go to the Russian revolutionaries' camp.

Getting rich was proving more deadly by the minute.

19

Lucas almost drew his pistol. He had fired it a couple times already. What did it matter if he fired it again into the belly of the man lurking across the street from his boardinghouse? It had been too long since he had stretched out on the too small bed and gotten even a rocky night's sleep on the hard mattress. Dunbar kept a constant watch on the room. A single shot could eliminate that. Lucas was tired enough to consider committing cold-blooded murder, although that wasn't his style.

Forming what words to say to the watcher got him nowhere. Nothing he could say would be adequate. This was a trap he would never talk himself out of. The smallish man did not know what he looked like—Lucas had never seen the man before. Even if he decoyed the man away, it would be only minutes before he realized he had been tricked and return to find his quarry asleep on the bed in the room at the rear of the house.

All such notions fled when a second man came up and spoke with the man lounging across the street. Lucas remembered seeing this one before. The first man left, turning over his watch to one who knew better than to be duped by the very man he sought.

Lucas's shoulders sagged as he retraced his steps and mingled with the crowds going about their daily business. Gallatin might provide him with a stall where he could sleep, but that held dangers to both of them if Clifford's men spied on the stable hand. Lucas had no illusions about how good an actor Gallatin was. The filibusters had to suspect he wasn't a down-and-out guerrilla hunting for a new army.

"Actors," Lucas said to himself. Returning to the Emerald City held a certain appeal, especially since Carmela's departure was imminent.

But Lefty avoided trouble at all costs. Just by asking for a place to curl up and sleep screamed danger to the saloon and everyone in it. Lucas wished he had slept there when he wasn't in such dire straits. That would make such a request now seem more innocent.

Hardly knowing it, he wound through the streets and came into the alley behind the Great West Detective Agency. Opening the door faster now than if he'd used a key, he slipped into the back room. He looked into the office. Finding Amanda there would have given him a real surprise. She had lost the dog again and needed help finding it, if she had dodged Dunbar's henchmen.

But she wasn't there.

Lucas spread out the blanket on the back room floor and lay down. Before he had stared at the cracked ceiling, imagining all manner of things. This time he slept like a dead

man, awakening sometime in the afternoon with his belly
grumbling for food. He stretched and felt better for the few
hours of sleep.

A rattling of the front door sent him scuttling on hands
and knees to look out. A ragamuffin tapped insistently on
the glass and held up a paper.

The boy had spotted him. Rather than send the newsy
away with possible gossip on his lips, Lucas went to the
door, fumbled it open, and found a paper thrust into his
hands.

"You ain't the usual guy." The dirty boy, all of ten, spoke
accusingly. He tugged at his ratty checkered cap and thrust
out his chin.

"Mr. Runyon's not here right now."

"He always buys a paper. You're gonna buy a paper, ain't
ya, mister? When he gets back, he'll want to know all the
news. He always does. He's a detective and keeps a close
eye on goings-on in town." The boy winked broadly. "I keep
a sharp eye out for him, and he pays me if I see anything he
might make a dollar off. You a new detective?"

The determined look and the peppering of questions further convinced Lucas the only way to rid himself of the
capitalistic brat was to pay him off. He fished about in his
pocket and found a quarter.

The coin disappeared along with the boy. Lucas sighed
and closed the door. Before he could toss the paper into a
corner, an article below the fold caught his eye. He sat at the
desk with the newspaper spread out before him so he could
read the smeary print one line at a time and not miss a single
word.

When he'd finished the article about a train wreck down
in Durango, he read it again. He rocked back and shook his
head sadly.

"Our paths will never cross now, Mr. Runyon." He glanced a final time at the article detailing how a Mr. Jacoby Runyon of Denver had been one of seven killed when a narrow gauge train derailed, the act of road agents intent on robbing the mail car.

Lucas went to the file cabinet and leafed through the folders until he found one with the railroad's name on it. On the top of the papers in the file lay a contract hiring the Great West Detective Agency, Jacoby Runyon primary detective, to bring to justice a gang of outlaws terrorizing the entire region of southwestern Colorado. Lucas let out a low whistle when he saw how much the detective was to be paid for his work, whether he brought the outlaws to justice or simply drove them off. Being a detective paid better than he would have thought.

He closed the file and leafed through other papers, stopping at one that had BILL OF SALE bannered across the top. Holding it up so the sunlight made the fine print easier to read, he quickly saw this was proof that Runyon had purchased the company from one Lawrence Duckworth. Lucas ran his finger over the signatures and smiled. At the desk he pushed aside the newspaper and carefully examined the way the bill of sale had been written.

Only a fool signed a legal document in pencil. He used his lock pick to open the desk drawer and took out a pencil. Next to it a spirit gum eraser begged to be applied to the bill of sale. Lucas had watched the Preacher forge documents of various kinds, but none of the techniques he had witnessed were needed here. A quick swipe of the eraser removed Duckworth's name. He signed his own in ink, with a flourish, then realized more had to be done. As it stood, the sold to and bought by were reversed.

Correcting this required the used of a straight razor he

found in the back room, a few minutes application of the steel to the printed words, and then a careful replication of the print style by hand. The ink didn't match well and his hand was a trifle shaky, but at first glance, he had just become the owner of the Great West Detective Agency, as sold to him by a deceased man.

Lucas felt a glow of pride at his skill. Dealing cards required manual dexterity. Forgery pushed the limits of that ability and added in a steady hand and more than a touch of audacity. He had no desire to own the agency, but the forgery had taken his mind off other, deadlier matters. He pushed the fraudulent bill of sale aside and scoured the newspaper for any hint as to Jubal Dunbar's plans. The man wasn't even mentioned, although a lengthy article about the gala the night before graced the social column.

He had to laugh when a single line told of a disturbance at the dance when a vagrant had intruded, intent on a free meal and some booze. Without a more detailed description, he reckoned another might have crashed the festivities, but he doubted it. He was the vagrant and the mention of food reminded him that he had yet to eat.

As he stood to go find a decent meal, he saw two figures fill the doorway, vying to be the first inside. He touched his pocket, then continued the movement to smooth out his vest.

"The agency isn't open."

"The door was unlocked," the woman said sharply. "We have come in response to your ad." She held up a newspaper turning yellow with age.

"The position is no longer open."

"What? You've hired someone else? That's not possible. We have come by repeatedly and have seen no one in the office." The man looked to his wife, as if he needed her approval for such a bold statement.

They were the couple Lucas had seen loitering about, arguing over whether to pursue this position or try something else.

"I am Mrs. Northcott," the hatchet-faced woman said. Her left hand made a chopping motion, using her right palm as a cutting block. Lucas doubted she even realized she made the gesture. "This is my husband, Mr. Northcott."

"Felicia and Raymond," he said timidly. She silenced him with a harsh look. Her dark eyes bored into his very soul until he fell silent.

Lucas sized them up quickly. Felicia Northcott wore a plain gray dress. It might have been the same he had seen her wearing earlier, but small differences told him that an examination of her wardrobe would reveal nothing but this color. It fit her personality. Or rather, it dictated the personality of her husband. She stood for a moment and glared at Raymond, who finally realized she was waiting for him to hold the chair for her. She sank down and folded her bony fingers in her lap before fixing her death skull gaze on Lucas.

"This position has not been filled. As Mr. Northcott said, we would have seen other employees in here while we waited for you to open. You are Mr. Runyon?"

"I, uh, no," Lucas said. "Mr. Runyon is unavailable."

"Then you are his office manager?"

"Not exactly. I—" Lucas tried to take the forged bill of sale off the desktop, but Felicia Northcott made her chopping motion and her hand held it firmly. Her quick eyes scanned down the page and came to the signature line.

"You purchased the agency from Mr. Runyon." She sniffed. "You need our assistance quite badly, it appears."

"Why's that?" Lucas wanted nothing more than to be done with these two, but her statement sparked his curiosity.

"This is a poorly drawn legal document. The signature lines are reversed from the standard form, and the date, well, I doubt you bought the agency two years ago."

"Why's that?"

"It was specifically stated in the advert for office help to report to Mr. Runyon. Why would a man who sold the company two years ago place such an ad?" She lifted her chin and looked superior.

"Because Jacoby continued to work for the Great West Detective Agency," Lucas said. He felt torn between matching wits with the woman and her sharp-eyed observations and getting the hell out of there. Revolutions boiled all around him, dogs and lovely ladies were missing, and a mountain of gold needed to be found.

"See, dear, there is a reason for him not being Mr. Runyon."

"Quiet, Raymond." She pushed back the bogus bill of sale and looked hard at Lucas. "We are perfect for the job."

"Both of you?"

"We will work for the price of one," Raymond said quickly. Again his wife silenced him with a quick hand gesture.

"You require an office manager. From the condition of the building, you also need a handyman. Raymond is capable of such repairs, in addition to being a trustworthy errand boy and, should the need arise, an armed guard. This agency protects banks and stagecoach shipments, does it not?"

Lucas stared at Raymond, trying to picture him with a six-shooter in his hand, shooting it out with road agents. The timid, unassertive man would likely throw the money into the air and run. As that thought crossed his mind, Lucas had to smile grimly. He had done that very thing back at the rat arena when Makepeace had come for him.

"I am a skilled secretary, know filing, and can take dictation and draft letters of suitable legibility. I taught school for two years and know grammar."

"She knows business, too. There's none better, which is why I married her."

Felicia made no effort to quiet her husband when he uttered those words. Lucas wondered why Felicia had married Raymond because he had no doubt she was the one who had insisted on exchanging rings. If she hadn't wanted a personality clash in her marriage, that would explain a great deal. Raymond had almost no personality to clash with.

"The business isn't making a great deal of money right now," Lucas started.

"Poor cash flow," Felicia Northcott said primly. "I understand such things. We will work for one week without pay to prove our skills. At that time, we can negotiate salaries and—" She tried to brush off her husband's insistent hand on her shoulder, but he wouldn't budge. "What is it, Raymond?"

"There's a savage in the doorway."

Lucas looked past the couple to where Good stood, arms crossed over his broad chest. Dirt smeared on one cheek looked like he had applied war paint. He had two six-guns, one on each hip, both with butts forward. A knife thrust into his belt turned him into a one-man army.

"That's one of my . . ." Lucas tried to find the proper word to describe Good. "He's a scout. Come on in, Good. These good people were just leaving."

Good stepped forward, then spun to one side, hands crossing his waist so he gripped both six-shooters in the cross-draw holsters.

"You, you're the one I want to see!" A man came in from the street and pushed Good aside.

Lucas tried to imagine how crazy anyone could get to irritate Good. Then he saw two others who remained outside in the street, tapping clubs against their palms. Good versus three men evened the odds, Lucas suspected.

"What is it, sir?" Felicia Northcott stood and interposed herself between the intruder and Lucas.

"I got a bone to pick with him. He's the owner, ain't he?"

"He is."

Lucas groaned. The woman was tying him down to the agency when all he wanted was to snatch the gold out from under Clifford, Dunbar, and Vera Zasulich. And Amanda. He couldn't forget her.

"I'm gonna sue!"

"Mrs. Northcott, why don't you and Mr. Northcott take care of this matter?"

She fixed him with her gimlet stare, then smiled just a little. Lucas felt a cold chill at the sight. He knew what a happy vulture looked like now. She pointed to the chair she had just vacated, ordering the man to sit, then circled and sat where Lucas had been only seconds earlier.

"Tell me what you feel is your problem. We will discuss the matter."

Lucas left Felicia Northcott to work out the problem, whatever it was, and inclined his head, indicating Good should join him in the back room. Good moved as if he rolled, no sound of his moccasins as he preceded Lucas. Once there, Lucas heaved a sigh of relief.

"She'll take care of everything," Lucas said.

"There is trouble," Good said. "We must return to the Russian camp immediately."

"What's wrong?"

Good scowled then said, "Everything."

20

Lucas Stanton wanted to moan but kept the misery to himself. He was more suited for riding in a stagecoach or on a train than by horseback. Aching and building blisters where there should never be any, he shifted in the saddle and pointed to a cut in the foothills.

"That leads to the Russian camp. Why are we going farther into the mountains?"

"Moved camp."

Lucas hadn't minded Good's silence or even the curt answers to the few questions he had asked on the ride from Denver, but now he felt as if they'd thrust their heads into nooses and all the Indian had to say was "drop."

"I understand why you think the Russians are in trouble with Clifford's gang. It's the gold. Each wants it, Vera Zasulich thinks they are going to use it to hire Clifford's army to overthrow the czar while Clifford has other ideas."

"Dunbar wants it, too."

"So do I," Lucas muttered. He looked at Good. Was there another runner in the race to find the gold? Five people wanted the gold. Did Good make number six? Watching his back when Dunbar's men, Clifford, and the Russians were about had become second nature to him. He found it harder to think of Amanda as an adversary willing to kill him, too, though she had double-crossed him and shown how little she wanted to share the bounty.

For whatever reason, he felt a little sorry for her. She had recovered Tovarich and lost him. So much gold must have turned her fingertips yellow and then . . . gone.

But how he felt about her had to be tempered with more caution. Not only was she the only one to have double-crossed him by making off with the dog, but she might be responsible for murdering Vera's brother and stealing the dog in the first place. Not a one of those struggling to find the gold was trustworthy. And Good? He had plans that didn't include any gambler. They had crossed paths accidentally and Good's insistence that he owed for saving him hardly held water.

Lucas usually knew when to fold a hand, but even if Clifford was wrong and the gold wasn't worth a million dollars, he would be happy with only a hundred thousand. That would give him a solid stake for the highest stakes games at the Union Club. Lucas stared ahead as he rode but he didn't see rock and scrubby vegetation. He saw San Francisco's richest men gathered around a green felt-topped poker table. A lovely lady in evening attire dealt to him, Huntington, Stanford, and other railroad magnates worth millions. He could risk a few thousand—more! He could take the deeds to their railroads and—

"Sentry."

He jerked around and hunted for the guard Good warned of. All he saw was acre upon acre of rocks and emptiness.

"There." Good pointed, lifting his chin to indicate the proper direction.

Lucas still didn't see anything and said so.

"Outline against sky gave him away. Gone now."

"Was it one of the Russians?"

Good grunted, which could mean anything. Lucas took it to mean he didn't know.

"What are we riding into? What's the big problem?"

"Dog escaped back to its pack."

"The one Amanda Baldridge had? Tovarich? How could the dog possibly have found the pack over such a long distance?"

"Dogs are good at sniffing out trails."

Good imitated a dog, his nose wrinkling up as he sniffed out a trail. Lucas had to laugh. To his credit, Good laughed also. Too late Lucas worried his companion might have simply left his body for the buzzards if he considered the laugh a blatant mocking.

"What do we try to achieve when we find the Russians? What do *you* intend to do?"

"Find dog, find gold."

"How do we divvy it up? Do you want half?"

Lucas worried that Good would double-cross him and take it all. He was a fair fighter and a decent enough shot, but the breed was better than fair at fighting, and from the look of the weapons he carried, he was a better than decent marksman. They had been used long and hard but were in top-notch condition.

"First, find the dog."

"That is reasonable enough. Do you know how the dog can sniff out where the gold is hidden? Metal doesn't have any scent unless it's heated. I can't imagine there is a pot of melted gold sitting around anywhere."

"Dog can find its way back to pack. Why not find gold?"

Good abruptly left the trail and worked his way up the steep side of a hill. Lucas stayed well behind, occasionally looking along the ridges for any sign of the sentry that Good had seen earlier. As far as he could tell, they were the only humans within twenty miles.

His horse began struggling with the steep climb, forcing Lucas to dismount and walk alongside. The blisters he had accumulated pained him with every step until they reached the top of the hill. From here they looked down on the Russian wagons, and all discomfort vanished as he spotted a half dozen wolfhounds cavorting about, snapping and barking, playfully wrestling and then running away, only to skid to a halt and charge back into the fray.

"Which one's Tovarich?"

"Why do they camp here? It is not far from other encampment."

"You think the gold is nearby?"

Good pursed his lips but said nothing and never took his eyes off the dogs. Lucas forced himself to stop trying to identify Tovarich in the pack. At this distance they all looked the same. He studied the location of the wagons and their occupants. Two low fires kept tea brewing. Even at this distance he caught the scent and remembered the sharp taste of the cup offered him by Vera.

"Sharp scent," he said aloud. Good paid him no attention. His mind raced as things began to make more sense.

The strangely pungent perfume both Amanda and Vera wore was distinctive. No other woman in this country was likely to use spikenard. Tovarich might have found his way back to Vera's camp following her unique scent. If the gold—or the crates or sacks it was stored in—was similarly treated, Tovarich could sniff it out.

Lucas sagged. Why Tovarich? Why not any of the wolf-hounds? Then he remembered how bloodhounds could be trained to go after individual animals exclusively, bears or deer or other creatures. Tovarich alone might have been disciplined to find that odor, no matter how faint or distant.

"Go into camp and warn her of Clifford and Dunbar."

"Why me? If you want to warn Vera Zasulich about them, do it yourself." Lucas doubted his reception would be cordial after he had ripped out the flooring and run off.

"She will listen to you. You talk like an eagle flies." Good made a smooth, sweeping motion with his hand.

"Thanks for the vote of confidence." He thought over what had been said. "You don't care about Dmitri or any of the others? Just Vera?"

Good stood a little straighter but said nothing. He stared into the camp below.

"Where did the two of you meet before?"

"Go, warn her. Clifford will kill her if he finds the dog. If you do not, I must kidnap her to get her away. That would not be good."

Lucas pondered this. Whatever their history, Good and Vera had not parted amicably. She wouldn't listen to Good, but the Indian still felt some obligation toward her. This made Lucas trust him a bit more, even if his relation with Good was unlikely to ever be as intense as between a Native American and a Russian revolutionary. He was a man who honored his commitments.

"I have to think about how to approach her. If I say the wrong thing, she'll think I'm only after the gold."

"Clifford will come soon. She thinks they are still allies. When he sees the dog, he will kill her and the others."

"I know, I know. Let me think."

Lucas felt as if his head was about to explode. His body ached—hurt!—and his life was on the line if Vera didn't speak up for him to keep Dmitri at bay. Being fed to the pack of dogs that had once attacked him wasn't the fate he had ever envisioned for himself. He doubted he would die in bed, but something more heroic than being ripped to bloody strips ought to be in the cards. Even if he had to stack the deck, a noble end should be his.

He mounted and started down the far side of the steep hill.

"You know what to say?" Good looked anxious.

"Hell, no. I'll think of something before I get to their camp."

But he didn't.

Lucas rode in with a half dozen Russian rifles and shotguns trained on him. Not being killed outright meant something. He feared it was torture and then death rather than a clean shot through his head.

"Good day," he greeted as Vera rushed from her wagon looking flustered. "I wish to speak with you on an important matter."

"Kill him," she ordered.

"Wait! Good sent me to tell you—"

"Good?" Vera came over and put her fists on her hips. She glared at him. Her breasts rose and fell with heavy, angry breathing. "Good?"

Lucas knew he had no way to retreat. In for a penny, in for a pound, as the saying went.

"Yes. He has a warning for you."

"He is too cowardly to speak to me himself? I thought there was a yellow streak in him!"

"Are we talking about the same man?" He was honestly startled at her denunciation of Good as a coward. The man would walk through hell backward and never flinch, though he had wanted Lucas to speak with Vera.

"Get down. We talk over there."

She pointed to a spot where the grass had been torn up by a half dozen paws digging at the ground. The sharp white of a broken bone poked up from one hole. What or who the wolfhounds had buried there was something he hoped never to discover. He swung his leg over the saddle horn and dropped. He held back a groan when he hit the ground. Never show weakness. That gave your opponent an edge.

Lucas fleetingly wondered how much more advantage Vera could gain over him. The revolutionaries all kept their weapons trained on him, the dogs yelped and barked, and after the long ride, he wouldn't have licked a newborn kitten.

"Why do you commit suicide returning?" She stared at him with a mixture of curiosity and outright hatred.

"Good wanted me to tell you that Clifford is going to kill you. He's a double-crossing son of a . . . czar. Trust him and you'll end up dog food." He couldn't keep his eyes from roving to the sharp-edged broken bone poking out of the ground where a wolfhound had buried it. It looked suspiciously like a human thighbone.

"Good, Good, is that all you can say? I should kill you out of hand, but I won't."

Lucas relaxed a little, then went numb all over when she added, "I won't kill you immediately because I want to torture you. When I am finished, Dmitri will take his turn. You are not likely to live long. He is brutal where I am subtle with my infliction of pain."

Lucas yelped when she came over and gave him a swat to his rear end. Blisters popped. He went weak in the knees from the lancing pain but she pulled him erect with surprising strength.

"So, do not talk to me of Good. Talk to me of other things."

"What do you want to know?" Lucas saw no reason not to spill everything he knew—or thought he knew. If he couldn't get the gold, he wanted to walk away with his hide in one piece.

And all his bones exactly where they belonged. The dogs edged closer, baring their fangs and eyeing him like dinner.

"There is so much hidden from me."

Before she said anything more, a loud shout went up. She reached for one of the knives sheathed at her belt and stepped back. With a quick lunge she poked the tip into his belly less than a quarter inch, but he got the message. Move and he would be spitted like a shish kebab.

Vera erupted with a long string of Russian, then drew another knife and left Lucas standing alone. He took a single step and found himself in the center of a ring of snarling wolfhounds. He carefully twisted his head around and saw two of the Russians flanking Good. There went any hope of salvation.

"I tried to tell her, Good. I tried," Lucas shouted.

He waited for a reaction. The smallest distraction could be turned into an escape. The Russians were too well trained to pay him any heed. He started to try again when he heard a rapid exchange of Russian—between Good and Vera. Whatever the Creek said infuriated her. She slashed at him with a knife. He stolidly allowed her to cut his cheek. The shallow scratch leaked blood.

The instant she cut him, she dropped her knives and hugged him. Then she shoved him away and spoke in English.

"You are too easily captured. Why?"

"Where is the dog?"

"Dog, dog, is that all you care about?" Vera picked up her knives and drew back as if she intended to gut him with two swift cuts.

"Dmitri stole the dog."

"That is not so. Tovarich!" She let out a piercing whistle, then called the dog by name.

Lucas realized how well trained the wolfhounds were. Although attentive, not a one of them budged at her call. They remained on duty around him, waiting to sink their fangs into his body and bury him out in the sward.

"Tovarich!" This time Vera spun about, hunting the dog. "Where is Dmitri?" A new burst of Russian sent the others in the camp scurrying away.

Lucas hoped that Good would take his unexpected freedom to jump Vera. He stood motionless, not even touching the cut that continued to leak blood down his cheek and onto the ground. In less than a minute, Vera and two others returned to stand directly in front of Good. She was six inches shorter but not a whit less aggressive. She bumped into him and barked, "What of Dmitri?"

"He stole the dog."

"He would never betray me!"

"He had no stomach for revolt. He stole the dog and tried to sell it to Clifford."

"He wouldn't do this to me. We—"

"Clifford took the dog and shot Dmitri. Once. In the face. Here." Good touched the spot just above the cut on his cheek and tapped.

"Put them in chains. I will see if this half-breed lies to me again!"

Lucas and Good were shoved back and forth and finally

knocked to the ground. In turn they were dragged to different wheels and chained securely.

Lucas watched Vera rally her troops and ride away, the pack of dogs barking as they ranged ahead of the revolutionaries. There was going to be more bloodshed. Lucas hoped it was Clifford's. Then he realized what that meant for him. In a game where everyone lost, there were no winners.

21

Lucas rattled his chains and studied the rusty padlock. It would take only seconds for him to pick the lock, but those few seconds were denied him because the two Russians that Vera had left as guards sat across from him and fixedly stared at him. They weren't inclined to leave.

"Good, how long before Vera comes back?"

"How can I know?"

"Where did you meet her? You speak Russian."

"Not much."

"More than I do, and enough for you to argue with her." Lucas waited for the Creek to fill in all the empty spaces and satisfy a gambler's curiosity. Good remained silent, staring directly in front of him. "Do these two speak any English?" Lucas finally asked when it became apparent Good was not going to indulge a random need for answers about his personal life.

"They understand enough."

"So it isn't too smart for us to make plans to escape when they can overhear us."

Lucas recoiled when one guard snarled and half rose, hand going to a knife at his belt. The other watched him closely but made no threatening move.

"All right, that's settled. They understand enough to keep us prisoners. How did you find out about Dmitri being killed?"

No answer.

"Are you sure Clifford has the dog?"

"The dog ran back here to Vera. Dmitri put muzzle on the dog and stole away to make a deal with Clifford. He had no stomach for revolution and wanted to stay here."

"Stay here rich," Lucas said. "Why didn't Dmitri use Tovarich to get the gold himself?"

Good stirred, rattling his shackles. He partly turned to look at Lucas.

"Only Vera knows how to set dog onto the proper trail."

"But she doesn't know where the gold is. Only the dog can find it?" Lucas thought his head would explode as if dynamite had been detonated in each ear. The harder he tried to make sense of it, the less sure he was that this wasn't a huge hoax.

But a hoax that men as pragmatic as Clifford and Dunbar bought into? Vera and her revolutionaries had come a long way to follow a will-o'-the-wisp. Greed might drive Amanda but Lucas thought she had a practical streak, too, and risking her money and even her life to find something that might not exist was a stretch. Lucas knew the profit possible in selling fake maps to imaginary gold mines. Like the Lost Dutchman, they had to have a decent story attached to make the mark believe he and only he had special information. Otherwise, the mine would have been found a long time since.

He tried to force away the throbbing in his head as he considered how little of that "story" was attached to this gold. Clifford and the others might believe the story, but no one was spreading it around.

"Has Vera told you where the gold came from?"

Good shook his head.

He leaned back, closed his eyes, then forced away all thoughts of Tovarich, Vera, and the filibusterers. It was harder to get rid of his mental image of Amanda.

"Ask them if they have a deck of cards and want to play some poker."

"You will win?" Good strained at his shackles. He examined them closely, then locked his gaze with Lucas. The silent communication was what the gambler needed.

Lucas shifted about and got his legs folded under him. Moving around, he could bring his hands out in front of him. He made shuffling and dealing motions.

"Will they steal my money if I show it?"

"Yes, but they like to gamble. If they win, they will not steal your money."

"Tell them I want to play poker."

Good picked his way through a small speech. Lucas realized the Creek didn't speak Russian as well as he had thought originally. Maybe all he knew were sweet nothings to whisper in Vera's ear. It took several minutes for him to get the idea across to the guards. The smiles on their faces showed they were anxious to play.

"I'm getting out my money," Lucas said slowly.

He moved to pull out a few greenbacks from his coat pocket, realizing he still had his pistol. A quick shootout might be the road to escape, but Lucas wasn't up to gunning the men down if another way worked better. And for him, a few hands of poker always provided a better solution to what ailed him.

While one guard left to get the cards, the other remained, keeping a close eye on both men. Lucas shifted around some more, moving to get his hands lower. The chains were long enough to rattle and give him some mobility. He made a few gestures intended to distract the guard to give Good a chance to slip his shackles. The Creek hadn't pulled free by the time the second guard returned with the deck of cards.

"Interesting pattern," Lucas said, studying the backs. He looked closely at them, holding them high so the light from the fire caught the geometric decoration. He flipped through, then shuffled. The cards were marked. A spoked wheel in one corner seemed to turn as the cards flew. After a few hands, he would learn the meaning and be able to cheat as well as either of the guards.

Considering his expertise, he would be able to clean them out in a hurry.

The pots started small, and Lucas won those, as the stakes mounted, he bet more. The guards grew more excited, telling him they were using the markings to cheat now.

"How're you doing?"

Lucas might have directed this to the guard clutching his cards, two pair, jacks over eights, but he wanted some progress report from Good. The single grunt told him the Creek was ready to make his break.

"I think you're bluffing," Lucas said, knowing the guard wasn't. All he had in his own hand was a pair of aces.

"No bluff," the guard said. He grinned, showing a shiny gold tooth.

"I should up the ante and force you to bet that tooth," Lucas said. He restlessly moved his cards in his hand, slipping one on top of the others to keep the guards' attention focused on his hands and not Good. "All right. I'm going for broke. Ten dollars to call." He shoved his entire stake forward as far as he could.

If he had intended to win, he would have palmed a third ace and taken the pot. What he wanted to win was time, a diversion, the chance for Good to get away. Lucas forced himself not to even glance away from the cards.

"Beat that," he said, laying down his losing hand.

The guard laughed and showed his hand. He reached for the money. Lucas grabbed the man's wrist and yanked him forward, off balance.

"You're cheating! Those cards are marked! Look!" He sent the deck flying through the air, cards fluttering all around.

"Won," the guard said, shoving Lucas back against the wagon wheel.

He clanked his chains and made a spitting sound like a stepped-on tomcat. As he thrashed about, he glanced over. Good was gone. The shackles were still closed. How he had escaped was something of a poser, but Lucas felt his lost money had been well spent. He continued to kick and grab to engage the guards, but he overplayed this hand.

One guard grabbed the other and pointed to Good's dangling, empty chains. A stinging blow knocked Lucas back. He hit his head against the wagon wheel. He let out a howl of pain, but the guards had already left, hunting for the escaped Indian.

Lucas grinned. The escape plan worked better than it had any right to. He slipped out the slender steel picks and had the padlock open in a flash. After rubbing his wrists to get circulation back, he reached over and picked up the pot the guard had left behind. Good's disappearance had flustered the man to the point that he left his winnings.

"A cheater never prospers," Lucas said softly, stuffing the money into his pocket and then heaving to his feet.

He started to run off and find his horse, then stared at the wagon. Vera's wagon. He rattled the lock on the door and considered picking it, then slipped underneath and found the floorboards he and Good had pried loose before. They hadn't been nailed back into place, only laid down. Pushing upward, he got into the wagon.

He fumbled out a lucifer, lit it, and found a coal oil lamp to give him light enough to search the woman's belongings. He admired some of her jewelry, but he wasn't a thief. Not a sneak thief, at least. He left it in the velvet-lined cases and worked over to her vanity dresser.

A small round jar caught his eye. With a quick twist, he unscrewed the top and took a deep whiff. The cloying scent made him cough. Spikenard. If this scent put Tovarich on the trail of the gold, he intended to have enough to make the wolfhound stand on his hind legs before racing off.

Lucas tucked the jar in his pocket, then retreated through the floorboards, carefully positioning them. Vera would never suspect anyone had rifled her belongings. Ducking out from under the wagon, he set off for the crude tether the Russians had used for their horses. A rope strung between two scrubby trees bounced about as the dozen horses fastened to it reared and tried to escape. Two belonged to the guards out hunting for Good. The others were used to pull the wagons.

With quick, nimble tugs, he unfastened the rope and set all the horses free. Some ran off and a few remained. He made certain to grip the bridle of his horse while he tried to shoo those away. Distant angry shouts warned he had only a minute or two before the Russians returned. Painfully, he swung up into the saddle and made one last effort to chase away the horses. He was partially successful. The three remaining were draft animals meant to be hitched to the wagons and wouldn't be much good chasing him down.

He hoped that was so.

Heels tapping his horse's flanks to urge it to a quick trot, he shot off, found the trail out of camp that led to the road back to Denver, and then slowed to preserve his mount's strength and to give his own blistered bottom some relief.

Good had gotten away. The revolutionaries might be Cossacks and princes on the steppe but neither was a match for Good, not here in the mountains or anywhere that demanded frontier skills. Lucas had no idea when but he knew they would get back together. Something about Vera Zasulich held the Creek in arm's reach, and Vera wanted to get Tovarich back. He patted his pocket where the jar of perfume rode safe and secure.

Good was safe. Vera might have ended Clifford's life by now—or the filibusterer might have ambushed her, along with the pack of dogs. Whatever happened, since both sides wanted him, Tovarich was likely to be safe and his keen nose would be set along the path to the gold.

Tovarich would find the gold for Lucas Stanton.

22

Good had gone after Vera, who hunted for Clifford since he had Tovarich. Trying to sort through his own options gave Lucas a new headache. He rode steadily to reach Denver before dawn. Not knowing where to search for any of those who had been in the Russian camp, he stopped at a café for breakfast. His spine ground up against his belly. If he'd had his throat slit, he couldn't have taken in less food than he had in the past few days.

He wolfed down a thick steak, boiled potatoes, and enough applesauce for a small army. Washing it down with poisonous coffee cured his headache and let him think more clearly about what to do next. He leaned back after finishing the meal, picked at his teeth, and stared out into the street where Denver citizens had come awake and hurried about their commerce for another day.

He had no way to get in touch with Good. If he returned to the Russian camp, the two guards would lock him up again, if he was lucky enough to escape their wrath. If not, they would kill him and leave his body where he'd never be found. He doubted his death mattered much to Vera when her plans were collapsing around her ears. Without Tovarich, she couldn't get the gold to finance her revolt. Worse, her brother had died and her right-hand man had betrayed her to a bunch of mercenaries intent on invading Nicaragua. Her sortie into the American West had brought her nothing but failure and death.

Unless she got Tovarich back, found the gold, left the United States, and financed her revolution. Lucas was a betting man. He didn't like her odds. Dennis Clifford, though, held all the wild cards in his hand. The filibusterer had a far better chance to use the dog to sniff out the gold—but did he know the spikenard was the key to the dog's prowess? It was only a guess, but in his gut Lucas thought it was close to the truth.

Lucas took out the glass jar and idly opened and closed it. The scent rose and made his nostrils flare, reminding him of the first time Amanda Baldridge had come into the detective agency office. He had been taken with her beauty and her plight. A lost puppy. He sniffed at that now. Tovarich was a full-grown wolfhound capable of holding his own in a ratter's death pit. Amanda had played him to find the dog, using her wiles and not a little bit of money. That had been her mistake. She should have relied on one or the other, her appeal to his chivalry and charity or to his greed. Not both. He had begun questioning her motives and that had led him here.

He closed the perfume jar and replaced it in his pocket. When he found Tovarich, he could use it to put the hound on the road to finding the gold.

How did he find the dog? He finished his coffee and stepped out into the street, his mind racing. Amanda had lost Tovarich and would still be looking. She had to dodge both Clifford and Dunbar. One would kill her, the other would imprison her until he learned the whereabouts of the dog—and then he would kill her.

"Jubal Dunbar," he decided. This was the end of the thread to follow back to Amanda, to Clifford, and to the dog. All he had to do was tug a bit to start everything unraveling.

He considered riding to Dunbar's house, then realized the saddle and sway of a horse under him would hurt more than walking. Lucas went by the stables where Gallatin worked inside. He led his horse in. Gallatin looked up, his eyes wide with fear. He calmed when he recognized Lucas.

"They've been after me," Gallatin said. "The men ridin' with Clifford. They got it into their heads I was a spy."

"You were," Lucas reminded him. "Have you learned anything more about them?"

"I ain't goin' near any of 'em. They're killers through and through."

"You've done well, Lester. You're an unsung hero." He handed the reins to him. "Don't be seen for a day or two. By then Clifford's gang will have moved on and you'll be safe. Come by the Emerald City then and I'll buy you a drink."

"Thanks, Lucas, that's mighty kind of you." He looked past Lucas's shoulder, obviously edgy about anyone riding past. "I might wait a spell. A week maybe."

"Whenever you come by and I'm there, that drink's yours." He paused, then asked, "You hear any gossip about Jubal Dunbar or Amanda Baldridge?"

Gallatin denied it, but Lucas wondered. He preferred the straight dickering with Little Otto for information. Otto feared nothing and had sources impossible to duplicate, but Gallatin had given him enough information.

"If you're sure, I'll be going."

"To Dunbar's place?"

"Is there something there that interests me?"

"Her. The pretty one with the black hair. Miss Baldridge. Heard tell Dunbar and her was seen behind his house this mornin'."

"By his carriage house?"

Gallatin didn't know, but Lucas suspected Dunbar had once more imprisoned the woman in the root cellar. Whether she had gone to him for help getting Tovarich back or he had discovered her hunting for the dog on her own hardly mattered. Dunbar had no intention of sharing the gold with her when his ambition to pry Colorado out of the Union hung in the balance. Her wiles would avail her little since she pitted herself against the drive for power. Lucas had seen how much more powerful that was than simple greed.

He left the livery stable, checked his pistol, and saw he had only five rounds remaining. That sufficed if he sneaked Amanda away without a shoot-out. Dunbar wasn't likely to post a guard outside the root cellar door. Someone might ask why an employee loitered there for no good reason.

Walking became less painful as he exerted some effort to stretch and get cramped muscles to relax. The blisters bothered him but not enough to take his mind away from fanciful schemes to free Amanda. He wanted her to be grateful for the rescue. If she helped him find Tovarich, he might even cut her in on a share of the million dollars. That would make her *very* grateful, which benefited them both.

The front porch of Dunbar's house was empty. His usual guards were elsewhere. Lucas gripped the rosewood handle of his Colt and went around the side of the house. If Dunbar had stationed them at the carriage house, an exchange of gunfire might be the only way to get Amanda from her prison.

He caught his breath when he looked inside the carriage house. Dunbar and his two strong-arm henchmen formed a half circle around Amanda, effectively pinning her against the rear wall. Lucas edged away from the door and circled to the outside wall. The plank where Amanda leaned inside bulged out and snapped back. Dunbar was repeatedly slamming her against the wall.

Lucas pressed his ear against the wood a few feet away. Every word uttered inside sounded loud and clear as if he used an ear trumpet.

"That son of a bitch has the dog," Dunbar said. "Where is he?"

"I don't know. I never had anything to do with Clifford." Amanda sobbed. "I got the dog from the Russian woman's brother. I've never had anything to do with any of the others there either."

Lucas knew she lied. He touched the perfume jar in his pocket. Amanda had gone to Vera's camp at least once to steal the spikenard so she could set Tovarich on the scent to the gold.

"One of the Russians had the dog and tried to sell it to Clifford."

"Tovarich got away from me after I got him back. You know that! He gnawed through his leash and escaped. He's like trying to grab water."

"He returned to the Russians," Dunbar pressed. "How did the dog know where to find them?"

"I don't know."

The loud slap and Amanda's gasp told him Dunbar was building enough anger to do more harm to her if she kept lying.

"How's the damned dog supposed to find the gold? Why'd it go straight to the Russians?"

"A perfume, a special scent. Gregor said the dog had been trained."

"He just told you that?"

"Of course not. I . . . persuaded him, Jubal. You know how convincing I can be."

"I know how conniving you are. The Russian who tried to sell the dog to Clifford got his comeuppance. And Clifford got the dog."

"He doesn't know how to put Tovarich on the scent. Not unless Dmitri told him."

Lucas held no affection for Dmitri, but the man was a revolutionary and not likely to be overly trusting, even of another he considered a fellow revolutionary—maybe especially of another man in the same pursuit of treachery and death. He offered Tovarich to Clifford but held back the secret of getting the dog hunting. That was all that kept the location of the gold a secret.

"The man who told me about Clifford getting the dog wasn't able to tell where the filibuster camp was." Dunbar paused, then said in a menacing voice, "He died before he could give my men that information."

"I don't know anything about Clifford, I tell you!"

A sound like a loud slap echoed from the carriage house. Then the plank next to Lucas bowed out repeatedly as Dunbar slammed Amanda against the wall. Lucas doubted his success in a shoot-out, but the secessionist might kill her if he didn't try. Then he settled down and thought through the problem. Amanda afforded Dunbar his only chance of getting the gold he needed for his revolt. The man might kill her by accident, but he only bluffed with his dire threats. That didn't save Amanda from a serious beating.

"Stop, please, Jubal, no more!"

"Where's Clifford?"

"I . . . I don't know, but I can take you to where I had the dog for a while. Clifford might go there, if he knows about it."

"I know the place. My men told me." For a moment no sound came from inside the carriage house, then Dunbar said, "Let's go. If this is the best you can offer up, I'll take it."

"Oh, Jubal, I can offer you so much more."

"Shut up."

The sound of feet scuffling was quickly replaced with the sound of a horse whinnying and the clatter of wheels. Lucas chanced a quick look around the corner and saw Dunbar's carriage driving away. He waited. In a few minutes, his two henchmen rode after him. With a deep breath, Lucas set out. He knew where the shack was in Cherry Creek. Cutting through yards and ignoring the streets might get him there before Dunbar.

It didn't. Lucas had been chased by dogs and chased by a maid with a broom and had still arrived after the carriage. Both Dunbar and Amanda were nowhere to be seen but the two thugs rode aimlessly around, as if they might find Clifford lurking behind a pile of trash or somehow walking up unaware. Neither was going to happen.

Dunbar came out and barked orders to his men to take the carriage away and to lay a trap. Lucas watched them carry out their orders and then find places for an ambush when Clifford came. If he came. The filibusterer had to come to the conclusion only Amanda knew how to put the hound on the trail, realize she would be here, and then come after her without any fear of a trap.

Lucas doubted any of that would happen.

He settled down, knowing Dunbar wasn't going to harm Amanda until he got the dog. Lucas dozed in his hiding place behind a pile of lumber and only snapped awake just before sundown. Dunbar's men stirred, exchanging whispers loud enough for him to hear. He drew his Colt, cocked it, and chanced a look over the top of the wood.

Clifford and two men rode slowly toward the shack. Muzzled and with a rope knotted around his neck, Tovarich trotted alongside the filibusterer. Lucas rose up to get a better look when a strong hand clamped around his right wrist and forced his pistol upward. Another hand clamped down over his mouth and nose, shutting off any outcry. With incredible strength, he was pulled backward, unable to twist to either side because of a knee in the middle of his back.

Fury coursed through his veins and then faded as the lack of air going into his lungs robbed him of all strength. He sank to the ground, defeated.

23

Lucas gagged and tried to sit up. A strong hand held him down, then crushed down over his face. He fought weakly, then blinked his eyes into focus and saw Good above him. When he stopped fighting, the Creek released him and put his finger to his lips, cautioning Lucas to silence. He scooted erect and braced himself against the woodpile.

Good reached down, took his forearm, and pulled him to his feet. He pointed. Lucas felt a rush of anger, but the Creek's hand on his shoulder held him back. Dunbar's men thought they had chosen strategic positions for an ambush. Both of them never saw Clifford's men creep up behind them. A quick slash across each neck left them dead. Only then did Clifford's soldiers slip closer to the shack where Dunbar held Amanda prisoner.

"We have to save her."

"Patience."

Lucas sighted along the barrel of his Colt and centered on one filibusterer. He heard Good swear under his breath and held back from pulling the trigger. Good had something in mind. Since he had so quickly found and identified all the players in the unfolding drama, Lucas was willing to wait. As long as Amanda knew how to put the dog on the trail of the hidden gold, she was safe. When she revealed the information about the perfume, no one needed her any longer. Lucas had to be there to save her.

He scowled as that thought crossed his mind. She had paid him to find the dog but hadn't bothered giving him vital information. He had found the dog, only to have her spirit Tovarich away at the first chance she got. His obligation—his paid job—should have ended there. Amanda had the dog back. But he felt something more toward her and wondered what it might be. Misguided chivalry played a part, but he reluctantly analyzed his own motives and knew there was more.

Carmela had spurned him in favor of Little Otto. Amanda was a lovely woman and not as completely crazy as Vera Zasulich seemed. Let Good deal with the Russian. Lucas needed to prove to himself he still had everything a lovely woman could want. She just hadn't had the opportunity for him to work his masculine magic on her. He closed his eyes for a second and remembered how their bodies had fit together so perfectly during the gala ball. That waltz had shown they worked together well, bodies and thoughts in synchronicity. All they needed was a chance to build on that start.

Dennis Clifford dismounted and walked to the door, tugging on the rope around the dog's neck. He kicked open the door and stepped inside, six-shooter drawn.

Good moved. So did Lucas, aware that the idea wasn't to take out Clifford's men but to eavesdrop. That suited him just fine. Gathering twilight hiding their advance, they got to the shack's rear wall. Good dropped to his knees and found a crack. Lucas had to stand on tiptoe to find another big enough to see inside.

"It took you long enough to show up, Clifford." Dunbar waved his arms around like a cavalry semaphore flagman. He spoke loud enough to draw attention.

He wrongly believed his men were lying in wait and would come to his aid.

"I brought the dog." Clifford yanked on the rope around the dog's neck.

Tovarich whined. He was securely muzzled.

"Has she told you how to make the dog find the gold?" Clifford stepped closer, pulling the reluctant Tovarich behind him.

"She has," Dunbar said. "Go on. Tell him."

Through his peephole, Lucas barely saw Amanda to one side. She had backed into a corner. When she reached out, Tovarich ran to her. She scratched the dog's ears. The spikenard perfume worked to identify her to the well-trained dog. That was how she had been able to run off with Tovarich so quickly after Lucas had rescued the wolfhound from the rat pit.

"The scent," Amanda said. "There's a scent the dog has been trained to sniff out."

"That's it, eh?" Clifford drew his six-gun and cocked it.

"Wait!" Dunbar let out a scream of help for his men to come to his aid. Clifford pulled the trigger.

Lucas flinched, then hastily looked back, fearing that the filibusterer would gun down Amanda. He had his six-shooter leveled but didn't make any move to cock it again to drill her.

"What's the smell? What is it the dog will hunt down?"

She moved into Lucas's field of view. She opened her mouth, then closed it and shook her head. Clifford whistled. Both of his men came in, bloodied knives in their hands.

"They can make you talk. That'd be a real shame, messing up a lovely woman like that. What's the dog trained to sniff out?"

"You'll kill me if I tell you!"

"Now, lady, I can't do that. I won't. What if you lied and the dog doesn't find the gold? I'd need to be sure you weren't lying. After I get the gold, might be you'd want to come south with us."

"And if I didn't want to live in Nicaragua?"

The gunshot startled Lucas. He frantically peered in, thinking to see Amanda dead on the floor. Instead Clifford had shot Dunbar a second time.

"That'll teach him to keep his filthy mouth shut. You can't think he stood a ghost of a chance prying Colorado free of the Union? No, I didn't think so. Me, now, with the gold, I can be king of my own country. I'd be needing a queen to share it."

"When you find the gold, could you just let me go?"

"I reckon," Clifford said. "What's the dog trained to go after?"

"This. It's this. It's a Union officer's coat. The captain who wore it found the Southerner's gold while on patrol in Oklahoma Territory. Rather than turn it in, he and some of his men deserted and moved the gold here to Colorado. He . . . he murdered his men so only he'd know."

"How'd the dog get trained?"

"He bought it from some Russians, but they're revolutionaries and wanted the gold for themselves, to take back to their country and overthrow their own government. Gregor—that was his name—tried to steal the dog. He and the captain shot it out. Both died."

"And you happened along and took the dog?" Clifford laughed. "That's rich."

"That's the way it happened. I wanted to be rich, but I'll settle for being let go free."

"Dennison, you stay with her while Lorry 'n' me see where the dog takes us." Clifford shook out the officer's jacket, then cried out.

Amanda had pulled off the muzzle, and with a deft move, she unfastened the collar. The rope tied through it fell away—and the freed Tovarich bolted for the door.

"You bitch!" Clifford and his henchman ran from the shack.

"Looks like me and you got time to spend," the one named Dennison said, moving toward her.

"Get the horses. We'll have to get the dog," Lucas said to Good. But the Creek had disappeared.

Lucas ran around to the shack's door and thrust out his Colt, ready to shoot. Dennison lay on the ground. He inched in and checked. The man had been stabbed in the heart with a thin-bladed knife. Lucas looked around, but Amanda was nowhere to be seen. He spun about, pistol leveled, when he heard a hard rap at the shack door.

"Here's your horse." Good dropped the reins and wheeled his own around.

"Wait, wait."

Lucas painfully mounted. From horseback he looked around for Amanda, but she had vanished in the night. If he didn't go after Clifford right away, he would lose him for certain. How Amanda had gotten away so fast, he didn't know, but Good was out of sight already. Lucas tapped his heels to the horse's flanks and rocketed off after the Creek.

Amanda must have been all right. Finding Clifford before Tovarich located the gold was more important. He put his head down and rode even harder after Good.

24

How he did it was a mystery. Lucas rode hard and barely kept up with Good. He had to believe the Creek followed the trail left by Tovarich and the pursuing filibusterers, but in the dark all spoor disappeared. For him, at least. Good might be faking his ability to trail but Lucas doubted it. The Indian didn't seem like the type who would puff himself up like that or lie about his abilities.

"How can the dog run so far?"

"Clifford hunts for the trail. He has no idea where the dog went."

"South," Lucas said. "The dog lit out going south toward Colorado Springs. Does that mean anything?"

"Yes," Good said. "It means the dog is running south."

Lucas fought the feeling of helplessness and outright ineptitude. He was out of his pond. Give him a poker game and he was prince. Put him on a horse and blisters popped up where they shouldn't and made him less efficient dealing with life. He was a crack shot but carried a small pistol unable to match the .45s men like Clifford sported. And on the trail, Good showed supernatural power tracking men and a dog in the pitch black of night.

"Is it actually hunting for the gold?"

Good didn't answer. If anything, he rode faster in an attempt to leave Lucas behind. Realizing he would be dealt out of receiving any of the gold if he let Good capture the dog and he was nowhere near, he lifted his butt off the saddle to remove some of the friction, put his head down by the horse's neck, and rode like a jockey. This put intense strain on his legs but allowed him to keep from sliding back and forth along the saddle.

Eventually his legs began to shake and he sank back down with a moan. Good had outpaced him and wasn't near enough to caution him to silence. Then Lucas knew being quiet didn't matter since the pounding hooves alerted anyone ahead along the road. When this occurred to him, he slowed and finally came to a complete stop. The blood pounded in his ears and then he became aware of the night around him. The sounds came to him so that he turned toward a spot far ahead and off the road.

Hooves. The sound of horses neighing. Then his heart jumped in his chest. A dog barked.

Lucas walked his horse away from the road across the rocky ground, trying to make sense of what he heard. The sharp yelps of a dog drowned out the other sounds. He wanted to hurry but kept the pace steady to save his horse from blundering into a gopher hole or otherwise stumbling and throwing him. It was a long way back to Denver, and Lucas wasn't inclined to walk if he could avoid it.

Ahead he heard loud voices and more barking. He looked around, wondering what had become of Good. The Creek had been so intent, it hardly seemed possible a citified gambler had found Clifford and his gang and an expert frontiersman had not. When he was a few hundred yards away, Lucas dismounted. His legs almost collapsed under him. Riding like a jockey might not have been the smartest thing he'd ever done, even if it had saved his inner thighs and rear from more blistering.

He secured his horse, drew his Colt, and advanced as carefully as he had ridden. The horse could break a leg in an unseen hole. So could a human. He approached the dismounted riders in a ravine. Flopping onto his belly near a cottonwood, Lucas steadied his gun hand so he could get Clifford in his sights. The leader of the filibuster had roped Tovarich and avoided the dog's nasty snaps at him.

"Stop him," Clifford called. "No, you idiot. Don't shoot the damned dog. Get another rope around his neck and hold him back."

The man who had ridden from Denver with Clifford made a loop in his rope and easily tossed it. Tovarich snapped at the rope but freedom wasn't to be had. The dog was easily held between Clifford and his henchman. A dozen strategies ran through Lucas's head. Gunning down both men would let the dog run free and forever ruin any chance of finding the gold. He had no illusion about his chances of ever finding Tovarich once the dog raced off into the night.

But Clifford used the free end of the rope to lash the wolfhound. Being held so securely prevented Tovarich from dodging the punishment.

Lucas centered his pistol on Clifford's back. What the man had likely done to humans probably made this torture pale, but Lucas had never thought well of cruelty to animals. It was hard enough shooting rabid dogs or injured animals to put them out of their misery, but what Clifford did had no purpose other than to vent his own rage.

Before he squeezed off the shot, he heard horses behind him. He scrunched down amid the gnarled roots, and in the dark, he became a part of the tree.

"That you, boss?" The challenge came from behind Lucas. A half dozen riders passed by him, made their way down into the ravine, and joined their would-be general.

"Took you long enough to find us," Clifford said.

"We got bad news. Dennison was dead when we got to that shanty. The woman was nowhere to be seen."

"None of that matters. I got the dog."

"Might be the dog's got you. He don't seem too inclined to let you scratch his ears. Not without you losin' a hand."

As if on cue, Tovarich renewed his ferocious barking and snapping. Clifford used his rope lash while the others jeered and shouted. This only further infuriated the dog. Clifford showed no sign of understanding how he needed the dog to find the gold. Everything he did drove the wolf-hound even crazier with fear and rage.

Lucas considered a shot at Tovarich to put him out of his misery, but if he did that, the gold would be lost forever. Without thinking how suicidal it was, he stood and fired his pistol. The tiny *pop!* was barely heard above the din, but Clifford noticed.

"Get him. Cover him!" Clifford whipped the end of the rope he had been using to beat the dog around a rock and secured it. The man holding the other rope did the same, then slapped leather to get his pistol drawn.

Lucas realized then he had only postponed the dog's torture—and had signed his own death warrant.

Desperately, he shouted, "Wait! The officer's jacket isn't

the way to find the gold. The dog can't follow that. I know how to make him hunt!"

Clifford drew a bead. His cocked pistol never wavered.

"Toss down your gun, if you call that pea shooter a gun. Don't ventilate him yet, boys. I want to hear what the man has to say."

Lucas did as he was told. With his pistol too far away for him to hope to dive, grab, aim, and fire at even one of the filibusterers, he slid down the bank and kept his hands high in the air.

"Who the hell are you?"

"That doesn't matter, Clifford."

Using the man's name almost got him shot. The guerrilla motioned for him to move around closer to Tovarich. As he did, the dog quieted his frantic barking.

"Sounds like he's taken a shine to you, mister. Why'd you want to tell us a damn thing about finding the gold?"

"I want a share. It's a million-dollar cache. Give me a few thousand and I'll be happy."

"Now then, it might be you're gonna be happy if you don't end up with a few ounces of lead in your gut. Tell me how to find the gold."

"Promise me," Lucas said, forcing himself to hold down the desperate tone in his voice. "I want a share. What do you have to lose? You get the bulk of the gold and sally off to Nicaragua."

"Boss, he knows too much to have just come on us," one of the six who had ridden up said. "Let me shoot him right now. He might have the cavalry on us."

"I don't cotton much to the law, marshals, or soldiers," Lucas said. This carried a ring of truth since it was gospel. "I got on to the treasure because of Amanda Baldridge."

"Dennison was dead," said one. "Might be he killed him and let the woman go."

"She wouldn't run to the law. And Dunbar's all ready for the bone yard. I saw to that. She doesn't have anywhere to go—except maybe for this one." Clifford lifted his six-shooter and aimed straight for Lucas's head.

"I know how to make the dog find the gold." Lucas looked at Tovarich. The wolfhound had stopped its frantic barking and just stared at him, as if he understood everything going on.

"Do tell." Clifford's six-gun never wavered.

"It's a scent," Lucas said. "I have a jar of the perfume here in my pocket. Let me get it out."

He reached slowly for the spikenard and drew out the glass jar and held it up. In the dark it was indistinct.

"What's that?" Clifford looked away from Lucas when the dog sat on its haunches and let out a long howl. "You just might have the key there, after all. Throw it to me."

"You might drop it in the dark. You don't want to do that."

"Bring it to me. I'll shoot you down if you make a funny move."

Lucas hesitated. Curious noises reached his ears. He closed his eyes to better focus on the distant sounds, trying to make sense of them. Opening his eyes again, he looked at the knot of Clifford's men. The number had been whittled down by one. Where had the filibusterer gone?

Then the night ripped apart with fierce howls and snapping. He looked at Tovarich. The dog came back to his feet and snarled again but was still firmly held by two ropes around his neck. Motion from the corner of his eye told the story. A pack of wolfhounds stormed out of the black night. One of Clifford's men got off a shot that wounded one dog.

Two others attacked him, one going for his crotch and the other his throat. He died before he collapsed to the sandy ravine bottom. But the hounds never slowed to rip and tear at the flesh of their victim.

They charged on and grabbed at wrists, legs, and exposed parts on the other filibusterers.

"What the hell!" Clifford swung about and fired. He missed the lead dog.

The wolfhound took to the air and crashed hard into the man, driving him backward so he landed flat on his back. Lucas tried to look away but couldn't. Clifford had fallen directly in front of Tovarich, where the dog could sink its fangs into his throat. Tovarich gripped powerfully, then gave a toss of his head. Strong neck muscles corded as the dog pulled away. Blood flew into the night.

Lucas knelt and scooped up his Colt, not sure who to shoot. All of Clifford's men had died or were so close to death that it didn't matter. He held out his pistol if any of the wolfhounds came for him. His experience with the big, powerful hunting dogs told him of the futility of shooting them and hoping to escape, but he had done stupider things that night.

Showing himself to Clifford to save Tovarich from being tortured was as dumb as it got.

"Don't move."

"I won't." Lucas put his hands in the air but still clung to his pistol in the futile hope he might use it to save himself.

Tovarich stood with blood dripping from his jowls. The dog's eyes fixed on him but Tovarich made no move to come for him. He wished that could be said of a half dozen other wolfhounds. They circled him, backed him against the ravine wall, and began coming closer. Snarling, drooling blood from jaws that had already killed all of Clifford's expeditionary force, they advanced.

A sharp command in Russian stayed the dogs' attack. They remained in a ring around him but only barred his escape.

"You saved Tovarich."

"Good evening, Vera," he said. Taking his eyes off the dogs was hard but he did. The Russian revolutionary strode out. Trailing her were several men from her band. "Sorry to hear about Dmitri."

She spat. "He was a traitor. How dare he sell out to *them*?" She spat in the direction of Clifford's body.

She went to Tovarich, used a knife, and slashed at the ropes holding him. He nuzzled her, and she patted him, soothing him, trying to rub away the torture already endured.

"Could you call off the other dogs?"

Vera called something in Russian that caused the wolfhounds to back away, then trot over and lie down beside her. As she turned, Tovarich broke free and ran for Lucas. He lifted his Colt but wasn't able to fire before he was bowled over. The dog pinned his shoulders to the rocky ground with both paws and started licking him with a bloody tongue.

"You have made a friend. Tovarich is the smartest of them all and knows you saved him."

"I'm glad," Lucas said, meaning it with all his heart. "How'd you know where to find Clifford and Tovarich?"

Good moved into his field of vision, arms crossed over his chest.

"I thought you'd left me. You went to fetch Vera and her men—her dogs?"

The Indian nodded once.

"You made it just in time." Lucas shifted his weight, but

Tovarich refused to let him up until Vera threw her arms around the dog's neck and pulled him away.

"He likes you," she said.

"What are you going to do?"

Vera looked at Good, smiled a little, then dragged Tovarich off. Lucas climbed to his feet.

"You're going after the gold, aren't you?"

"I will see that she finds it, then get to the coast."

"What's there?"

"There is a Russian colony at Fort Ross. She and her friends will take ship back to her home."

Good tried but could not keep the sadness out of his voice.

"Are you going with her?"

"There is no place for me in Russia." Good spun and strode away. The pack of dogs sprang to their feet and trailed him as he disappeared into the night with Vera Zasulich.

Lucas stared at the carnage. Clifford and his men were all dead. How many of Vera's had died, he had no way of guessing. The pack of wolfhounds roved at full strength, and now that Tovarich had returned, they would trot along and sniff out the gold.

At that thought, he had to laugh. Lucas held the jar of perfume and started to unscrew the lid, then thrust it back into his pocket. No matter how sensitive the dog's nose, it could not sniff out hidden gold smeared with the spikenard. Too many questions cropped up as he thought about Good leading the way to some hidden cache.

Who had put the perfume on the gold and then thought to train the dog? A simple map made more sense and required less effort. Even the best trained dog might leave the trail to go racing after a rabbit. After all the tribulations the dog had been through, death would have left the gold forever hidden. Tovarich was a fierce fighter, but eventually the rats or other dogs would have killed him in Makepeace's rat pits.

Amanda had somehow gotten the perfume from Vera's wagon, but how did she know this was the key to unlocking the dog's sensitive nose? Lucas shook his head sadly. There wasn't any way. No way at all.

In the silence of the night, Lucas looked up at the crystalline stars. The dogs were long gone, and not even a breeze stirred the bushes. Bodies strewn all over the ravine began to smell, forcing Lucas to climb back to the bank of the ravine. From here he found his horse, mounted, winced, and then settled down.

Tovarich might be the key to finding the gold, but the perfume had nothing to do with it. In spite of the pain in his butt, back, and legs, Lucas trotted back to Denver because he knew how to find the gold.

25

Lucas got more excited with every mile he rode on the way back to Denver. When Amanda's Cherry Creek shack came into view, he let out a whoop of glee. He was right. He had to be since nothing else made a lick of sense. With a quick move, he dropped to the ground. His earlier weakness had passed, and the certainty he'd gained while turning over every possibility in his mind gave him renewed confidence and strength. Even his legs were strong and worked well as he kicked back the door and went inside.

The interior was too dark for him to find what he wanted. He lit a match and held it aloft as it sputtered and flared. He turned slowly until he found the corner where Tovarich had been chained. The mute testimony to the dog's confinement lay on the dirt floor. He dropped to his knees and pawed through the debris, hunting for what had to be here. Amanda had freed Tovarich from the collar and dropped it. When he pushed aside a pile of offal, he touched the thick leather strap.

He fell back and found a dirty rag to wipe off his hand and Tovarich's collar. A second match provided enough light for him to examine the collar. Along the inside the thread had been ripped away. His fingernail completed the cut so he could peel back the leather to expose a metal strip. By the time Lucas pried it away from the collar, his match had burnt to a black, charred stick. He went to the door and held up the metallic strip so starlight shone off it.

More by touch than sight, he made out lines and dots stamped into the metal. Holding it close, he got a good look at it. A slow smile came to his lips. Tovarich had been the answer to finding the gold, but it had nothing to do with the dog's keen nose. The map had been sewn into his collar.

Lucas ran his fingers over the metal strip until dawn broke and gave enough light for him to get a better look. The small triangles had to be mountain peaks. Dots showed a river or perhaps a road. But where? It took him another few minutes to understand the final part of the map. Corners on one end had been folded back and a notch on the bottom cut out. An arrow. An arrow like a compass needle.

He aligned it with north, then studied the Front Range as sunlight struck the mountains fully. Was it intended to be magnetic north or should he find the North Star? Lucas realized that hardly mattered since the map lacked detail. This was a broad hint where the gold had been cached and nothing more. He pressed his thumb down over the X that would make him fabulously wealthy.

Anxious to get on the trail, he realized he needed to prepare. He needed supplies for at least a week, and more immediately, he needed food now and rest.

Lucas got his supplies and ate in the saddle as he rode into the foothills. Excitement kept him alert and on the trail until he fell asleep and almost toppled from the saddle.

Realizing how dangerous it would be to tumble off his horse and down the increasingly precipitous drop-offs along the trail, he found a cave, gave his horse what grass he could pull up, and then lay down out on his blanket, intending only to take a quick nap.

Ten hours later, he came awake with a start. He stretched, moaned a little at the effort, and made sure his horse got more fodder before eating some of the food he had brought along. The time it took to prepare galled him, but his hunger had grown to the point his hands shook and dizziness hit him whenever he moved suddenly. That might be due to the increasing altitude, but Lucas had pushed himself to the edge of exhaustion.

He told himself he needed to be sharp, alert, and able to appreciate the treasure trove when he found it.

After eating, he took out the thin strip map. He pressed his thumbnail into it. The metal might have been tin or some other malleable metal. The map was plainly punched into the strip that had been hidden in Tovarich's collar. He almost wished the dog could be here to share his triumph. Then he realized how little he liked dogs. Vera's pack had attacked him in town, even if it had saved him from Clifford and his men.

He oriented the strip and found the highest peaks to the left. Only the loftiest 14,000-foot mountains had been used as markers on the map. His heart raced when he realized he was getting closer. The cache had been placed remarkably close to town, but from what he had overheard, this was Confederate gold so had to have been moved from its original hiding place.

In places he had to walk. This caused him to worry how the gold had been moved this route in the first place. More and more he checked the metal strip to reassure himself he wasn't going in the wrong direction. Then he went down a steep slope and into a grassy valley feeling winter's first bite. Snow dotted the ground. He caught his breath when he saw how a horse had come from the other end of the valley and turned due west—the direction his map showed. He dismounted and studied the tracks. They weren't too recent, but he wasn't much of a frontiersman and couldn't be certain. It had been several days since it had snowed. The icy crust that formed in the warm autumn sun had folded over some of the hoofprints. Or maybe he was only minutes behind the other rider. How anyone else knew of the location baffled him, but he was willing to fight for his share.

He was willing to fight for it all.

He lost the tracks across a rocky patch. Lucas stopped looking for the other tracks when he saw what had to be the hiding place. Twin rocky spires rose on either side of a narrow valley entrance. In spite of gasping from the altitude, he ran forward. His horse balked, but he tugged at the reins. Lucas dropped the reins and scrambled up a rock-strewn slope to what had to be the hiding place.

The dirt and frozen mud had been disturbed. He wasn't the only one who had been here. That didn't mean whoever had entered knew anything about the gold. He had slept in a shallow cave the first day out. This might be another pilgrim on the trail to—where? Lucas had no idea.

Anxiously entering the cave, he took a deep whiff to be sure there wasn't bear or wolf spoor. Finding nothing, he pushed deeper. At this point, he would have wrestled the bear and the wolf, both at the same time, to get a million dollars of gold bars. Or was it coins? How had the Confederates poured their gold?

He moved to one side and let the light from the cave mouth show him the way. The only possible spot where anything might have been hidden was a narrow crevice jammed with loose rocks. He tore at the rocks and threw them to the cave floor until he came to a wooden box. Small enough to hold in his hands, it could not possibly hold even a few hundred dollars in gold, much less a million dollars.

Hardly daring to act, Lucas summoned the courage and pried open the lid. Nothing inside. Nothing. He carried the box outside into the bright sun, where he could better examine the box. It had once held fine Cuban cigars. Now not even dust was inside.

He turned the box over and over, then discarded it. Whatever had been here was gone. The rider whose tracks he had seen had come here and beaten him to the contents. Another map? Why would anyone create such a chain of clues? He had no answer for that.

Lucas leaned back, closed his eyes, and let the warm sun soothe him. He had dared everything and lost. But so had others who were less inclined to have stardust blind them. Dennis Clifford had given his life hunting for this. So had Jubal Dunbar. Gregor and Dmitri. He tried to imagine the tracks coming here as belonging to Good or Vera Zasulich. That hardly seemed possible. All of them had hunted for gold and lost far more than he.

He opened his eyes and squinted. Not everyone had lost. There was one other player in this treasure hunt who might not have lost.

Lucas picked up the cigar box, tucked it into his saddle-bags, and then mounted. His search wasn't quite at an end. Not yet.

26

Lucas moved his pile of belongings and rolled over onto his back. The crack in the ceiling had grown larger in the week since he'd been thrown out of his boardinghouse. The landlady complained of Dunbar's henchmen being rude to her, demanding to know not only where he was but where all her other boarders were. No matter how Lucas tried to assure her that Dunbar and his men would never be a problem again, she would have none of it. He had picked up his belongings on the street and considered where to stay.

The Great West Detective Agency had an empty store-room. He'd bedded down there, getting up before the North-cotts came in to work at 9 A.M. Felicia Northcott had proven almost as insistent as his old landlady, wanting to open the office at seven. Lucas tried to fire her and Raymond, but the conversation always twisted away from it. Looking at Raymond and seeing his hangdog expression kept Lucas from pressing the point, although Felicia finally relented and agreed to open the office at a time when Lucas could reasonably be awake after working at the Emerald City all night long.

He closed his eyes and tried to picture Carmela Thompson, but already she faded in his memory. She had continued her tour while he was out in the mountains trying to get rich from a hoard of Confederate gold. Lefty replaced her with a half dozen cancan dancers, real crowd pleasers, but not a one of the dancers had the talent or stage presence of lovely Carmela. When he finally sidled up to the faro table for work once more, he expected to see Claudette. Lefty said she had pined for him and disappeared after a couple nights. Lucas tried to picture the two of them together, but couldn't.

Lefty had been distant, probably because he had been sweet on Claudette and blamed Lucas for her going.

And his run of luck had been poor. Losing at the faro table meant he not only cost the house but wasn't being paid since there weren't any earnings to share. After his shift, he had tried his hand once more at the poker table. No matter how he played, loose or aggressive, he simply could not win.

That summed up his life from the minute Amanda Baldridge had walked through the door. He hadn't heard a whisper about her either. Or anyone unearthing a huge trove of gold.

He wished her no ill though she had involved him in a world of trouble and double-crossing. If anyone found the gold, he wanted it to be Amanda.

The rapping on the front door brought him to his feet. He looked out and saw Good pressing into the plate glass until his nose flattened and his face took on an otherworldly aspect. The Creek knocked again. Lucas padded over, not bothering to put on his boots, and opened the door to let the Indian in.

Good stepped in and stood, arms crossed and looking glum.

"I never expected to see you again," Lucas said. "You didn't find the gold."

"No." Good glared at him. "The dog did not hunt. Vera tried everything but nothing."

"A shame. Where is she?"

"On her way back to Russia. Revolution means everything to her."

"You aren't up for overthrowing the czar?"

Good glared at him.

"It's not my fault you—Vera—didn't find the gold. I came away empty-handed, too."

Good grunted.

"You could always catch up with Vera," Lucas suggested. He wondered why Good had stopped by like this, but he lacked the will to ask. He was a bit intimidated by the man.

"She is gone. All my Russian tongue is wasted now." Good looked around, grunted, then said, "You stay here?"

"I'm bedding down in the back room until I find a new place."

"You have no money."

"That's a fair way of putting it. I spent everything Amanda gave me in bribes, for information, getting supplies." He considered leaving the office before he had to pay the Northcotts because he barely had two nickels to rub together. That wasn't fair, but then they hadn't done much more than file papers left by Runyon. There hadn't been any new business to generate money to pay salaries.

"I will work for you."

Before Lucas could do so much as laugh, Good clapped

him on the shoulder, smiled wickedly, then said, "She will be at Governor's Ball tonight."

"Amanda?" Lucas spoke to thin air. Good moved with surprising speed and lost himself in the crowd outside.

He closed the door and considered how much he wanted to see Amanda again. He went to the storeroom and pulled on his boots. The door opened again, and he heard Felicia berating her husband. He settled his coat, walked out, touched the brim of his bowler to them, and said, "Carry on. You're doing a good job."

Before Felicia Northcott could reply, he followed Good into the street and put as many people between his back and the detective agency as possible. Lucas spent the day walking around Denver, taking in the brisk air, enjoying the crush of the crowd about him, even stopping on the edge of the crowd and listening to the Preacher spin a wondrous tale of rejuvenation and all for the price of a two-dollar bottle of Professor Drosselmyer's Somatic Potion, straight from the Old Country and responsible for men and women in the Black Forest living to age one hundred and beyond.

Whatever the Preacher sold probably had a bitter taste— it was medicine, after all, and medicine had to taste bad. Otherwise, only the cheapest of ingredients went into that bottle. Lucas walked on, whistling now. Somewhere during the day he came to a conclusion.

That night he found himself outside a large private house on Capitol Hill. He remembered the last gala he had crashed. Amanda had been there, too, but this time she wouldn't have Dunbar escorting her—as a prisoner. Lucas had never come to a satisfactory conclusion as to whether she had been a willing prisoner or he had coerced her. Now Jubal Dunbar was moldering in a grave and she was free.

He caught his breath when he saw a carriage stop and a

tall, slim man in a tuxedo reach up to take Amanda's gloved hand. She was resplendent in a gold dress decorated with tiny pearls. The neckline was daring, even for a frontier ball, and she still made him stare at her face. She was achingly pretty. Moving like thistledown, she floated up the flagstone path on the man's arm, paused on the porch, and turned to look back. For an instant their eyes met. Lucas thought she opened her fan and waved it a few times as she studied him, then laughed and went inside amid orchestral music billowing out into the night.

Lucas went around back. A dozen servants worked to bring in cases of liquor and prepare food to maintain the flow of gaiety inside. He found a carriage house and opened the door partway. The carriage seat was comfortable enough to sit in while he waited. An hour later he heard the soft whisper of cloth brushing the ground and looked up.

"Hello, Amanda," he said. "I figured I would find you where there was a party—or rather, when you were heading out for a grand ball."

The woman stood silhouetted in the carriage house door, the bright lights from the house behind her. The light highlighted her dark hair and turned it into a halo. Here and there a sparkle betrayed a hidden gemstone. She had done well for herself in the last week.

"Hello, Lucas. I never thought I would see you again. I'm happy to say that I was wrong."

"Are you?" He stepped down from the carriage and went to her. "You are still using the same perfume." He pulled her closer and took a deep whiff.

"Spikenard," she said.

"Perfume you stole from Vera Zasulich."

"That is a bit strongly worded. Let's say I sampled her exotic scent."

"You hitched a ride with her caravan?"

"I was down on my luck." Amanda shrugged her shapely bare shoulders.

"So you stole it. Is that when you heard about Tovarich, Gregor, and the gold?"

"How's a girl supposed to close her ears to such wild talk? The Russians gathered around their campfires."

"They'd be speaking Russian."

"Not when your friend joined them. He spoke poorly so they often used English, even when he wasn't nearby."

"Good?"

Amanda smiled. She pressed against him and put her arms around his neck.

"That's all in the past. What are your plans?"

"You didn't find the gold, did you?"

A flash of disgust crossed her face, then she smiled again.

"No. If there ever was gold, it is long gone. More likely, it is only another tall tale built up by retelling."

"A million dollars," he mused.

"See? Never did anyone claim a million dollars in gold had been hidden away. They began by saying 'a prize beyond value.' That translated in the revolutionaries' minds as gold. What else could it be?"

Lucas laced his fingers in the small of her back. Whenever she spoke, he imagined soaring dreams and honeyed lies. He kissed her. This took her aback. She tried to push away, then melted into his arms and pulled his head down for an even more passionate kiss. They broke off.

Her bosom heaved, and he thought she was flushed.

"If only it could have been different between us," she said.

"Fate can be cruel, but we are both penniless. We—"

He looked up. Amanda's escort stood a few feet away.

Lucas had sought out the man most likely to have a future and knew that Amanda would end up at his side. Hearing of the gala tonight made this the likeliest time and place to find the woman. Lucas wished her new beau had dallied just a few minutes longer.

"There you are, my dear. I missed you." He stepped closer, studied Lucas, then said in surprise, "You're the one she won't stop talking about. It's so good to meet you, Mr. Stanton."

Lucas tried to find words to give him a few seconds to think. His thoughts tumbled and churned. Nothing came but a tiny ulp.

"He came to give a final report about . . . the matter we spoke of," Amanda said.

"Dunbar," the man said angrily. "What a yellow dog. The state of Colorado owes you a great debt of gratitude."

"I should send my bill to the governor," Lucas said. Amanda hid a grin.

"Don't do that. He is up to his ears in dealing with other matters affecting our statehood. If the Eastern politicians caught wind of what Dunbar intended, it would put us in a bad situation."

"Certainly," Lucas said. "I can understand that."

"Send your bill to me. Mark it personal."

"Yes, send it to Lafe."

"Lafe?" Lucas was adrift.

"Lafayette Head, our lieutenant governor." Amanda clung to the man's arm. He beamed at her.

"I'd never heard you called that," Lucas said. "Only the lucky gent with the lovely woman on his arm."

"From all my darling Amanda has said, the state would be willing to entertain a bill of, oh, say, one hundred dollars for your efforts." She squeezed his arm and stood on tiptoe to whisper in his ear. He nodded. "Becoming a state has turned everything into a morass of paperwork. It might be some time before payment could be made. Send along your bill, and I will see to it personally."

"That's very generous." Lucas couldn't take his eyes off Amanda. She flashed him an impish smile.

"Considering your part in this sorry matter, it would be well to keep your agency on retainer."

"The Great West Detective Agency," Amanda cut in. The look she gave him was undecipherable.

"Yes, that," Head said. "I am sure we can find new investigations to keep you busy. Colorado is a brand spanking new state and corruption will be rife. Where there is opportunity, there is also excess."

"I can appreciate that, sir," Lucas said.

"We must get back to the ball. Governor Routt wouldn't understand if we weren't there to greet him when he makes his grand entrance."

Lucas watched them go, arm in arm, back to the house. On the back step Amanda blew him a kiss and then disappeared. If he collected the promised money, his luck had indeed changed, and it was at least partly due to Amanda Baldridge. He touched his lips. The wine of her kiss remained all the way back to his pallet in the back room of the detective agency.

By sunrise, he found himself wondering if Amanda had made off with the gold, then decided it wasn't possible. The tracks weren't what he'd expected from carrying out a great amount of gold. He yawned, sat behind the desk, and looked at the cigar box on his desk. Whatever had been inside had been taken. Small, not a million dollars if it had contained a few gold coins.

The sudden wind of the door opening startled him. He was sure he had locked it the night before. Good had his hand on the knob. Before Lucas could say a word, the Creek half turned, waited a moment, then closed the door.

Lucas heard the click-click of claws on the floor and then Tovarich jumped up and pinned him back in the chair to lick him.

"Down, boy. Down." He pushed the wolfhound away and shouted for Good. The Indian had left. "I can't keep you. I don't want to keep you." The dog barked once and dropped to the floor beside the desk, head on outstretched paws. Mournful, accusing eyes stared up at him. "I can't keep you around. I'm going to take what I can out of this place and—"

Lucas turned and clumsily banged into the cigar box with his elbow. His arm went numb because he had hit his funny bone. He rubbed circulation back, then reached for the box. It had been empty when he brought it here from the mountains. The weight now belied its being empty.

He flipped it open. Inside lay an oilskin-wrapped package. String had been tied around it, and then retied with big knots. He turned the box over and looked at it. Tovarich climbed to his feet and sniffed. He shoved the dog away and unwrapped a thick manuscript.

He held up the book so it caught a slanting ray of sun. In faded ink he read the title. *Wealth Beyond Imagining.* He carefully opened the cover and saw it had been written by Jefferson Davis during his two years of imprisonment by the Federals.

"No gold, just this?" He rocked back and stared at the memoir.

When Tovarich growled, he looked up, thinking Good

had returned. Little Otto came in. The huge man stared down the dog, then marched over to the desk.

"I heard you had it."

"It?"

"This." Little Otto reached over, turned the book around, and began leafing through the pages. Only when he had examined each page of the manuscript did he look up. "How much?"

"What do you mean?"

"This is a valuable book. The only copy of Davis's memoir. Rumor has it he is writing another, but not mentioning his years in prison. How much would you sell this for?"

Lucas scratched his head.

"How did you know I had it?" Then he realized it was a silly question. Little Otto was the spider in the middle of the web. The slightest vibration along the strands communicated directly to him. Lucas changed the question. "How did I get the book?"

"Her. She's found a gold mine and isn't interested in such dross. I am."

"Did you enjoy the Twain novel?"

"Two hundred dollars."

"For this?" Lucas put his hand on the book.

"It's one of a kind. I am working on its provenance. Men died smuggling it out of prison for Davis. It was lost when a courier died somewhere in Kansas on his way to New Orleans. I need to learn more of its route to our state."

Lucas saw how those trying to recover the book would spin tales of how valuable it was. Even the title lent to the legend. Someone had mistaken the title for real gold, and another had built on that until the value grew to a million dollars. Boomtowns grew from a few lost souls to thousands in a week. The prattle over the book would cause those who wanted to believe to kill to retrieve it. Clifford and Dunbar had staked their lives on the booty being gold. So had Vera Zasulich. She had lost a brother and others before returning to her home country.

"She?"

"Three hundred," Little Otto said.

"Sold," Lucas said. To his surprise, Otto pulled out a thick wad of greenbacks and peeled off the money before showing a delicacy of touch surprising in one so large as he wrapped the book in the oilskin, placed the package in the cigar box, and then left.

"Tovarich, old friend," he said, "I have a decent stake. Let the Northcotts collect the bill from the state as payment for their services. I can walk out of here and leave everything behind to—"

The door opened again. Lucas came to his feet. The woman was small, a face like Dresden china, ruddy cheeks, and lips meant to be kissed. Her eyes darted about before locking on his. He had never seen a lovelier woman.

"Can I help you?"

"Why, yes, I am looking for the office of the Great West Detective Agency."

Lucas remembered his intent on walking away from the detective agency.

"Please, have a seat."

"Oh, what a handsome dog. Such an intelligent look." Tovarich let out a woof. "But then such a dog would be invaluable to a clever detective such as yourself."

"You think I'm clever?" Lucas said. "You're in need of the services of a detective?"

"I am. A family heirloom has gone missing. A sword. It should take only a few days of your time to recover it. I would be grateful." She batted her eyes. "I would be *very* grateful."

"Tell me more," Lucas Stanton said. How long could it take to find a missing sword? And the young lady would be *very* grateful.

NEW IN THE
GIDEON RYDER SERIES

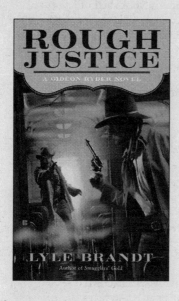

You never hear the shot that kills you...

Available November 2014

penguin.com

M1533T0714